AROUND THE EDGES

CRYSTAL CHARD

CCBooks

Published by Crystal Chard Books 2020

www.crystalchardbooks.com
Editor: Diana Simmonds
Cover: Daniela Di-Benedetto @design_by_daniela

Title: Rough Around The Edges
ISBN: 978-1-5272-6006-1

CCBooks

Out beyond ideas of wrongdoing and rightdoing, there is a field. I'll meet you there. – Rumi

PROLOGUE

I LEANED IN TOWARDS THE vanity mirror and took one final look at my reflection. Christ, was I even in there? All my life I'd been told I have my grandma's eyes, it's the only thing that made me feel a connection to the woman I never met, but at that moment, as I stared back at the inch-thick liner, black shadow, and Mac lashes, even my mum wouldn't have recognised those eyes. I slumped back on the chair and scanned the dressing room to see if any of my colleagues had witnessed my distaste, they hadn't. They were all too busy getting themselves ready for their set, which was exactly what I should have been doing. I wondered then – just as I had before every shift – what the hell I was even doing there.

The room was pretty much as you would expect: four dressing tables lined against the back wall, cluttered with aerosol cans, hairbrushes, hair straighteners, wigs, and enough make-up to keep Cirque du Soleil going for the next ten years. Two clothes rails in the middle of the room held some of the sluttiest dresses known to man, and Ariana Grande played on loop as it had every single bloody shift since I had started there.

"Rox, you're up." Paul's cockney accent bellowed from where he waited at the stage side.

Okay, so, if I were going to change my mind and not go out there, then that was my cue. I stared at the mirror, tucked in my top lip and watched my nostrils flare. Shall I? Shan't I? Oh, forget it, who I was kidding. I applied a layer of cherry-red lipstick, cursed as it smudged beyond my lip-line and rubbed at the smear until it was fully removed. I lifted my left leg onto the chair and pulled a lacy black stocking above my knee.

"Roxy, get your arse out here!" Paul's thinning patience was evident in his tone.

"Jeez! Paul, I'm coming!" I caught my reflection one last time and sighed.

Okay, let's do this.

CHAPTER 1

SOMEONE WISE ONCE TOLD ME, if we live until we're eighty, then we only get to live for four-thousand weeks. *Four-thousand*. That's not a lot. And of course, that's if you're one of the lucky ones. Some people are not so fortunate. Some people have far fewer weeks, and when you know they're dwindling, believe me, they tend to go by even faster. That's when you find yourself starting to count.

I guess then, as I stood outside her door with my forehead resting against the cold wall, that's how I was able to recount off the top of my head, that forty-nine weeks had passed since the specialist had sat her down and delivered her second diagnosis. Twenty-five weeks ago, we made the decision to condemn her to that home, and three weeks back was the last time she left her bed unaided. What I could never have known, however, was how the weeks to follow were about to start a ripple effect that would determine the rest of my life.

"Come on, Rox, get your shit together." My whispered words bounced off the wall and were enough to prompt an affirmative nod. "You've got this."

I slipped into the room and closed the door gently behind

me, aware that even the smallest of creaks would wake her. The rubbery squeak of my Converse on the hardwood floor echoed up to the high ceiling as I crept over to the windowsill. Attempting to be as stealth-like as possible I removed the wrapper from the purple freesias I had bought for her and slipped them into a vase before stopping to look out at the view of the lake.

Chislehurst manor house had been converted into a luxury care home back in the early sixties. Its tranquil expanse included four acres of woodland and lakes and was in stark contrast to the built-up area of my patch in Greenwich. On such a scorching summer's day, when the birds tweeted their afternoon song and the sun bounced off everything it touched, I wondered how a place so lovely could make me want to rip my heart from my chest.

To describe the room as extravagant would be an understatement. It oozed extravagance, the space itself screamed lavish. The bed, king-sized and made of solid oak, towered over her and swallowed up her frail frame. The furniture was spread out across the room; a bedside table, two chairs next to the bed for visitors, and a dressing table in the far corner which sat as a reminder that my once beautiful mum no longer took care of her appearance. For the most part, though, the room consisted of a whole load of space – just a whole load of extortionately priced space.

I arranged the flowers as best I could, and tiptoed over to the bed where I sat beside Mum and studied her while she slept. She must have lost another three pounds over the past couple of weeks, and for someone already excessively underweight, this was not good. I rubbed my tense shoulders and watched the rise and fall of her chest with every laboured breath she took. I wondered where her dreams went, whether she dreamed about my siblings or me, or if she drifted back to a time when she wasn't confined to this room, to this bed, a time before her antibodies had taken early redundancy. I wondered too if she wished she had lived her life differently, whether she feared the inevitable or had resigned herself to it, whether–

"Boo!" Her eyes sprung open.

I leapt back in my seat. "For Christ's sake, Mum! You nearly gave me a bloody heart attack." I struggled to stifle a smile.

"Well, you shouldn't stare at someone while they're sleeping, it's pissing creepy, and I didn't drag you up to be creepy."

I rolled my eyes. "You didn't drag me up, Mum."

"Yeah, yeah, if you say so." She struggled to prise herself up on her elbows.

I fluffed the pillows behind her and helped manoeuvre her so she was upright. As I lifted her body, she pressed a hand to her chest and winced. I paused, but Mum flicked her other hand, ignoring her pain. "So, whatcha get up to after you left here yesterday, kid?" Her thick Essex accent croaked in her throat more than usual.

I poured her a glass of water and carefully avoided looking at her. "Oh, this and that. I worked from home in the afternoon, then the bar in the evening, nothing too riveting."

When I eventually did look at Mum, she was squinting and it was the same sceptical look I had been privy to before. I wondered if today would be the day she'd call me out on her suspicions. I thought too about what I would tell her if she ever did. It's not as though Mum would have given a shit what I did for a living. In fact, before she became ill, she probably would have come by to watch. I had visions of her telling anyone who would listen, "That's my baby girl up there", while whooping and cheering. It's not as if she was a prude, it's just that Mum wouldn't have wanted me doing *that* for *her*, she would never have allowed her illness to be the reason.

"So, how are you feeling today? You seem brighter?" I was

keen to steer us onto safer ground. I handed her the glass and watched both hands tremble as she took it from me.

"Yeah, not arf bad. Doctor fancy bollocks upped my meds which are knocking me out for most of the day." She leaned in, and her sunken eyes sparkled with a look I had come to recognise, "'Ere, you'll never guess what I found out yesterday?"

I rolled my eyes, already anticipating where the conversation was heading. "Go on."

"Well, you know your ol' mum, I'm not one to gossip, but Jan next door, the new one with the lazy eye? She's only got herself a lover. Her husband visits her during the week, and on the weekend, her bit on the side turns up, what a slut, eh?" She chuckled at the titbit, and it soon turned in to a rough rattly cough.

"Hmm, not one to gossip, my arse."

Before Mum could cough or snort at me the door creaked and swung open. A husky yet flustered voice filled the sudden silence.

"Oh. Erm. Sorry, I didn't mean to barge in. You don't usually have visitors at this time. Ignore me, I'll pop back later." The figure turned and began to head back out the door.

"No, wait. It's fine," I called after her, "It's just a flying visit, don't let me interrupt you, do what you have to do." I beckoned the visitor back, expecting to see a nurse, but as she stepped into the room, the nice clothes and absence of a nurse's uniform was evident. The girl – correction – woman walked towards me in two long strides and held out her hand. "Hi, I'm Josie Calhoun. I'm sorry for barging in. I read to Susan a couple of times a week, and she's usually alone at this time." She took my hand and shook it with assurance.

I turned to face Mum and narrowed my eyes at the revelation. "News to me." I struggled to keep the accusation from my tone.

Mum became fascinated by her glass of water. I shifted my attention back to this Josie Calhoun.

"Did you just say you read to my mum?" I didn't give her time to answer. "What type of thing do you read?"

Josie hesitated and looked at Mum, who shrugged and remained unusually quiet. Josie turned back to me. "Poetry mostly, sometimes stories too, anything I come across during the week really that I think she might appreciate. Haven't told me to piss off yet have you, Susan?" Her affectionate smile revealed two perfectly formed dimples.

"Poetry, huh?" I raised my brows at Mum before remembering my manners and turning back to Josie. "Sorry, I don't mean to be rude. I've just not heard about any of this, and if you know my mother dearest, you'll know it's unheard of for her to not share. I'm Roxy by the way, I probably should have already said that."

Josie feigned shock. "Huh? Your mother? Susan, you never told me you have a daughter. I'm sorry, Roxy, but I'm afraid I've not heard a thing about you." A smile tugged at her lips.

"Oh, really?" I found her little dig kind of amusing.

"No, not really. She literally hasn't shut up about you since the day I met her. I feel like I've known you for years. It's nice to finally meet you." Josie's eyes crinkled at the corners as they held on to mine.

I looked away. "Hmm, well, as long as she hasn't told you too much. I know what she can be like."

Mum's croak from the bed interrupted our exchange. "If you two have finished talking about me as though I'm not bloody here, I wouldn't mind you getting on with it."

I mouthed "sorry" to Josie.

Josie smiled. "It's fine." She spoke from the side of her mouth, "I've got used to her ways over the past three months."

I smiled back at her, masking my internal dialogue. *Three months?* She's been reading to my mum for three months and not once has anyone mentioned it? I shot Mum a curious look as Josie walked past me, leaving an exotic woody scent behind her, which I thought made a pleasant change from sickly sweet "floral" air freshener.

She drew up the other chair next to Mum on the opposite side of the bed and removed a worn-looking book from her bag. I took a moment to study her while she flicked through the pages. She was wearing cut-off denims, which came to just above her knees, a faded yellow t-shirt, and an emerald green silk scarf draped around her neck. The scarf was an unusual choice given the heatwave London had been hit by all week. A pair of dark sunglasses straddled auburn hair which was in a haphazard bun as though she had thrown it together yet had somehow mastered the art of a perfect mess. She sat upright, ankles crossed, owning an air of confidence that seemed to reach across the bed and bitch slap me.

I had stared for too long.

"So, do you work for the home?" I rested my elbows on my knees and leaned my chin on my clasped fists.

Josie's eyes flicked up from the page and at Mum, her expression curiously unreadable. She went back to the book before answering. "No, I just volunteer here a couple of days a week after my late lectures." Her tone was almost dismissive.

"Wow, good for you." My surprise was blatant as I wondered why in the hell anyone would choose to spend their spare time in this place. "So, what do you study?" I was, perhaps bordering on nosey but this poetry-reading-stranger had me intrigued.

Mum's snigger didn't go unnoticed.

An amused smile curled Josie's lips as she looked up from her book and met my gaze. "I'm a *lecturer* at the University of London."

"A lecturer?" The words escaped me a little too quickly. "You look so…young."

Josie smiled, exposing the dimples once more. "Thanks, I'll take that, but I'm thirty-three. Still pretty young to be doing what I do, granted, but I'm one of the lucky ones who knew what I wanted from an early age."

I nodded, impressed, and about to ask what she lectured on when Mum cut in.

"Huh-hum." It was a growl that demanded attention. For someone as poorly as she was, the woman sure as shit still knew how to control a room.

Josie's eyes widened, and we shared a smile. "Sorry, Susan. I'll just get right on with it, shall I?" Josie sat straighter.

"That would be good. Roxanne needs to get to work anyway, don't you, dear?" Mum flicked her eyes at the door, telling me in no uncertain terms to do one. I stood up and stretched out my back, wondering why the hell she didn't want me around.

"Well, hint taken, I guess. I'll just be going then." I leaned over to peck Mum on the forehead and attempted to sneak a look at the book on Josie's lap. It was a hardback, its spine so worn the gold lettering had practically disappeared, and I couldn't make out the title. Josie's eyes shimmered with amusement as she caught me looking. I screwed up my nose in response and gave up.

"Love you, Mum." I tucked a stray wisp of hair behind her ear before addressing Josie, who had already risen and was holding her hand out to me once more. Another handshake. It felt like a formal gesture for someone wearing cut-offs and Timberlands, and I figured it must be part of the whole lecturer thing, it probably explained the scarf too. I held out my hand, liking the warmth of Josie's palm against my own.

"It was nice to meet you, Roxy. Perhaps I'll see you again some time?" Our eyes locked for a split second longer than might be expected. I nodded, acutely aware of the voice in the back of my head that quietly whispered, "I hope so".

What was it with me and red-heads?

MY FINGERS CLOSED AROUND THE pole as I forced a smile in time for the curtains to open. The maroon drapes receded to the beat of INXS's "Need You Tonight", revealing the crowd as I elevated my body from the stage, praying that just this once my smile would reach my eyes. It didn't.

Chace's is a popular strip club in the heart of London's business district, Canary Wharf. I had worked there for six months, and on a good night, I could expect to take home anything between £300 and £350. Not bad for someone who, at best, just pushed above average in the looks department. But what I lacked in pretty, I made up for with my hour-glass figure. I was blessed with a naturally toned physique, a good pair of tits and a pert arse, and as it turns out, that's exactly what the suits angled for after a rough day at the corporate sharp end.

I continued to mount the pole, giving them an eyeful of six-pack and skin and moved into a basic climb by pushing up with my feet. I reached the top and let my head fall back and slid effortlessly into a fireman's spin while my pony hung towards the floor. I pulled myself back up into a seated position and clasped the cold pole between my thighs, ready for my dismount.

Over those past six months, I had developed a muscle memory sufficient to get me through my routine without so much as a second thought. This pleased me. It allowed my mind to wander – specifically – to the poetry-reading stranger I had met earlier in the day, and even more specifically – why the hell she was the one reading to my mum. I'm a writer for Christ's sake. Well, I was. Why did Mum never ask *me* to read to her?

I loosened my grip on the bar and allowed my body to glide down, feeling a slight sting from the pole as it chaffed the tender skin of my inner thighs. My feet met the floor, and I belly-rolled up into a standing position before I stepped out from the pole and teased the buttons of my red dress. Although grotesque and nothing like I would ordinarily wear, the little leather babydoll was fastened together by popper buttons all running down the front. This made it easy for me to remove it in one swoop, which is precisely what I did.

And who was this woman anyway? This lecturer woman, I reminded myself. She seemed like a kind person. Why else would anyone choose to spend their free time in a place where people go to die? And look, I'm not going to lie, her attractiveness had caught me off-guard. I couldn't remember the last time I had even thought about someone in that way. There was just something about the way she held herself, something more than looks that I couldn't quite put my finger on, and it had a small part of me wanting to see her again.

Left wearing only suspenders, an excuse for a black thong, and a lacy bra to match, I prowled about the stage to the sultry beat, throwing an exaggerated wink at anyone who caught my eye.

And what was that look they gave each other, my mum and her reader chick? Her lecturer chick? As though they had a secret between the two of them. Mum had never kept a secret in her life, what was she playing at?

I moved back to the pole and repeated the same routine as before. It's all I knew. Pole dancing tears at your muscles like nothing else on this earth and leaves every part of your body on fire if you're not careful, so I tried not to stretch too far from the basics Stacey had taught me on my first day. I worked my way to the top of the pole and spun around with my head dangling again, only this time, something else went on. The blood would usually rush to my head as I made that move, I was hanging upside down after all, but the pressure that built felt like a balloon was expanding inside my skull. I hauled myself up and slid down the pole until I landed back on my feet once more. I had missed out half the routine. I pressed my forehead against the beam for a moment and made sure I continued to sway my hips, so the customers bought it as part of the act. I regained some balance, and after a minute or so, felt able to continue. I unhooked the back of my bra with a ridiculous flourish and descended into a slut-drop, a move which never failed to make me cringe from the inside out, but the punters liked it, and I didn't exactly dislike the tips. As my bra dropped to the stage, I pushed up through my heels and squinted as the dizzying lights induced a weird heaviness behind my eyes. I paused for a moment and drew in a long breath, determined to continue. I would not be the one who left the stage mid-set, knowing it drove the clients insane with booing and general displeasure.

My thumbs dipped below the elastic of my thong, doing all I could to arouse the ogling faces beyond the stage lights. Their lechy stares told me how oblivious they were to my queasiness. That was a relief, albeit short-lived. Against my will, my head began to make small involuntary circles. Around. Around. And around again.

I leaned forward and attempted to remove the thong from my foot. The number of customers at the bar had doubled, and the room circled crazily. I stood up, way too fast, and froze. The reeling sensation in my head, coupled with the nauseating churn swirling in my stomach, overpowered me. I closed my eyes and held my hand over them to block out the fluorescent blue light from the bar, but that made it worse. A sudden tropical heat radiated from my skin and within seconds everything turned to…

Black.

CHAPTER 2

I HAD ALREADY FAINTED THREE times during the month. The first had been on the grounds of the home after visiting Mum, and the second after a long shower. Both times I was alone. After the second occasion, I visited Dr Shah, who told me that I more than likely suffered from something he called psychogenic faints. This meant that whenever I found myself under an unusual amount of stress, my mind basically said, "fuck this" and went into shutdown mode. I'm paraphrasing a little here, but that's the gist of it. He suggested several things: counselling, pills, long walks in nature, blah blah blah, but the fact was my life had invited stress in as its nearest and dearest, and until that changed, I would be prone to the occasional blackout.

Club manager Paul dropped me home, and was actually pretty sensitive about what had happened, even though I had lost him both custom and money. I assured him for the third time that I would be okay and that he could go back to the club. When I got in, I found my flat-mate stretched out across the leather sofa. She wore short cut pyjama pants and a white camisole which accentuated her naturally tanned limbs. Clara's parents were of Spanish origin, and although born in north London, she looked every bit the Mediterranean goddess, even in her jammies.

She looked up from the bowl of crisps resting on her lap and stared at me for a moment. "Girl, you high?" She cocked an eyebrow.

"No, I'm not high." I yanked at the strap of one of the shoes I hadn't changed out of since my rudely curtailed set.

"So, what's with the passing out?" Her perfectly shaped right eyebrow remained elevated.

I narrowed my gaze. "How did you-"

"Paul just texted me, he asked me to keep an eye on you. Said you dropped like a pair of saggy tits. I can't believe I missed that shit." Her eyes widened, and she grinned as she patted the sofa with her foot.

"Yep. You would've loved it. Me humiliated within an inch of my life. It's the stuff your dreams are made of." I plodded over to the sofa.

Clara lifted her legs, and I sat on the end and she laid her feet on my lap. "Seriously, you okay, though?"

Although I appreciated the unusual hint of sincerity in Clara's voice, there were just some things I was not willing to go into. Not just yet, anyway. I laced my fingers behind my head and leaned back against the headrest. "All good. I skipped dinner and haven't been sleeping too great."

Clara eyeballed me for a moment, unconvinced, then shrugged and reached into her crisp bowl and threw a Wotsit at me.

"Hey!" I flicked the cheesy crumbs from my forehead and stuffed the Wotsit in my mouth.

Clara smirked. "That's the first part taken care of, and if you're struggling to sleep, I've got some pills you can take. I usually pop a few after a night out. They're in my top drawer, help yourself."

I snorted. "Nope, I'm good, and even if I were to indulge in your probably-not-even-legal meds, if you think for one minute I'm rooting through your underwear drawer, you're even more delusional than I thought. Christ knows the kind of rank shit you keep in there."

Clara smirked again. "Okay, valid point. If you need them, ask, and I'll get them for you."

I laughed a genuine laugh even though I still hadn't fully recovered from the blackout.

Clara had been living with me for the past three months. We met on my first night at Chace's, and within seconds she took a dislike to me. Throughout my first shift, she didn't even bother to say so much as hello. Instead, while all the others introduced themselves and busied around me making a fuss, Clara sat at her dresser narrowing her eyes at me in the mirror with an expression that encapsulated everything I already knew – I didn't belong. Her frostiness went on for a good couple of months until one night, a bald business type who looked a lot like Mr Monopoly, got severely handsy with me instead of shoving a note in my thong elastic. Clara came to my rescue like a banshee, dragging me off the stage while the bouncers dealt with the bloke by throwing him out on his arse. After I thanked her profusely and she snorted dark opinions about handsy blokes, we got to talking and, although we were an unlikely pairing, we actually hit it off. I felt grateful to her for having my back and later learned that the whole chilly arsehole thing she had going was more of a tried and tested defence mechanism.

One evening, when I visited her shithole flat in Hackney with its piss-stained lift and mould spores on the walls, I found myself compelled to ask her to move in with me. Coming from a relatively deprived upbringing, it pained me to see her living in such squalid conditions, and I figured that no one should have to live like that, even someone who liked to come the mean bitch act. Besides, it made sense. I had a spare room closer to work for her, and it meant we could keep each other company and go halves on the rent. My "flat" was really more of a luxury apartment, which was quite costly, so having her there would leave me with even more disposable cash for my mum.

Clara didn't know about Mum, though. I had chosen to keep that part of my life separate from her. I didn't want her sympathy, and I certainly didn't want her treating me any different. I liked the whole frosty bitch thing she had going on, it made me chuckle and kept some normal in my otherwise abnormal life. As far as Clara knew, I went out for the best part of two hours every day to meet my writer friend Cayden, so we could discuss each other's work, and that's the way I wanted it. Occasionally, she would question me on my "story", insisting that everyone who worked at Chace's had one.

"There's no way a brainiac like you just chooses to strip for a living," she'd said.

Clara shoved her phone out to me, holding it inches from my face and snapping me back to the room. "This is it; this is what's going to shake you out of this weird woe-is-me thing you've got going on."

I read the post on her Facebook page:

Ladies night at the Lounge. This Saturday. No men allowed.

2 for 1 on all cocktails.

I shook my head vehemently and batted the phone away.

"No way. I'm not going to that." I couldn't think of anything worse than a night out after the evening I'd just had.

"What? Why?" Clara looked like someone had just stolen her last Wotsit.

"Because I'm not, that's why. It'll be the same old faces, shit music and no one I'm even remotely interested in."

Clara sat up and tucked her hair behind her ears.

"Okaaay, I think there's been some kind of misunderstanding. You're clearly missing the point." She grabbed my chin and looked me straight in the eyes. "Two for one *all cocktails*." She dragged out each word.

I pursed my lips, stifling a smile. "Nope. It's not happening."

Clara let out an over-exaggerated huff. "Fuck! I'm not asking you to find a wife, just have drinks and a dance, you know, lighten up a bit. I've never been to one of your lezzy nights, it might be fun, and you never know, *I* might get lucky." She flicked her tongue and wiggled her eyebrows.

I laughed. "You're the worst, the actual worst, you know that, right?" I could feel my resolve caving.

Clara feigned shock. "So, that's a yes?"

I internally debated the pros and cons of a night out with Clara, knowing deep down that I probably did mope around too much, and it might be beneficial to let my hair down just this once. "Fine, I'll come."

"Yes!" she screeched before shoving a handful of Wotsits into her mouth.

"But you better promise not to be a total knob like you were last time."

Clara spoke through her mouthful, covering her cleavage with crumbs. "I resent that. The only reason we got kicked out was that muppet of a barman. He couldn't take a joke."

I sniggered. "Clar, you stuck a pool cue in his arse! Just promise me, okay?"

"Scout's honour." She held her fingers to her forehead in the Brownie salute, and I couldn't be bothered to mention her mistake.

~

THE LOUNGE, LAID OUT OVER two floors, had been a theatre back in the early '60s. The décor hadn't changed much since then, with gold pillars, chandeliers, deep red drapes and black and white photos of the theatre's most famous productions filling every space in between. It seemed a shame really, for such a building to now be home to a load of sweaty, drunk lesbians out on the pull. The first floor, where most of the women danced to club classics from the '90s, was where the older crowd had gathered. The top floor, an R&B room which overlooked the lower dance floor, was where the younger clubbers congregated and where, if I knew Clara, we would be spending most of the night. She wasted no time in elbowing her way through the three-deep mass at the bar. I followed close behind her.

"Better double up on drinks," I shouted over the thumping bass.

"Six mojitos!" Clara yelled to the skinny-tat-covered sourpuss while holding up the right number of fingers in case she couldn't hear her over the racket.

I rested my chin on her shoulder. "I said, *double* up!"

She shrugged. "Fuck that! It's two for one, and I can't be arsed with queuing all night."

I rolled my eyes, knowing it was pointless to argue with Clara about anything to do with alcohol. We waited for what felt like an hour for our cocktails to be crushed, pulped and mixed then made our way upstairs, trying to balance the drinks between us.

"Genius idea to get six," I teased as half of one of my three sloshed down my front.

"Stop your whining and just drink it, you pussy! Or suck your shirt front!" She slurped up an entire drink through the straw in a matter of seconds.

"I wish you would stop calling me that. It's pretty vulgar, you know?"

Clara took a swig of her second mojito. "Well, you know what they say: if the cat fits?"

"Sorry, they say what now?" I wondered if I had misheard her through the heavy beats.

"If the cat fits, wear it. It's a saying, Rox." Her tone was obnoxious as ever.

My mouthful of mojito shot out my nose. Clara looked at me, clearly not getting it.

"Cap. It's cap," I managed, beginning to think that maybe, just maybe, having a night out wasn't such a bad idea after all. We offloaded the drinks on a table next to the dance floor where we could keep an eye on them and, without needing to wait for the alcohol to take effect, began to dance.

Given our occupation, it's no surprise that Clara and I both knew how to get down, admittedly Clara more so than me. That Chica moved like she left the womb swinging her hips, and there was no doubt about it, she was a showgirl through and through. It wasn't long before we built up a bit of an audience. Clara was rocking a black lace bodice trouser suit, which accentuated a killer cleavage. That, coupled with her lush dark hair, scorching Mediterranean looks and the whole Shakira arse thing, she was literally a lesbian's wet dream, and she knew it. Not to me, though, funnily enough. I had never thought about her in that way. To me, she was just Clar, my good mate.

Clara leaned closer to my ear. "Anyone that makes your minge twinge?" There was a naughty glint in her eye.

I blew out a breath on a snort of laughter and looked around halfheartedly. I recognised a handful of faces from around town. A group of rugby players, who I'd had a couple of fun nights with when I first moved to London, hung out in a booth. They were a cool bunch, up for a laugh, but after the fifth drinking game, usually became too rowdy for my liking. Two attractive women stood over by the bar, but the sour glare on their partners' faces pointing in our direction told me they were out of the question. I shrugged, I just wasn't that interested.

"C'mon, you're being picky, lower your standards a bit. There must be one?"

I rolled my eyes and did another scan, knowing that if I

didn't at least show willing, I would never hear the end of it. Again I scoped the dance floor, the bar, and even the booths, but no one caught my eye. To me, most of them looked like they had just passed their GCSE's and were out celebrating scraping a couple of C grades. Then, I caught the briefest glimpse of a familiar face engrossed in conversation with the DJ over the far side of the room. I did a double-take just to make sure I hadn't imagined it. Although I had only met her once, she was unmistakable.

"Shit, it's her." I moved to hide behind Clara.

"Who? What? Who?" Clara swivelled her head like in *The Exorcist*.

"Let's go downstairs." I dragged Clara over to our drinks and began gathering up glasses.

"What the hell? I like it up here." She continued to crane her neck in several directions at once. I ignored her, peering over my shoulder, making sure I hadn't been spotted and tugged her downstairs to the smaller dance floor.

"What the hell was that about? Who'd you see?" Clara was not willing to give it up.

"No one, just someone I met once. Forget it."

"Ahh yeah, I get it, didn't call her the next day?" There was more pride in her tone than there should have been. "She's over here! Roxanne Mackenzie's right here!" She stretched onto her tiptoes and pointed at me, finding herself hilarious.

Clara and I continued to dance, but I hadn't forgotten about the redhead's presence. Every once in a while, my eyes flitted around, almost of their own accord, like automatic radar. I knew why I ran when I saw her, but I couldn't quite figure out why, even after scarpering, a large part of me actually wanted her to still be there. I hadn't touched a drop of alcohol for at least six months, and after more mojitos, than I could count, I was beginning to remember why. The night was starting to tail off. The music had become that low late-night drone I generally associate with narcotics, and although a handful of people still danced, Clara included, most had petered out. My feet throbbed, even through the copious amount of alcohol consumed, and I knew I would be in pain the following day. Clara had persuaded me to squeeze my feet into her three-inch heel brown boots, and I decided to kill her for it later. That's if she ever stopped dancing.

I sat in a booth nursing the dregs of my final mojito and watched Clara lap up the attention of the older regulars. If they were men, I would have seen her mouth "save me," but because the attention came from women, she skipped the S.O.S and actively encouraged the mauling. She stretched her arms above her head as she moved her hips, pressing up against anyone within close proximity. Every once in a while, when she had her back to the women so they couldn't see, she would flick her tongue at me with wide eyes. Sexual politics and Clara have never been on speaking terms. I removed one of Clara's boots and massaged the part of my heel that hurt. Damn Clara.

"So, if I were to ask what a nice girl like you is doing in a place like this, would you cringe?" A familiar voice shouted in my ear above the music. I turned and took in the close-up image of Josie Calhoun standing above me. Christ! She had light makeup on, a touch of gloss on her lips and black eyeliner which made the impossibly deep brown of her eyes glisten. She wore a tan corduroy jacket, cinched at the waist, a tight mint-green top underneath, a vintage-looking scarf around her neck and skinny Levi's. She looked hot. It was official, Josie was hot.

I grinned. "Put it this way, a bit of vomit just found its way up to my tonsils." I cringed. "Sorry, that was gross. I have no idea why I just said that. It appears I've had one too many mojitos." I was slurring my words, suddenly feeling the effects of too much alcohol.

"I can see that." A smile tugged at the corners of her mouth.

I gestured for her to take a seat beside me, and she obliged.

Although I had avoided Josie earlier that evening, I had to admit, my stomach had done a small flip to see her.

"I was going to come over earlier and say "hi," but you looked like you were having fun with your girlfriend, so I didn't want to interrupt. Nice moves by the way." She sipped her white wine.

"Wait. What? Who Clara? No, she's just my housemate, thank god." I nodded towards Clara, who was now snogging the face off some woman who wore a suit jacket, a thin black tie and black cufflinks to match, looking a lot like a casino bouncer. Josie and I shared a laugh.

"Ah, I see. I guess I just thought because you dashed away when you saw me that–"

"You saw that?" I interrupted, my cheeks prickled from the heat. "Shit, I'm sorry, you must think I'm so rude. It's just, Clara doesn't know about my mum, and I was worried you would say that's how you know me, and it would open up a can of worms. Also, she's a nightmare when she's drunk, and will do anything she can to embarrass me. It's nothing personal."

Josie cocked her head and held my eyes for a second or maybe two. "So, I can keep my inferiority complex in check then?"

"Yeah, honestly, it's not you, it's me." I immediately scrunched my face at the line I'd just dropped.

Josie's expression was playful. "I think I'm feeling a little of that vomit myself."

I laughed. "Yeah, sorry, bad line. I haven't drunk like this in ages. I really am too wasted to have a grown-up conversation."

"And I'm guessing dancing's out of the question too?" She signalled at my feet.

For a fleeting moment, I considered it. It would have been nice to dance with her. To press against her body and feel her moving against me, her hands riding up my back and in my hair and…I shook my head.

"Honestly, I would love to, but my feet feel like they're on fire and I'm already going to pay for it the minute the alcohol wears off."

Josie shrugged. "Fair enough. I'm not sure if I would even know how to dance to this crap anyway. Is this really what they're calling music nowadays?"

"Nowadays?" I was amused by her choice of words.

She let out a small laugh. "I don't get out much."

"Well, Clara seems to be doing a pretty good job, in fact, I don't think she's ever going to want to leave." We both looked at Clara and found her still locking tongues and grinding against the poor bouncer woman who I suspected had no clue Clara was straight when sober. An ever so slightly awkward silence fell between us for a moment before Josie spoke.

"So, listen, in the interest of taking advantage of the universe having placed us together for the second time this week, I'm wondering if you would be up for grabbing something to eat sometime?" She swallowed hard as her deep brown eyes watched me expectantly.

I paused before answering, feeling my alcohol mind slip slightly out of focus. Numerous questions flashed through my mind in response to what she had asked. Was she asking me out? Like on a date? Why? Would I be good company? What would I wear? Did she always wear scarves? I held her gaze, taking her in.

"Can I ask you something?"

"Of course."

"How did you know I'm gay? Other than the fact I'm here at an all-girls night. It's just, people generally say they can't tell, but obviously, you can?"

She wrinkled her nose and closed one eye. "You're wearing a thumb ring. Studies have shown that nine out of ten women who wear a ring on their left thumb are attracted to the same sex."

I gazed down at my hands where I did indeed have a ring on my left thumb. I looked back up at Josie, scrunching a frown. "What and you could tell..." I began before I caught the shimmer of amusement in her dark brown eyes. Very dark brown, shimmery eyes.

"You're messing with me?" I was feeling like a tit for being so drunk and so off-guard, I would never have fallen for that if sober.

"Yes, I'm playing with you. You're right, you're not exactly transparent, and I wouldn't have known if I hadn't had a little heads-up from someone."

"Who?" I asked just as the obvious answer sprung to mind. "Ah, let me guess, my mum?"

Josie held up her thumb and finger, showing a small space between the two. "Maybe."

"Un-fucking-believable." I huffed, grabbed my drink and took a large swig through the straw.

"Are you mad?" Josie looked at me, curiously.

"At her? Yes. She tells everyone everything. Honestly, that woman knows no boundaries. I'm sure you've heard my bloody life story, and not once has she even mentioned that you read to her. I just find it weird, that's all."

Josie reached out and lightly touched her fingers to my knee. "Roxy, I haven't heard your life story, just little snippets, barely anything really. Go easy on her, she talks about you because she's proud of you."

I stared at the fingers that were still resting on my leg and let her words sink in.

"Right. Yeah, sorry. Perhaps you're right." She was right. But Mum happened to be a touchy subject for me, and it was probably best to avoid going there when drunk.

Josie cleared her throat. "So, erm, what do you say?"

I looked up in time to see her gently biting on her lower lip.

I took another pull on my straw, clearly too far gone to know I should stop.

"To what?"

She chuckled, and it was low and sexy. "You really are drunk, aren't you?"

I mirrored her action from earlier, showing a small space between my thumb and finger.

"What. Do. You. Say. To. Going. For. Something. To. Eat. Sometime?" She pronounced each word carefully in a playful but slightly mocking tone.

I nodded, getting lost in those smoky eyes. "I think that would be–"

I was about to say yes to the appealing offer. Of course, I would say yes. After scanning the club for most of the night, under Clara's strict instructions, it quickly became apparent that Josie played in a whole different league to any of the other clubbers. However, I didn't get to finish my sentence. Clara suddenly plonked herself on my lap, draping an arm around my neck.

"Roxanne Mackenzie, I love you, this place is the bollocks. Did you see my girlfriend?" She slurred her words, even more than me. She wobbled about on my lap before holding her hand out to Josie.

"Hola Chica. I'm Clara, the drunk friend. If you're taking my friend home, give her a good seeing to, god knows she needs it, but keep the noise down because I'll be just next door. Oh and don't expect a phone call the next day cos that's not how she rolls."

My head snapped back, sobering me almost immediately. What the fuck was that? I squeezed my fingers into Clara's sides, enough to make her screech and jump from my lap. Okay, so my history with women isn't exactly blemish-free, but firstly, Clara didn't know that; she had only been in my life for a matter of months, during which time I had remained entirely celibate. And secondly, she made me sound like a complete and utter arse which wasn't fair. I had always been upfront with the women I slept with.

"Thank you for that." I stood up quickly and whispered sharply into her ear through what I felt were gritted teeth. I turned to Josie, who was looking up with a slightly uneasy smile. Clara teetered about, and I gripped both her arms to steady her. I looked at Josie apologetically.

"Well, on that warm and fuzzy note, I think we should probably get going. I imagine I have about five minutes before this one chucks up all over me." It was a half-truth. Really, I was more concerned about the thought that any minute Clara could drop another bomb which would cover me in an even worse shade of shit, if that were possible. I don't know why it bothered me so much, but I cared what Josie might think of me.

Josie got up and helped hoist Clara's arm over my shoulder. If she was deterred by what Clara had just said, she was hiding it well.

"It was good to see you again." Her smile was warm and showed off those damn dimples again.

I reciprocated her smile and let out a small but audible sigh of disappointment.

"Yeah, you too." And it really had. "I'll see you around?" I took my first step with Clara hanging off me.

Josie nodded slowly. "It certainly looks that way."

CHAPTER 3

I WOKE EARLY THE NEXT day with my head throbbing like Conor McGregor had used my brain as a punchbag. Any small movement sent a sudden reminder of the stupidly too many mojitos the night before. As predicted, a blister the size of a fifty pence piece had formed on my heel, and the skin had stuck to the bedsheet. I winced from the sting as I peeled my foot away. The room was light. Way too light. Even diffused by the wooden blinds, the strength of the sun bounced off every wall. I turned over and groaned as my face met the kitchen bucket, which I had a vague memory of taking to bed with me the night before – just in case. I peered in and sighed in relief to see it empty. I tentatively lowered my head to the pillow again, afraid to get out of bed in case the toxins swishing around in my stomach made their way up and out. I cursed myself for drinking as much as I had. There was a reason I had avoided getting wasted all this time, and this was it. My skin was clammy from sweating it all out in the night. My mouth tasted like I had gargled paraffin and my head…my god, my head. It was official, I was hanging out of my arse, and I only had myself to blame.

After at least twenty minutes of swearing an oath I would never drink again while the threatening gurgling noise in my belly sounded off, Clara burst into my room and slumped beside me. The force of her collapsed body shook the mattress, and it amplified the acidic internal swishing I had been trying to avoid.

"Eurgh," was about all I could muster out of my clacky mouth.

Clara buried her head in my pillow. "I vommed in the Uber, didn't I?" Her voice was muffled and thank god it muffled her breath too.

"Yup."

"And I snogged the face off someone, didn't I?"

"Yup."

"Was she wearing an actual suit?"

"Yup." The side of my mouth curled upward, against my will.

"And did I screw up your chances of getting laid?'

I spun round to face her, instantly regretting it. "Who? Josie?"

"Yeah, whatever her name is. The redhead in the scarf drooling over you."

I narrowed my eyes. "No, she's just a friend. In fact, I barely know her. I've only met her once. She wasn't drooling anyway. What makes you think she was drooling?"

Clara lifted the pillow from her face, she was smirking.

"What? She wasn't drooling." Maybe I protested a little too much.

Clara replaced the pillow, but I heard her clearly. "Yeah, if you say so, Mackenzie."

I thought back to the night before and was pretty sure Josie hadn't drooled. She *had* asked me out on a date though and, I had to admit, once I paid the £60 fine to the Uber driver for Clara chucking up all over his back seat, tucked her into bed, and snuggled into my own, Josie's face *had* been the last thing I pictured before dropping off.

"I didn't mean to be a dick," Clara said through the pillow.

I laid my arm across my face, covering my eyes and exhaled, "You never do."

"Seriously Rox, it's just..." She was silent for a moment. "Ah, fuck it, it doesn't matter. Am I working tonight?"

I couldn't be bothered to press her on whatever excuse she was about to give. I knew what she was like and didn't need her pitiful explanations.

"Uh-huh, we both are, so we need to get our shit together. And that's going to start with breakfast." I rolled off the bed, changed out of last night's clothes into ripped jeans and a vest top and slogged to the kitchen. We needed to eat something if we stood any chance of getting through the day. I opened the fridge, still straining to keep my eyelids from opening too much and peered through the slits. Half a pint of skimmed milk, two tomatoes, half an avocado – which looked about three weeks past eat-by – and a cheesecake. Hardly a recipe for breakfast, or brunch as it had become. I closed the door and set the coffee machine going. While I waited for the milk to heat, I trudged into the bathroom and rustled my hair into a bun, while groaning at my reflection. I scrabbled a face wipe out of the package and began the sad task of removing last night's mascara which had found its way to literally everywhere but my eyes. The elimination of the make-up made me look a lot worse, revealing dark under-eye bags and blotchy cheeks. The sight made me glad it was summer so I could hide behind my Ray-Bans. Once semi-ready to leave the house, I poured Clara a coffee – a strong coffee – grabbed my denim jacket and shades and set off en route to Manney's.

MANNEY'S IS A SMALL DINER JUST five streets down from our place, and serves the best pancakes in the whole of south east London, or so it says on TripAdvisor anyway. Because we lived just off Finchley Drive, I had to cross the market to reach it. Greenwich Market has been going forever and pulls in about seventeen million visitors a year. Summer weekends – like this one – made it feel like all seventeen million had arrived at once. Walking through bumbling herds of people was not exactly at the top of my list of favourite things to do, and especially when I both felt and looked like crap, and the temperature had already soared to about twenty-eight degrees. I wiped at an itchy trickle of sweat on my forehead. Although clearly t-shirt weather, I hitched the hood of my jean jacket over my head, hoping to make myself inconspicuous to the market-goers. Which just showed how hungover I was because, of course, I looked like a yeti among the t-shirts and shorts. The nausea that had gripped me earlier still lingered and the scents from the food stalls didn't help. A conglomeration of Indian, Chinese and vegan paté whiffs put my gag reflex to the test. I held my sleeve over my nose and mouth and dodged my way between the stalls.

By the time I reached Manney's, the queue was outside the door. Most of the people in it mirrored how I felt: a younger crowd who'd been out the night before, looking to nurse their hangovers with pancakes and a strong latte. No way was I waiting in that queue, and fortunately, I didn't have to: I knew the chef. I snuck around the back and unsurprisingly found Cayden leaning against a wheelie bin, taking a drag on his – wait, was that a vape pen. In all the time I had known Cayden, he had smoked twenty-a-day and carried a bit of extra weight. He wasn't huge but could have been described as a little bit podgy. Yet as I stood there looking at him, even through his chef clothes, it was clear he had shifted the podge. His jawline, something I'm not sure I had seen before, looked chiselled and shaven and his hair was cropped short on both sides. He looked good. Really good. I cleared my throat to get his attention. Cayden looked startled at first before recognition took over.

"No way! Roxanne Mackenzie rears her gorgeous head." He held his arms out for a hug.

"Shush, not so loud." I was still sensitive to any sound louder than a whisper. I fell into Cayden's arms and let him cuddle me.

Cayden Lawrence was one of the first people I had got to know when I made the move from Essex to London. After starting a job at an independent bookshop in Camden, where Cayden had already worked for two years, we soon discovered we had heaps in common, including our love of writing. Our friendship had formed effortlessly and it wasn't long before we became each other's writing buddy, meeting up every week to critique our latest work. He took me out and introduced me to people on the gay scene and helped make my transition from nowhere to somewhere easier than I could ever have imagined. We were both heavily into our writing and hyped each other with the possibility that we would be the next big thing, encouraging each other and cheering us on. When the shop owners, Cath and Bob, had to sell up because they could no longer compete with Amazon, Cayden and I continued to see each other to go through each other's writing, but it had become less frequent. By the time Mum's condition worsened, our meet-ups had dwindled almost to none. We hadn't seen each other since my birthday in November, but I still considered him one of my best friends.

"Rox, it's been too long, girl." Cayden continued to squeeze the life out of me. I managed to peel him off and took a step back so I could appraise him properly. I lifted my shades and squinted into the brightness of the midday sun. "Cayd, you look insane. What are with these guns?" I pinched at his bulging bicep.

Cayden beamed, flashing his almost luminous teeth. "Ah, Rox. I've been meaning to catch up with you for months now, it's been crazy. So much has changed."

"You've met someone?" I guessed from the grin that was literally taking up half his face. Cayden nodded excitedly, and I picked up on the slight flush of his cheeks.

"Cayden Lawrence, are you blushing? Shit. You're in love, aren't you? Tell me everything."

He leaned in close again. "Okay, well, I've got to be quick because we're manic, but his name's Dean, and he's a personal trainer down at Healthkick, hence the new me, and my God, Rox…" He blew out his cheeks, unable to find the words to describe this Dean of his.

"We met at Christmas in the West End, and it's still early days, but honestly Rox, I think he's the one." Cayden's face lit up as he spoke. It was really quite special, I had never seen him looking this good or this happy. "You haven't heard the best part." He clasped his hands together.

"There's more?" Despite lingering nausea, I found his excitement infectious.

"I wasn't going to say anything until it was all in print and I had the proof in my hands because I still can't believe it's happening, and I don't want to jinx anything, but remember the book I was working on just before Cath and Bob sold up? *Pink Ribbons*?"

"Yes." I drew out the word as my stomach did a peculiar somersault.

"Well, Mainline Books have only offered me a publishing deal. It's going to be released next month. It's been a quick turn-around because they wanted it released before national pride day and…"

Cayden continued to talk, but his words became background noise to the squawk of my own thoughts and the raging pulse in my ears. It wasn't that I wasn't happy for Cayden. As one of my best friends, of course, I wanted him to be successful. He worked hard and put his all into his writing, and unlike me, didn't quit when the going got tough. But none of this stopped the overwhelming current of jealousy slithering its way through me. That was my dream. I was supposed to be the one with the published book and I –

"Hey, Rox, you still with me?" Hearing my name snapped me out of my wandering, to my good friend sharing his incredible news.

"Oh my God, Cayd that's amazing. I'm so happy for you." I drew him into my arms and hoped if he couldn't see me, he would remain oblivious to the loser-at-the-Oscars smile that was making my face feel like it was about to crack and crumble. Just as our embrace came to a natural end, one of Cayden's colleagues shouted out that they needed his help with a sticking dishwasher.

"Cayd, can you grab two lots of pancakes and syrup, please?" I asked apologetically before he dashed into the cafe kitchen. He thumbs-upped and disappeared.

I waited outside, propping against the same bin Cayden had been leaning on, and five minutes later, he came out with two polystyrene trays and handed them over.

"On the house. Listen, I've got to scoot, it's a shitstorm in there, but I'm having a launch party to celebrate once the book's out, and you have to be there. I'll text you details nearer the time. Feel free to bring whoever you like." He rushed his words out, looking at the door behind him.

"Great, I'll look forward to it, and thanks for these." I held up the trays. Cayden gave me a quick kiss on the cheek and hurried back to the sounds of crashing pots and panicky voices. When he was out of sight, I slumped against the wall, and the smile slid down my face and disappeared. I wanted to be happy for him. I really did. My mind drifted to one of my favourite memories of Cayden. We were at the back of Beans, a small privately-owned whimsical tea shop where none of the furniture matched and cross-stitched pictures decorated every wall. Cayden had just finished reading a letter I received from *Litro* magazine, and I was staring at him eagerly for his response.

"Oh my god! Rox, this is amazing! They're printing it. They're actually printing your work." There was nothing disingenuous about his excitement.

"Isn't it? I nearly pissed my pants when it came through. I've been dying to tell you all morning."

"Well, this deserves a celebration. Wait here." Cayden made his way to the cake stand while I sat grinning from ear to ear. Okay, so, it wasn't getting a novel published, but it was an acceptance letter for a three-thousand-word short story about a family who woke one morning to find all electricity across the earth had been cut. It was a piece highlighting the powerful effect the breakdown of interconnectivity had on the family relationship. Cayden had been the one to convince me to send it off and I was so glad I listened because that acceptance letter was the first bit of validation I'd had in a long time that my writing was actually any good. Cayden had returned to the table carrying not just a slice of cake but an entire carrot cake with a small candle sticking out the top. He proceeded to sing at the top of his lungs "Congratulations to you" to the tune of *Happy Birthday*, until the café owner and a few customers joined in. I sighed, bringing myself back to the present. It was the sweetest thing, the way Cayden had been able to celebrate my success as his own. It was one of the things I loved most about him. He would get so worked up every time he read my writing, and he believed in me more than anyone I knew. So, I struggled to understand why, in all his happiness and reasons to celebrate, all I wanted to do was curl up in a ball and cry.

I tried to blame the hangover, that the lack of serotonin to my brain had put me on a downer, but beneath it all, I knew the truth. I felt sorry for myself. It was that simple. Hearing

Cayden's good news served up a reminder of how little I had achieved. I scoffed as I made the comparison between those early days at the café and now. What was I doing? Sleeping for most of the day, getting myself ready to visit Mum and going off to a job where I stripped naked for a room full of desperate pervs because I was too proud to accept help from my siblings to pay for Mum's care. Yay! Go me! I shuddered at the thought of who I had become.

"Pull it together, Rox," I told myself, shaking out from the pity-party. I knew I had to change my train of thought. I couldn't take this moment away from Cayden and sincerely hoped by the time his celebration came around, I would be grown up enough to stop being so jealous and manage to be happy for my friend. And he *was* my friend, and it *had* been great to see him again.

WHEN I ARRIVED HOME, I found Clara still sprawled on the bed with the pillow draped over her face. The room smelled like stale alcohol.

"Here." I plonked the pancake box on her belly and cracked open the blinds, which let in fierce light before opening the window. Clara groaned and hauled the pillow from her face. Wow, If I thought I felt rough, seeing Clara made me realise it could be a whole lot worse.

"Dude, what the fuck?" She dragged herself up the bed and stared at the pancake box through squinted eyes. I sat beside her and handed her a fork.

"You're too old to be using the word "dude", that's what the fuck." I opened my polystyrene box and made a start on my own brunch. Clara peered under the lid of her box and stabbed at the pancake like it had done something to hurt her.

"Was Cayden there?" she asked through a yawn.

Although Clara hadn't met Cayden, I had talked about him a lot. I couldn't let Clara in on my shock at how much he had changed because it would have given me away. As far as she was concerned, I saw him daily.

"Uh-huh. He's just been told he's got a publishing deal." My voice seemed an octave or two higher than I meant.

"Cool." Clara's reply came through a mouthful of pancake. "When are you gonna get yourself one of those? You've been beavering away on that book since I've known you."

"Don't say beaver," I deadpanned, ignoring the lie.

Clara's fork stopped before it reached her mouth. "What?"

"Beaver, don't say it."

Clara frowned.

"You don't know what a beaver is?" I felt confident that I had steered the conversation onto much lighter ground.

Clara rolled her eyes. "Yes, of course, I know what a beaver is. I just wouldn't have thought *you* of all people would have a problem with that word."

"It reminds me of old lady minge."

Clara snorted, trying not to lose her pancake. "And you call me graphic?"

"Just saying. Anyway, Cayden's having a party to celebrate and said I can bring whoever I want. Wanna come?" I closed the pancake box, unable to face the last few mouthfuls and slid it under the bed.

"Tonight? No way. I would rather have thirsty hens peck the tears from my eyes than even think about drinking."

I shook my head, bewildered at the things she came out with.

"Not tonight, you muppet. Once his book's released."

Clara shrugged, nonchalantly, "I'll come." After finishing her food and whining some more about having to go to work tonight, Clara fell back to sleep, leaving me mulling everything over. I wondered whether, if Mum hadn't become ill, it would have been me with the publishing deal, throwing a party to celebrate *my* success. Was I really going to let it all just slip away? Could I live with myself if I did? If I really listened to my heart, I could hear it telling me in a gentle and loving tone to follow my childhood dream of getting a degree and becoming the best writer I could be. It was pointing me towards writing. It always had. As I fell back to sleep, I drifted off to the thought: Cayden and I could both follow our dreams, couldn't we? It's not too late, is it?

CHAPTER 4

I PULLED MY FIESTA INTO the monstrous driveway, parked between a shiny new BMW and a Jag and turned the ignition key to off. The twenty-five-minute drive from Greenwich to Chislehurst was horrible. I left it late enough in the day so I wasn't over the limit, but I still felt all kinds of fragile. I rested my head on the steering wheel and took in the peacefulness of the grounds. The only sound was the occasional calling of a wood pigeon. It felt nice just to sit like that for a while. I needed a moment before going in. Visiting Mum was difficult at the best of times and having a hangover was bound to make it more of a challenge than usual to keep my shit together. Once I had regained my equilibrium, I dragged my feet to Reception to sign in. Milly sat at the front desk, confirming her excellent casting for a place like that. No matter how low I felt, something about her round rosy cheeks and chirpy disposition made me smile, even against my will.

Without even looking up from her phone, as though she had familiarised herself with the sound of each visitor's footsteps, she practically sang the words, "Hey, Roxanne, good to see you, girl. Josie Calhoun asked about you earlier, you're a little later than usual, but I told her you would be here. I've not known you to miss a day yet." She was so engrossed in her phone, watching yesterday's episode of *Corrie,* she missed the grimace.

"No worries." I scribbled my name in the guest-book before checking to see if Josie had signed out yet. She hadn't. Eurgh. I said my goodbyes to Milly and sped, as fast as my hangover would allow, down the corridor. I looked like crap and really didn't need Josie seeing that. I arrived at Mum's door and could hear the faint sound of voices from her room. I recognised the second voice as Josie's. I paused so I could listen in.

"...he may be clearing you out, for some new delight. The dark thought, the shame, the malice, meet them at the door laughing and invite them in. Be grateful for whoever comes, because each has been sent as a guide from beyond."

I leaned my forehead against the cool wall and really thought about the words and their implications. They were beautiful. Had Josie written that?

"Is it that Rumi fella again?" Mum asked after a moment of silence.

"Who else?" Josie answered as the book snapped shut.

"He's alright, he is. I'm not gonna pretend to understand most of it, but I like what he says about the souls and that, gives me hope, you know?"

Josie's seat creaked as she got up from it. "And what a beautiful soul you have too. Now you get some rest, and I'll be in over the next few days, there's still plenty I haven't read to you yet."

Josie's footsteps came closer and I took a few steps back, attempting to make it look as though I had just arrived at the door. She walked out and came to an abrupt halt. Her eyebrow shot up, letting me know I hadn't quite pulled it off.

"You believe in all that?" I didn't bother to deny I had been listening.

She leaned her shoulder against the wall and met my eyes.

Unlike me, Josie looked good. She wore a high-waisted pair of striped trousers, a low-cut navy top and of course, a scarf. A cream scarf with owls stitched into the fabric. She was fresh-faced, and I could just make out a spatter of freckles across her nose and cheeks from where she had caught the sun. They suited her, I thought.

"Well, I think it's important to have faith in something at a time like this. There's a lot of research to show that it has exceptional healing qualities when a terminal patient finds faith and develops a belief that there's something better waiting."

I hesitated, digesting her words. "But, do *you* believe in all that?"

She dropped her head to one side and shrugged. "I know what I know through my own experience. If we say we believe in this religion or that god, I think it limits us. I guess I would say that it's better to just say 'I don't know.' it leaves it open to all the possibilities, but if you're asking if I think there's something more, then yeah, I would have to say yes."

Silence fell between us as I attempted to unscramble what she had said, but it was pointless, my hungover brain was unable to follow. "Wow, that's some profound shit right there." It was lame but it's all I had.

Josie beamed, "I have my moments."

I nodded at the book in her hand. "Well, whatever it is, she seems to be going for it."

"Your mum?"

"Yeah, not exactly the religious type."

"Oh, I don't know, she might just surprise you. You'd be amazed at how open she is to some of the spiritual teachings. Granted, sometimes she gives me a hard time, hiding behind her humour. The other day she told me she thought Jesus would be a good lay because he worked as a carpenter so he must be good with his hands." We laughed. "But for the most part, she seems to be engaged."

Josie's use of the word "engaged" jogged my memory that she worked as a lecturer. "I never did ask you what it is you teach."

"Oh, I'm a psychologist."

"*You're* a psychologist? *You*?" I didn't try to hide my surprise. She just looked so different from how I would expect a psychologist to look. So far removed from my stereotyped idea of a man in his fifties wearing tweed and stroking a beard.

Josie's eyebrow rose. "I'm a psychologist, not an alien."

"Just as intimidating if you ask me."

"You're intimidated by me?" Amusement danced in her eyes.

"I don't know, by your profession, maybe a little. No one likes the thought of every word they say being analysed." It was an honest answer.

"You think I'm analysing you right now?" She dropped her tone.

I lifted my shoulders and let them fall. "Maybe."

Josie leaned towards me a little and furrowed her brow, a concerned look on her face. "And let me ask you, Roxy, how does that make you feel?"

A moment or two passed before she grinned, and I got the joke.

"Sorry, I'm being an idiot, aren't I?" I scrunched my nose.

Josie smiled. "No, it's fine, I get it a lot. You wouldn't believe the crap my friends gave me about it once I qualified. I guess, if I'm honest, I do analyse, but don't we all? I'm just able to put my analysis into a box and call it something, that's the only difference."

I pursed my lips and nodded; she had a fair point.

"So, genuinely, how *are* you feeling today? You seemed pretty much the worse for wear last night."

"Yeah, well, I'd say that I feel about as well as I look."

Josie looked me up and down, lingering for the briefest of

moments on the dip of my chest. "Pretty good, then?" She rested her tongue on her top teeth.

I bit the inside of my cheek to sit on the grin that wanted to take over my face and dropped my eyes to the floor, having no clue how to even respond to that.

"And your friend?' The amusement in her tone remained.

I shook off my visceral reaction to her previous compliment in time to roll my eyes and answer.

"Clara? Well, let me see, after throwing up in the Uber on the way home and throwing up once she got in, I'm going to say, she's not the best."

"Oh, no. That bad?" Josie laughed and the sound it made, coupled with the way her eyes lit up, set off little sparks inside me. I tugged on my sleeves, geeing up for what I knew I was going to say next. I took in a breath.

"Listen, Josie, I'm sorry about last night, Clara was such an arse. She drinks way too much, gets out of control, and half the time doesn't know what she's babbling on about."

Josie shrugged, still smiling. "It's fine, honestly. We've all been there."

I rocked back and forth on my heels and plunged on.

"Well, I want you to know that what she said about me, it wasn't true, you know. Not anymore anyway, well not even before really, I never did the things she said I did, well not intentionally..." My god, was I babbling. I couldn't have screwed it up much more, but something about Josie not only made me feel I owed her an explanation but shit, I was nervous.

"Roxy, it's fine. As I said last night, it would be nice to make up my own mind about you. Not from your mum or your friends but from you." She looked at me, expectantly.

I nodded, holding her gaze, and she continued. "Look, I don't know if you remember, but we didn't exactly get to finish our conversation last night."

"I do remember, you asked me if I wanted to go for something to eat with you. Before we were interrupted by Clara."

"I did." She bit the inside of her cheek, showing a glimpse of something that resembled nerves. "And do you?"

I knew there were many reasons why going out together would not be the best idea and, for a split second, I let them all present themselves. But – and it was a big but – the intrigue Josie evoked in me, coupled with the obvious attraction I felt for her, had seeped through the pores of my skin, which didn't happen often, and frankly, I felt a little reckless.

"Yeah, I think I do. What do you have in mind?" My heart was racing as the words left my lips.

"You live in Greenwich, right?"

"Uh-huh." I wondered again precisely how much Mum had told this woman about me.

"Well, that's only twenty minutes on the tube from me. We could meet there if you know of a nice place?"

"Ciao Bella's good if you like Italian?"

She looked pleased. "Great. Say, Friday at seven?"

"I'll look forward to it." My nausea from earlier was suddenly replaced by excitement.

Josie grinned. "And maybe while we're there, you can tell me why your acceptance to our date had the word "think" in it."

I frowned and thought back, unable to even remember having said the word. It appeared as though the analysing had begun. We exchanged numbers, and before I knew it, and just like that, I was watching my date for Friday night saunter off down the corridor. And I knew, in that moment, I was in trouble.

THE SUN THROUGH THE BLINDS OF MUM'S room bounced off the walls and made me squint. I pulled the shutters closed just enough so I could see without having to put the Ray-Bans back on and settled my attention on Mum. In comparison to the previous day, she looked terrible. It seemed to go like that. One day she had strength in her and the next she looked beaten. Today was one of those days. Her complexion was as pale as I had seen it, the red rims around her eyes told the sad story of sleep deprivation, and instead of wrapping around her head, her headscarf was on the bedside table.

"About bloody time." Were the first words to leave her mouth as I leaned in to kiss her. "More interested in chatting up the staff than seeing you ol' mum are ya?" A wicked grin lit her face. She had been listening. *Of course,* she had been listening. I pecked her on the forehead and took a seat.

"Firstly, I was not chatting her up, and secondly, she's not staff. She volunteers her time here for free as you well know."

"Yeah, bloody loon," Mum mumbled under her breath.

I sighed and narrowed my eyes affectionately. "Mum, I know you don't think she's a loon. You're not the only one in the family who can eavesdrop. I know you like the things she reads to you, and you enjoy her company; otherwise, you would have told her to bugger off a long time ago."

"Fine, fine, you got me. I like the girl, she makes me feel better." She attempted to turn onto her side but struggled. I reached over the bed to help manoeuvre her, and she sucked in a sharp breath.

"Mum? You okay?" I watched a grimace take hold of her face.

"Will be, once I'm put out of my bloody misery."

I rolled my eyes. I hated it when she said things like that. To be fair to Mum, this kind of attitude wasn't something that came about with her illness. Mum had said things like that before her terminal diagnosis. She had never liked life too much, my mum. She was a bit of a tearaway in her younger days and as a result, fell into toxic relationships. She just seemed to ping from one shitstorm to another and never quite caught a break. She suffered from depression most of her life, and during a breakdown in the late '90s, she tried to commit suicide. She popped a tub of pills then panicked and called the ambulance. She told me and my younger siblings she couldn't go through with it because of us kids. I guess she never gave much thought to how bad we would all feel for her continuing to live out a miserable existence.

"So, you like Josie, then?" I asked, changing the subject.

Mum's eyes widened. "So, *you* like Josie then?"

I rolled my eyes for the second time in the space of two minutes. "Can you just stop!" I adjusted my tone. "Anyway, why didn't you tell me about her? She seems to know the ins and outs of a duck's arse about me, and you've never once mentioned her, not once."

Mum's shoulders slumped, and her eyes darted around the room to anywhere but me.

"Mum? What is it you're not telling me?" I was acutely aware there was something going on. She looked at the ceiling, I think to debate how much to give away and sighed.

"It's not my place to say, Roxanne. All I can tell you is that she's a good girl, but she's fragile…I just don't know if she could. I'm not sure that you two are a good idea that's all."

I frowned and felt confused. Not only by Mum's newfound ability to not share but because the woman she'd just described – that fragile "good girl" – was the confident, self-assured woman I had been privy to just minutes before.

"Mum, what the hell are you going on about? Why would we not be a good idea?" My tone was in direct proportion to the frustration that was building in my long-suffering gut.

Mum snuggled her head into her pillow. "I'm tired, I should probably get some rest, okay love?"

"No way! You're not using that one. What have you got against me getting involved with Josie?" I knew damn well she was trying to avoid talking about it and I was also aware I had just let on I *was* interested in Josie. She closed her eyes, pretending to snooze.

"Mum!"

She opened her eyes. "Ah, fine." She huffed like a petulant teenager. "Like I said, she's fragile. I don't like to gossip, so I'm not going to tell you why, that's up to her, but I know you, darlin', I've seen your track record, and no one gets out of a relationship with you unscathed. I would hate to see that happen to her, and I would hate to see what it would do to you to do that to her. I just think you should spare her, that's all."

I drew a deep breath, unable to do anything else but blink repeatedly. It wasn't unusual for Mum to be an arse. She could tear people down in a split second with her sharp tongue and total disregard for feelings. The number of blazing rows we'd had in the past over her lack of filter was in the dozens, but the more her health deteriorated, the harder I found it to challenge her. If our final words to each other were born from an argument, I would never forgive myself. I swallowed, trying to ignore the rate at which my heart banged in my chest.

"Let me get this straight. You're not wanting me to get involved with Josie because you think I'm going to hurt her?"

Mum shrugged. "She's a really good girl, Roxy."

"Yes, you've said that Mum! But I think what you're actually trying to say is that she's too good for me?" My jaw clenched as I fought back my deeper reaction to the sting of her words. She tentatively reached out her hand and placed it on my arm. Her expression softening.

"Now, that's not what I'm saying. No one is too good for you kiddo. You're incredible, and I'm so proud of how you've turned out. God knows I can't take credit for that. Growing up not knowing your dad and having to deal with the arseholes I brought into your life would be enough to make a shitbag out of anyone. But not you. You're good. But I've seen what you do, you don't believe you're good enough, so you sabotage everything that threatens to make you happy. I see this in you because I see it in me, it's my trait that I've passed on, and I'm so sorry I've done that. I guess I just don't want that sweet girl, who's been through so much, to become a victim of it."

Uninvited tears welled in my eyes, and I swallowed the lump in my throat.

"You mean you don't want her to fall victim to *me*? Like I'm some monster who just roams around breaking people's hearts. Great, thanks, Mum, I'm glad I know how you really feel about me." I ran my fingers through my hair, thinking that today of all days I didn't need this. Mum's grip on my arm tightened, she was using all of the very little strength she had. I left it there, even in my anger, I couldn't bear the thought of pulling away from her.

"Listen to me. I'm not saying you're a monster, darlin'. I'm just saying unless you can be sure you're not going to do the same to her as what you've done to the others, you should leave well alone."

I rubbed at my eyes with my free hand, not knowing what I could even say to that. And Mum continued, "You know, I don't know if I ever told you this, but you were born during one of the worst storms ever. The streets were flooded, trees blocked the roads, and the thunder was so loud that every time it roared I jumped so hard I thought you would pop out of me and shoot across the room." She paused for me to laugh, but I didn't laugh like I had whenever she told me that story before.

"Yes, you've told me this a hundred times." I was losing patience.

"Shush, I haven't finished yet. I was exhausted, it took the ambulance three hours to get out to me, and I was all alone. I ended up being in labour for seven hours, seven! I was so scared. I didn't know if I was coming or going. Then you gave in and decided to arrive, and I gave birth to you. You were the tiniest little thing I had ever seen and just perfect, but I couldn't hold you for long because I couldn't keep my eyes open."

I sat back and folded my arms over my chest while she continued.

"At six in the morning after a bit of sleep, I woke, and there you were, my beautiful baby girl. No one can explain in words what it feels like to stare into the eyes of a little person that has been living inside your belly for nine months. As I lay there looking at you in amazement, you reached out your tiny arm to me and..." Mum's words caught in her throat, causing her to cough. I held her water glass up to her mouth so she could take a sip.

"I knew at that moment that's what I'd come here on this earth to do. To give birth to this amazing little person. I tried to do my best for you and your brother and sister, even though most of the time it was me reaching out for you, wasn't it? I made you grow up too fast, and you had to be so strong, too strong. Your sister's different, she met Jake so young that he was able to steer her in the best direction before she was too damaged. But you didn't have that luxury, and I worry you're shut off from getting close to someone because of your fear of getting hurt. You're too scared to reach out like you did when you were that tiny little baby, in case there's no one there to take your hand."

I rested my face in my hands as tears threatened to spill over. I closed my eyes in the hope it might stifle them, but they were stubborn, they leaked out slowly and slid down both my cheeks.

"Oh, come here." Mum used all her strength to draw me into her. I let her grip me close where, for the first time in as long as

I could remember, she was comforting me. Her words had broken through. She was right. I was closed off. I did have to be the strong one growing up, and I guess a by-product of being strong was that I had shut myself off and avoided being in any situation where I could get hurt. What this meant for Josie and me, though, I was yet to find out.

CHAPTER 5

"YOU LOOK LIKE ABSOLUTE HORSE shit!" Were Clara's first words as I arrived back at the flat. "You can't go to work like that, the guys will be paying to get you off the stage."

I slumped next to her on the sofa and moaned. "I know, I'm not going, Stace said she would cover."

Clara paused whatever reality crap she had been watching and spun to face me. The fact that she had slept the entire day had worked wonders. She'd taken a shower, freshened up and put her face on, and aside from still wearing her PJs, she looked like her pristine self again.

"Oh, okay, bitch, take me out, get me wasted and leave me to take the shift without you. Nice." Her eyes widened, looking for an explanation.

I sighed. "Firstly, you took *me* out and got *me* drunk, remember? And secondly, just shush." My head still pounded, even more so since seeing Mum. I rubbed at both temples, hoping to ease some of the tension. Clara stood up, making a deliberate huffing sound and stomped into the bathroom as I continued to sit there, staring at the ceiling, seeing what pictures I could make out of the swirls in the Artex. I couldn't seem to shake

Josie from my mind. What did Mum mean by her being fragile? What had happened to her? Was Mum just being dramatic? Should I take Mum's advice and just not go there? I knew there were more questions than answers, but really, none of it mattered because when Josie's face entered my mind, the frisson of feelings won out.

My thoughts were interrupted by Clara's re-appearance. She entered the room wearing a pair of tight black jeans with slits in the knees, a black low-cut, lingerie-looking-top with a glitzy silver belt, and heels at least three inches high. I eyed her suspiciously. Why had she made such an effort just to go to work? We would usually wear old joggers, a hoody and sometimes even a cap because we liked to arrive incognito before we got ready at the club. Her choice of clothing rang alarm bells.

"So, you get to mope around here all night feeling sorry for yourself, and I'll go and make the rent." She sat beside me. I ignored her jibe. She knew damn well we split the rent regardless of who went to work. She looked at me, her eyes softening.

"You okay, Rox?"

I squinted, wondering about the imposter who checked on my wellbeing with that level of sincerity. Definitely a side of Clara that hadn't reared its head before.

"You getting all soppy on me?" I threw a cushion at her.

She threw it back at me with extra vigour. "Oh, forget it. I don't even know why I bother." She shot up from the sofa. "You want a drink, fuckface?"

And there it was, balance had been restored in the universe, Clara had slipped quickly and effortlessly back to her usual gutter-mouthed self.

"I literally could not think of anything worse," I moaned. "Surely, you're not drinking? What happened to rather having thirsty hens and all that?"

She strutted to the kitchen, ignoring my comment and poured herself a neat Scotch.

I watched her through the serving hatch. "Are *you* okay?" I looked pointedly at the drink in her hand.

"Yup." She necked the drink in one.

"No, seriously, what's up?" Her tone was definitely frostier than usual.

"If you're not sharing, I'm not either." Her eyes widened as she waited for me to speak. I hesitated for a moment, thinking that maybe I should just come clean and tell her everything that had been going on. It would be easier, but I just wanted to hold on to the little pocket of normality I had in my life that didn't revolve around the pain of losing my mum. I closed my eyes.

"I've nothing to share."

"Well, then neither have I." Clara slammed the empty glass down on the counter, grabbed her handbag and yanked it over her shoulder. "Laters Rox, don't wait up." Her tone froze the lightbulbs.

I let out a loud sigh as the door banged shut. Could this day get any worse?

~

"FUCK, FUCK, FUCKETY, FUCK." I bent over the sofa, wincing as the stabbing pain shot through my foot. My baby toe felt as though it had been squeezed in a vice. Without a doubt, there is nothing worse in the entire universe than stubbing your baby toe. Friday night had appeared from nowhere, and I flew around the place in a way that suggested I had thirty seconds until I had to be at the restaurant. In reality, it had just turned five o'clock, and we had arranged to meet at seven.

I had changed my clothes three times, each time ripping them off and discarding them into what was fast becoming a heap. Everything came across as either too casual, too dressy or too 'I'm trying not to be too dressy or too casual'. I styled my hair up, down, wavy, then straight. Each time I changed my clothes or hair, I wondered what Josie might think it said about me. I still wasn't sure how I felt about a date with a psychologist. I had strewn clothing all over the place as I couldn't seem to find anything I looked for – definitely Clara's fault. She gave herself permission to wear anything of mine she wanted and never bothered to return a single thing. I had hit my head twice on my bedroom shelf and tripped over a pair of Clara's shoes because she doesn't understand the concept of tidying up after herself, and now the stubbed toe. I was beginning to think that the universe was siding with my mum on this one. I knew Mum's words had affected me and had put pressure on the evening. Because of them, I *had* considered cancelling. I even picked up my phone to text Josie, I had planned some bullshit story about being called in to work, but I just couldn't do it. I knew I should, but sometimes the right thing to do goes against what the mind and body cry out for, and for whatever reason, everything told me to go.

I settled on a pair of tight jeans and low-cut olive-green top which I accentuated with a silver mid-waist belt. I wore my hair up, in the same style quiff Clara had sported the previous Saturday at the Lounge, and after much deliberation in the mirror, I decided that I just about passed.

Ciao Bella was only a ten-minute walk from my flat so I took a slow stroll there, appreciating the warmth of the evening. Greenwich had a certain buzz about it on a Friday night, different from other nights of the week. I walked past a group of young lads with their arms slung around each other's shoulders wailing a song I'd never heard but suspected had something to do with football. They were followed by a similar number of girls who took tentative baby steps trying to not ruin their heels. I couldn't help the small pang of envy at how carefree they all looked. I remembered those days, before Mum got her second diagnosis, before I turned my back on my dreams, and before I had chosen to sell my soul at the club. If I was honest, I longed for that feeling of hope and excitement again.

I arrived on the high street and stood outside the restaurant for a moment. The sign above the front window was black with large fancy white swirled lettering which simply said: 'Ciao Bella', giving it an expensive vibe. I positioned myself in the doorway of an independent bakery next door and took a moment to think about what I was actually doing. I knew if I was going to back out, these would be the last moments I had to change my mind. The thought occurred to me then that maybe Josie hadn't shown up. I peered through the restaurant window, hoping that if she were there, she wouldn't see me. The place bustled with customers and at first glance, I thought I had got lucky. All the tables were filled, and I couldn't see anyone sitting alone. I told myself she had cancelled, that I could just go home, change into my PJs, and forget the whole thing. That it was probably for the best. I had one last scan and was about to head home when a waiter moved, and I caught a glimpse of Josie's auburn hair. She was sitting at a table for two, checking out the wine list and her knee was jiggling in a way that looked a lot like nerves.

Although I had convinced myself to go home and forget about the date, everything changed the moment my eyes fell on her, alone at the candlelit table, looking more gorgeous than I could have imagined. Against my better judgement and against Mum's advice, I walked into the restaurant and crossed the room without waiting to be shown to the table. The mouth-watering scent of garlic wafted through the air, and soft music filled the spaces in between. It was…romantic. I slowed before reaching my date and allowed her time to notice me. When I was just a few feet away, she looked up and smiled an easy smile with a look in her eye that was a lot like relief. My breath caught, she was captivating. She wore a black wrap-around top which tied at the waist and green stud earrings that sparkled as they absorbed the candlelight. Her hair cascaded around her shoulders in soft waves and her eyes…what had she done to her eyes? They shimmered with the colours of polished mahogany. She was simply stunning.

Josie rose to greet me. I instinctively held out my hand to shake hers as she had done the first time we met. I hadn't noticed, however, that at the same time she had leaned in to kiss me on the cheek, which resulted in my hand brushing over her left boob as we awkwardly collided.

"Shit, I'm so sorry. I thought you were going in for the shake." I scrambled my words out nervously, feeling my cheeks set alight.

Josie's eyes sparkled with amusement as she sat. "You always shake hands on a date?" She sipped her water, still smiling.

"No, never actually, but when we met, it's what you did, so I thought it was a thing." I tried to hide my embarrassment and be done with my klutziness.

"Ah, I always shake hands when I first meet someone. Research shows it increases the chance of a favourable interaction." My god, that voice, I really could listen to that voice all day. I smiled, sat down opposite her and picked up the wine list.

"Well, I would agree our first interaction was favourable." I thought back to the immediate effect she'd had on me.

Josie did a small shrug. "There you go then. I'll add it to my qualitative data." And then she winked. She actually winked, and it did things to my insides that I didn't even know were possible. I cleared my throat and tried to get the attention of the waiter, while Josie went on. "You know, handshaking originated as a way of people letting each other know they weren't carrying weapons." Something about the matter-of-fact way she said it made me laugh.

"No, I didn't know that, but it's good to know you come in peace."

She smiled. "I do. But I would also like to put it out there that I'll take a casual grope of the tit over a handshake any time." She grazed her top teeth with her tongue.

I laughed again, trying desperately to not let my eyes wander. A short silence fell between us while I attempted to unscramble my thoughts. I wanted to come back with a witty retort, something that would show my fun flirty side, but I had nothing. Instead, I flicked through the wine list, apparently finding it the most compelling read of my life.

"I thought there was a chance you would stand me up."

I looked up from the list of Italian reds and appraised her curiously. "And why would you think that?" I attempted to keep my tone as neutral as possible.

"Well, I railroaded you into coming out with me, I figured once you had time to re-think the idea, you'd be a no-show." There was a question in her eyes. Of course, I *had* considered not showing, but it had nothing to do with feeling railroaded into anything, and it certainly had nothing to do with Josie. Christ, is that the impression I had given?

"Can I be honest with you?" I laid the menu on the table.

"Sure." Josie leaned forward and rested her chin in her hands. The shimmer of the candle reflected in her eyes.

"I did consider cancelling tonight. I even started typing out a text, but it had nothing to do with you–"

Josie lifted a finger, interrupting what I was about to say. "Is this going to be the whole "it's not you, it's me" line again?"

I sighed. "Kinda. It really is me, though. I've just not been myself lately, and I've had so much going on with Mum and work that the last thing I've been looking for is to…you know… get involved with anyone." I dropped my eyes, hoping I hadn't misread the situation and we were not just two friends meeting up.

Josie studied me, thoroughly. "Okay, well, in response to the second "it's not you, it's me" that you've thrown at me in the space of a week. I would just like to put it out there that I'm not exactly keen on getting 'involved' myself." She did the whole in-quotation thing with her fingers and added, "This doesn't have to be a big deal. It can just be two friends meeting for some food. Anyway, just because we're both gay and attracted to each other, it doesn't mean that something *has* to happen between us does it?"

I felt the twitch of my nostrils wanting to flare as I tried to disguise my reaction to what Josie had just said. She found me attractive, and this made my solar plexus clench in the most delicious of ways. Her comment about me being attracted to her, although a little presumptuous, was bang on the money and on top of that, she had thrown into the mix that nothing had to happen between us, all of these things made me want her even more.

"No, I guess you're right." My eyes locked on hers for longer than appropriate for people who didn't plan on acting on their attraction. The waiter arrived to take our drinks order, interrupting our moment. Josie ordered a glass of Pinot Grigio, and after looking at the wine list for the third time, I opted for half a house beer. Once the waiter left, our moment from earlier had been lost.

"So, your mum says you're an affiliate marketer?"

I swallowed and fidgeted a little. "Of course, she did. Is there anything mother dearest hasn't filled you in on?"

"As I said at the club, your mum's been pretty reserved when it comes to you, and any time I thought she might be about to cross a line and share too much, I intervened. I would prefer to get to know you myself. So, who are you an affiliate for?"

I picked up the menu. Shit, something in the way she asked the question suggested she knew her stuff. It was one thing fabricating stories for my family, who knew very little about the world of internet work, but quite another trying to pull the wool over the eyes of a bloody psychologist. I took a deep breath, worried any small thing I said or did would give me away. I adopted the most casual tone I could find,

"I'm connected to quite a few programmes, but I make most of my money as an Amazon affiliate." Good, that was good, casual and to the point.

Josie's eyebrows shot up, and she nodded a slow nod, "Good for you. That's not easy. When I was working on my dissertation, my roommate was an Amazon affiliate. She was always putting so much time in and never got a lot back. You must have a few tricks up your sleeve if you're doing as well as your mum says you are. What are your best sellers?"

I held my breath. Bestsellers? Let me see, bestsellers? What are my bestsellers? Erm…I had nothing. Literally nothing. Why hadn't I researched this in more depth? Why hadn't I asked Mum what she had shared with Josie about me and my life? Why on earth did the back of my neck burn like a furnace?

"Your drinks, ladies." The sweet sound of the waiter's voice appeared just in time. He placed the glasses on the table and removed his notepad and pencil from his shirt pocket. "Are you ready to order your food, Signorinas?" His luscious Italian accent was a welcome distraction.

"Yes. Please." I rushed the words out before he had even finished asking the question. This was perfect, this would buy me a little more time, and I needed it to come up with something, anything at all that suggested I had an ounce of a clue what I did for a living. I tried to steady the pulse that was pounding in my chest and speak calmly to the waiter. Even though I lacked any appetite, I ordered lamb cutlets with a red wine jus and Bella's famous garlic potatoes. Josie ordered a mushroom risotto. The waiter bowed and walked away, leaving my stomach clenching as heat continued to spread out through the rest of my body. It was time for a quick subject change.

"I also work another job." I blurted it out before Josie could follow up with more questions, it was the best I could do under pressure. "I do a bit of bar work over at Canary Wharf."

"Two jobs? That's impressive. Anywhere I know?"

I chastised myself for not only staying on the topic of work but for making it a whole lot worse. I explored my brain for the name of a bar, any bar, literally any goddamn bar would have done. Leading up to the date, I had been so bummed out by what Mum had said about not going near Josie, it's what I had given my full attention to, rather than anticipating what we might actually talk about over dinner. Of course, she would ask me where I worked – of course, she would do that. It had been seconds, and I still hadn't given her a name. She must know I was lying to her. Surely, she could read my body language or notice my eyes dart about, giving me away. It had been too long.

"Chace's." I held my breath as I waited for her response. I mean, could I really not have done any better than that? The truth?

Josie squinted while she thought. "Never heard of it. But I don't know Canary Wharf either!"

My stomach relaxed, and I released the breath I had been holding for far too long. That was a close call. Too close a call. Maybe I should have told Josie there and then what I did for a living. Who knows, she may have even been titillated by the idea, but it wasn't about that. It wasn't about how Josie would react to me working as a stripper. It was about how I felt about myself. I grew up on a rough council estate in Essex. I'm talking mattresses in the gardens and bars on the local shop windows type of estate. Women wore their dressing gowns to the post office and kids threw stones at greenhouses just for kicks, that's how rough it was. It was a total shithole, but it was all Mum could afford. From about the age of ten, I promised myself every day that it wasn't going to be my life when I grew up. I wasn't like my friends. While they were out chasing boys and getting high, I was at home either writing or practising a neutral accent in the mirror. I told myself repeatedly I wasn't going to be like them, that I would make something of myself one day and I hated how miserably I had failed at that. So, no. I didn't want to tell this gorgeous, educated woman in front of me what a mess I had made of my life and that I take my clothes off for a living, even if I *was* doing it for what I considered honourable reasons. It was time to steer the conversation on to safer territory.

"So, who's Rumi?" I remembered the name from my eavesdropping at the home.

Josie took a sip of her wine, and a wistful look lit up her face. "He was a Persian poet, a Sufi master and one of the best spiritual teachers who's ever lived. I don't think I have ever read a poem of his that hasn't cut right through to my soul."

"Wow, that's quite a review there." I smiled, getting enjoyment out of how passionate she'd become.

She adorably wrinkled her nose. "Sorry, I got a little carried away there, didn't I? It's just what he does to me, he acts as a constant reminder that we each have an eternal soul and I guess, as well as that, I'm just a sucker for words."

I didn't know how to comment on the whole soul thing, it was a little out there for me, so I let it slide. Instead, I smiled, finding it hard to not be affected by her enthusiasm. I couldn't remember the last time I felt that fired-up about anything. Also, her comment "a sucker for words" had not been lost on me. Had Mum shared with her that I was a writer? I chose not to ask, more interested in getting to know the intriguing woman in front of me. The rest of the evening needed to be about that.

CHAPTER 6

THE EVENING HAD GONE WELL, better than well, in fact, after my crap start-stop-start it had been effortless. Once I successfully dodged the questions about my current occupation, we moved on to other safer topics of conversation. And I have to admit, the more I heard and shared, the more compelled by Josie I became. In answer to my questions, she talked a lot about her job at the University of London. She had clearly worked hard to get there and expressed pride as she spoke. Her eyes widened with intensity as she shared stories about her students and how exhilarated she was when she knew they were fully engaged. It was impossible not to be in awe of her, and after just a couple of hours, I made up my mind that Josie Calhoun was one of those people who would attempt to change the world one student at a time. Much too soon, I found myself outside the restaurant on the street with Josie. I supposed it would have been the opportune time to say our goodbyes, but we hadn't yet. Instead, we said nothing. I studied her, noticing she had a look in her eye that suggested she wanted to say something or do something, or was waiting for me to say or do something, I couldn't tell which. I watched her curiously until she spoke.

"Hey, Rox?" She tilted her head, regarding me with the softest smile.

"Yeah?" My eyes remained fixed on hers.

"I've had a great time with you tonight, it's been a while since I–"

"Come back to mine?" I interrupted. The words blurted out from nowhere conscious. I had panicked. She was saying goodbye, and I didn't want that, not yet. I wasn't ready to watch her walk down the street in the opposite direction, knowing there was so much more I had to know about her, and I did *have* to know. I couldn't explain why and I'm sure if I tried, it would probably end up as a cheesy cliché, something like there being a magnetic pull between the two of us that I felt when I was in her company, and wondered if she did too. But no, I wouldn't go there. I just didn't want her to leave, that's all I knew.

Josie took a moment to digest the abrupt question. "Oh, erm..." She looked at her watch as a plethora of emotions flickered across her face. I had caught her off guard. She thought for a moment, chewing the inside of her cheek before she settled on her answer.

"Sure, why not? As long as I don't miss the last tube."

We walked back to my place in silence. Josie had a faraway look which I hadn't seen before, and I thought perhaps it was regret. I wondered if we had crossed the line from two friends meeting for food and a chat to two people who, by our own admission, were attracted to each other and were about to be alone together? We both slowed our steps as we reached the footbridge that crossed the Thames.

"Penny for your thoughts?" I wasn't entirely sure I wanted to know, but I figured if she wanted an opportunity to change her mind, then I should probably give it to her.

"Believe me, they're worth far more than a penny." The

sentence was said quietly, almost under her breath. I wasn't sure how to take that. There was a slight hint of playfulness in her tone, and when I turned to face her, one dimple was visible. Our slowed steps came to a halt.

"Is your flatmate going to be there?" Josie asked.

I studied her curiously. "No." I drew out the word. "Clara's at work."

Josie nodded, chewing the inside of her cheek again. "Right."

I touched her arm lightly. "Hey, you don't have to come back, you know. If you're having second thoughts. If you think it's a bad idea, then–"

"No, I want to." She smiled the softest, most sincere smile I had seen yet. "I want to," she repeated, nodding firmly.

I OPENED THE DOOR TO the flat, struck by instant relief that Clara hadn't been home and everything remained as I'd left it. After destroying the place earlier while getting ready, I'd had a quick blitz around – just in case. I had been caught out on that one before. I once took someone home with me and made her wait outside for fifteen minutes while I dashed around picking underwear off the floor, removing hair from the plug hole and hiding dirty plates in the oven. So, ever since, I tried to be mindful of the state I left the place in – just in case.

The scent of fresh-linen Febreze still lingered in the air as Josie removed her boots and jacket and followed me through the hallway. When we reached the living room, she let out a low whistle. "Wow, affiliate marketing's treating you well."

On my way to the kitchen, I called back to her. "Well, Clara pays half the rent and bills, and like I said, I'm working two jobs, so it's manageable. What would you like to drink?" I hoped the night was not going to consist of me having to dodge more questions about my job.

"I'll just have what you're having."

Josie was right though; it was a great place. The entire flat had been refurbished before I had taken the lease. And it came fully furnished to a really high spec. It was all creams and browns with authentic oak flooring throughout. I had added one or two of my own touches such as a pine bookshelf filled with all my favourite books and a tall Dracaena in the corner that we managed not to kill, but for the most part, it was still pretty much as it had been the day I moved in.

I studied the bottles in Clara's drinks cupboard and removed a half-full bottle of vodka. I took the tonic from the fridge and two glasses from the shelf and began to hum to myself as I sliced a lime. It had been a while since I'd had anyone back to my home, and I enjoyed the thrill of not knowing what could happen or how the night would end. Most women I'd asked back barely made it to the sofa before we were ripping each other's clothes off, but there was Josie, perusing my book collection while waiting for her drink and we hadn't even kissed yet. Maybe I *had* grown up.

Although the vodka tonics were ready, I remained in the kitchen, allowing myself a moment to study Josie through the pass-through. She plucked a hairband from her wrist and tied her hair back, exposing her neck. The sight of pale soft skin caused a little flutter in my stomach. It had been a long time since I had felt one of those too. I swallowed as my eyes drifted further down, following the route from her neck to her cleavage, she really did look stunning in that top. As though sensing my gaze, Josie turned around. I cleared my throat and averted my eyes to the drinks. It was apparent from the glint in Josie's eyes that she was aware I had been gawping.

"Is that you and your mum?" Josie asked, pointing to a photo.

I had just turned four in the picture. Mum was only twenty-two, it was a time before my siblings came along. We had spent the day together at the beach. Mum looked fresh-faced and full of life in a black slimline swim-suit, she was bent over, holding my tiny waist from behind, and I had ice-cream all over my face.

I smiled. "Sure is."

Josie picked up the frame and studied it. "Wow." She ran her thumb over the glass. "She was stunning, wasn't she? I can see now where you get your looks from." Josie replaced the frame and turned to face me. I handed her a drink, feeling her fingers lightly brush against my own as she took it.

"Well, I'm not too sure about that. My sister's kind of always been both the smart one and the pretty one, but I got some of the brains, so that's something." I smiled before continuing. "You look great tonight by the way. I probably should have said that earlier, but you really do look lovely."

Josie flashed her dimples. "Thank you. And you look..." She hesitated, her teeth grazing her lower lip as she took me in. "You look...like someone who most definitely got the looks as well as the brains."

I laughed, and it sounded awkward because I wasn't quite sure what to do with the compliment.

"You want to sit down?" I asked, finding the end of the sofa and tucking my legs under me. I gestured for Josie to sit at the opposite end. She took her seat and mirrored my position, resting her cheek on her hand.

"So, tell me about Roxanne Mackenzie." She took a sip of her drink and widened her eyes.

Maybe I had gone a little rogue with the vodka, but I was still sober and needed something to calm my nerves.

"You want more tonic?"

She took another sip, this time giving no reaction at all. "Are you deflecting?"

I laughed. "Are you analysing?"

She held up her glass and grinned. "Touché."

"So, what do you want to know?" I asked quietly.

Josie sat up straighter. "Well, why don't we start with your hopes and dreams. You moved to London for a reason, what was it?"

Okaaay, we're just going straight there are we? Not, what's your favourite colour or band or brand of toothpaste? What's my life dream? I sighed and shuffled uncomfortably. Talking about my dreams served to remind me how distant they had become and how, over the past year, I had done nothing towards them except feel sorry for myself and had pretty much resigned myself to working as a stripper until I was eighty. I shook that image from my mind.

"You ask very personal questions." I swirled the drink in my glass and watched it make a whirlpool.

Josie smiled. "I'm a psychologist, if it's not personal, I'm not particularly interested. For me, the conversation has to mean something. It has to be something I can't find in a textbook. I want to get to know *you*." Her dark eyes looked at me intently.

I set my glass on the table. "Okay, well, I came to the city to write. I am – was – a writer." My voice was small and hesitant.

"*Was* a writer?" Josie's lack of expression immediately told me that as predicted, Mum had already divulged this information.

"I haven't written anything for a while. Well, anything official anyway. I'm not working on anything specific. I guess with work and Mum and–"

Josie held up her hand, cutting me off mid-sentence as though about to say, "You don't have to give me your shitty excuses", but instead, she simply nodded and said, "I understand." And there was something so gentle and sincere about the way she said it, I believed her.

"Sooo, that's enough about me." I not so subtly attempted to escape the examination of my life failure. "Tell me more about you. Why psychology?"

Josie tucked her legs further beneath her and thought for a moment. "Well, I guess it comes from a place of wanting to understand people. I like to know what makes people tick, why they do the things they do, why I do the things I do, that kind of thing."

I considered that for a moment and nodded slowly with what felt like a sceptical look.

"What?" Josie squinted her eyes light heartedly.

Before answering I carefully constructed my sentence, not sure if I was about to cross a line. "Well…" I hesitated again. "It sounds to me like that's the same generic answer you've given to everyone any time you've been asked that question, but I expect there's a little more to it than that."

Josie tilted her head and smiled. "You're not bad at this."

"You're not the only one who can get personal, you know?" I felt a small smile spread over my face.

Josie sipped her drink and stared into her glass for a moment. "Okay, well, everything I just said is true. My yearning to know about the human mind does come from that place, I guess I just…" she squinted. "Chose to miss out one or two details."

"Which are?" I shuffled in my seat, getting myself really comfortable.

"Which are…" she circled the rim of her glass with her finger. "Not up for discussion tonight."

My mouth fell open. "That's so not fair!"

Josie grinned, and I found myself laughing out loud before stopping to look into her warm eyes. We fell silent, and she stared back at me with what felt like the same intensity. I became acutely aware of my breathing then; it had developed a raspiness that only I could hear.

"So." I slowly drew out the word.

"So." She gave the same elongation to the word. It wasn't an awkward silence, just a knowing on both parts as we considered how the night would progress. The moment felt heavy, a little too heavy perhaps. We hadn't even finished our first drink.

"Want to go out on the balcony?" I pushed up from the sofa. Josie's eyes were wide.

"You have a balcony? Wait, of course, you do. Had to have a view of the Thames, did you?" It was said almost to herself, and she smiled as she said it, but I caught a slight edge and suspected there was a dig in there somewhere.

"I'm sorry. You don't like my home?" I was more than a bit taken aback.

Josie shook her head. "Shit, no, sorry, it's not that. I didn't mean to say that out loud. It's lovely. Really lovely. I guess I just didn't have you pegged as someone so…" Her eyes wandered around the room, taking in her surroundings while she attempted to find the word.

"Materialistic?" I offered, sensing that's where she was going.

"Yes, I guess." She grimaced as she answered.

I looked around the room, seeing it afresh and could tell why she thought as she did. It was, perhaps, a little over-the-top, with the high ceilings and a luxurious fireplace whose gas logs ignited with the clap of my hands. Yes, it was definitely clear why she would think of me as materialistic. I let out a breath and cleared my throat.

"Do you want the truth?"

"Always."

I sighed. "Look, I'm not telling you this to win the poor-me vote, in fact, I've not told anyone this, not even Clara, but for whatever reason, I feel compelled to give you an explanation."

Josie straightened. "I'm intrigued. Go on."

I looked over at the photo of Mum and me. "Well, growing up, we never really had a lot, you know? Mum loved us and always did the best she could, but because of her depression, she didn't work, and our fathers were off the grid, so it was a struggle. I won't bore you with the details but let's just say that sometimes there were days on end when we would go without electricity because we couldn't afford to put money on the key meter. At its worst, some days we would go without food. I hated growing up without things. Our clothes were hand-me-downs from Mum's friends' kids and when it came to the weekly shop, we had to buy the cheapest of everything. Do you remember when Tesco did the blue and white stripe range?"

Josie nodded.

"Well, that's all we would buy, and I remember whenever I had friends visit, I would run around peeling the blue and white labels from the value products because I was so embarrassed and ashamed. So, I suppose now I'm in a position where I can afford it, I do try to have a nice home because it's all I ever wanted as a kid, you know?"

Josie released an audible breath, and her expression was compassionate.

"Okay, well, I don't feel like an arsehole at all now for calling you materialistic. Shit, Roxy, I'm sorry. I've really put my foot in it, haven't I? I should know better than to judge without the facts."

I shrugged. "It's fine. I just didn't want you thinking I was some extravagant, showy knob-head or anything, because I'm not like that. I just like a nice home, you know?"

Josie nodded, "Rox, I really am sorry."

My smile was genuine. "Sooo, you want to see the balcony?" I walked over to the patio drape, pulled it aside, and opened the patio door for Josie to go out alone while I fixed us another drink. When I returned, I found her leaning over the railing, catching her breath at the sight of London lit up.

"This is incredible." Her voice was a whisper.

I placed our drinks on the tiled table, went over to her and leaned on the railing.

"It's pretty special. Makes you feel like anything is possible, doesn't it?"

A long silence followed before she tore herself away from the twinkling lights and turned to face me.

"You know Roxy, anything *is* possible. All you have to do is believe it's possible for you and work your arse off to achieve it, and you really can make anything happen."

I faced her, catching my breath at how beautiful she looked with the ambient light highlighting her fair skin. I smiled.

"You have such a positive way of looking at the world, don't you? But it's not always like that, sometimes life–"

"Gets in the way?" she finished for me. "I know, I know, I get it. But is that the story you're going to keep telling yourself until one day life's got in the way so entirely that you don't have a life worth living?"

Whoa, that hit close to home. I sighed, exasperated. The streams of light from the Canary Wharf office towers hit the Thames, giving off a spectacular display of reflected colours.

"You don't hold back, do you?" It was a rhetorical question as the weight of her words still lay heavy on me. She placed a hand on my arm and moved in closer.

"I just want to see people living their best life. Maybe it's the teacher in me, I don't know. I can't stand seeing people give up on their dreams, and I especially can't stand it when I can see that person has so much potential."

I looked down at her hand and back up to her expressive eyes. "I think I'm going to put some tunes on." I said the words slowly and made no attempt to move. Josie tightened her grip on my arm and lifted her other hand to my cheek. I stopped breathing as she narrowed the space between us.

"Or not?" I whispered as we moved even closer to one another. Josie leaned in and pressed her lips to my ear.

"I would prefer it if you stayed out here with me." Her breath on my skin sent shivers down my spine in the most extraordinary way. I bit down on my lip and swallowed. Her perfume filled my nose, the same woody scent from the day I first met her. It was curiously intoxicating.

"You smell nice." It didn't sound as idiotic as it might have.

"Thank you." Her breath touched my face, forcing me to take in a deep breath of my own.

"Is it JOY by Dior?" This time it did sound idiotic.

Josie stepped ever closer, bringing our bodies together. "Do you really want to discuss the brand of perfume I'm wearing? Or?" She left the question hanging there.

My hands found their way to the small of her back where I applied just the tiniest amount of pressure, giving her my answer. It was all it took. Our lips came together, lightly at first, small tentative kisses, both unsure, both hesitant. I drew away, wondering what the hell I was doing, but quickly dismissed those doubts as Josie's eyes gave me confirmation: what we were doing was okay. I leaned back in, this time, our mouths came crashing together as we simultaneously searched for each other. I opened my mouth a little and felt Josie's tongue enter. A bolt of arousal shot through me. I moaned from the sudden rush and how quickly it had stirred something down below.

My hands moved up Josie's back and into her hair. I took hold of it and pulled her into me. She groaned, deepening the kiss and cupping my bum in both her hands. And I pictured all the things that could happen next, all the ways in which I was going to take her, because my god, she could kiss. It didn't take long for my breath and heartbeat to quicken. I pressed Josie back against the railings as our tongues continued to collide in the most luxurious way. I was surrendering to the moment. The throbbing between my thighs intensified with every brush of Josie's tongue over my own. I reached under her top, her warm skin was soft to the touch. I traced my fingers over her tight stomach before cupping her pert breasts. I applied enough pressure with my palms to elicit a small moan. That sound made me come undone. I pushed close against her, wanting – no needing – to gain as much contact as possible. My nerve endings were alert and engaged in a spectacular display of tiny fireworks, and with every stroke of Josie's tongue against my own, the desperation to touch and be touched took hold.

I moved my hand down from Josie's breast and found the button on her jeans, I grappled with it, trying to get the damn thing to come undone without having to look because that would mean breaking our kiss and that would just be unthinkable. Just as I found the right angle to pop the button from its hole, the unthinkable happened. Josie pulled away from my mouth, leaving only the sound of my ragged breathing between us as my brain began to unjumble itself from the sex-fest it was immersed in a second before. She moved her lips to my ear, just as she had done before. I closed my eyes in anticipation of what she might whisper, expecting something along the lines of "take me to bed." I was wrong. Only two words left Josie's lips: "Calm down."

It took a moment for my fuzzy sex brain to compute. Wait, what? Calm down? Calm down? Calm-fucking down? My eyes sprung open at the words. Now, *Slow down,* I could have lived with, *go down* would have been even better, but *calm down*? I froze.

"Hey, what's up?" She furrowed her brow, still a little breathless.

I remained silent. Calm down? Was she implying that I was out of control? That she was in control? I took a step back, my hands out in front of me, making a barrier between us. "I don't think this is such a good idea" I hesitated "Maybe you should–"

She interrupted. "Roxy, I didn't mean it like–"

I interrupted in turn, shaking my head. "No, it's cool, Clara will probably be back soon anyway, and I've got a long day tomorrow."

Hurt flashed in her eyes. "Just let me explain, it came out completely wrong." She took a step towards me.

I stepped back at the same time. "No, honestly, it's fine. You should probably get going."

She froze.

"Are you kicking me out?" Her face was awash with confusion. I said nothing and watched as Josie searched for some logic. At my silence, she took a step back, widening the gap between us and hesitated. After a moment or two, she nodded as realisation kicked in.

"You *are* kicking me out. Right, of course." She headed for the patio doors. Her steps were hesitant at first, as though waiting for me to change my mind. I wondered if I would change my mind too, but instead, I followed her to the front door. Josie took hold of the handle, but before letting herself out, she turned to face me.

"Roxy, I'm really not sure what just happened, I thought we were–"

"We were. I'm sorry, it's just me. I don't know how to explain it."

She stared at me for a moment as though trying to figure something out, then held out her hand to me. Shit. I had blown it. We shook hands and she opened the door and walked out. I closed the door behind her and leaned against it for a moment, debating whether to run after her like it was *Love Actually*, but let's face it, I wasn't that person, that just wasn't my style. I had blown it. And frankly, I wasn't surprised, it was my signature move after all.

Admittedly the pulling away would have usually occurred at a much later stage, conveniently after all the sex, but I supposed it was indicative of the feelings Josie sparked in me. She scared me, straight from the off. Something about being with her had me on guard, and just like Mum predicted I would, I had used a pathetic excuse to push her away. Had I really just asked the most intriguing and gorgeous woman I had met in a long time to leave my flat because she said two simple words which probably didn't even mean what I took them to mean? Crap. Was it too late to run down the street?

CHAPTER 7

I WOKE TO A TEXT bleep from my phone. I squinted one eye, trying to re-orient myself. My head swam as I lifted it from the pillow, reminding me of the copious amounts of vodka I had consumed – again. My head flopped back on the pillow as my mind began to churn. The vodka. Eurgh the vodka. Vodka. Josie. Shit. Josie! I groaned. I hadn't run down the street after her. Instead, I finished off my vodka, finished off Josie's vodka and proceeded to pour myself another two. I had sat out on the balcony lounger until gone three, looking out on the landscape of "possibilities" and thinking about what a mess I had made of the evening.

In my slightly worse-for-wear state I typed out at least four different texts to Josie, all in a roundabout way saying the same thing: "I'm an idiot, please forgive me", but every time I stopped my thumb hitting send. Something held me back. I just couldn't bring myself to do it. Or wait…had I? I really couldn't remember getting to bed, or the hour or so previous, maybe I had sent something. Shit.

With effort, I turned onto my side and grabbed the phone. I had two texts. The first was from Clara.

Won't be home.

And the second was from Cayden.

Hey girl, my book is on the shelves at Waterstones. Can you believe it? Don't worry about buying one, I'm doing a signing of free books at my party which, just to remind you, is Saturday night. Bring whoever, can't wait to celebrate with you xxx

I read the text once and then again. Waterstones? *Waterstones*! Wow, he really had done it. He had managed the dream – our dream. I inhaled a sharp breath, rested my head in my hands and closed my eyes. I needed a distraction.

"Alexa, play something I like."

"Shuffling songs from your playlist…" The robotic voice spoke back.

The first chords to Abba's "The Winner Takes It All" rang out around the bedroom. I sniggered, the irony of the lyrics was not lost on me.

"Alexa, Skip!"

Radiohead's "Creep" was next to play.

"Oh, come on, you've got to be kidding me. Alexa, skip!"

R.E.M "Everybody Hurts." Jesus! I really did need to re-think my music selection.

"Alexa, sort it out. Skip!"

"I'm sorry, I don't know that one."

I slumped back on the bed. "Alexa, play something that's not depressing."

"I couldn't find any depressing songs in your library, to ensure you have a music service linked to your account, go to the Alexa app, select settings and –"

"Alexa, please shut the fuck up."

"I'm sorry, I don't know that one."

"Argh." I sprung from the bed and whipped the plug from its socket. "Traitor."

I sat on the side of the bed and covered my face with my hands. What the hell was going on with me? I had taken to behaving like someone I didn't even recognise. I thought about Cayden's success and my reaction to it. I re-ran the previous evening with Josie, the way I had let her walk out thinking she had done something wrong. And, just for good measure, I added into the mix thoughts of Mum. I was angry. That much was clear. But my anger wasn't directed at Mum, or Josie and especially not Cayden. I was mad at myself. Cayden was my friend. I moved to London and hadn't known a single soul, and lord knows this city can make you feel like the only person on earth. He took me under his wing, taking me out and introducing me to his friends. He was my only friend. He helped me keep faith in my writing in the times when I lost it and he always supported me, blowing smoke up my arse and telling me I would make it big someday. Yet, here I was begrudging him his chance at writing happiness.

I knew what I had to do. Despite the vodka I bounced off the bed with purpose and threw on a pair of skinny jeans and a worn t-shirt, bunched my hair, grabbed my phone, and screwed up my face in the mirror on the way out. I raced down the high street to Waterstone's and scanned the gay section, initially unable to spot what I was looking for, but after a few choice words under my breath, I found it. There it was, in all its flamboyant glory, *Pink Ribbons* by Cayden Lawrence. I swiped the book from the shelf and opened it up to the first page 'Acknowledgments' and scanned. Dean, parents, teachers, yada yada, then right at the bottom, the last paragraph read: "My good friend Roxy for always believing in me and encouraging me during our times at the café. Your time will come." I swallowed back a surge of emotion. He really was the best kind of person.

I took the book to the counter, telling the young store assistant that my best friend had written it. His face told me that he couldn't care less, but regardless, I left the shop with a spring in my step, knowing I had said it with pride. Before I reached the flat, I extracted my phone from my pocket and took a selfie holding the book under my chin with the biggest grin. I sent the picture to Cayden and tapped in:

As if I wasn't going to buy a copy! I'm so proud of you. See you Saturday for celebrations P.S I can't wait to meet your new man xxx

Genuine warmth spread through me as I placed the book back in the bag and headed home. Stage one of "be a better person" was complete, and it felt good, *really good*.

~

MILLY WAS MANNING THE FRONT desk when I arrived at Chislehurst. Her eyes were glued to a double-page spread in *Hello!* Magazine, dedicated to one of the Kardashians, I couldn't tell which, I never did care enough to tell them apart. While she made no attempt to tear her eyes away from the glossy photos, I scanned the visitors' log for Josie's name. She hadn't arrived yet. That realisation was followed by a wave of disappointment. I knew I had to apologise for being such a dick, and I wanted to do it face to face.

"Hey, Mill, I don't suppose you've seen Josie today?"

She looked up from her magazine and studied me curiously. "No, she's not been in yet, but when she arrives, I'll tell her you asked?"

I shook my head – too vigorously for the residual vodka effects. I gulped on a wave of dizzy nausea. "No, don't worry. Don't mention me. I'll get hold of her." I scribbled my name in the book and crossed the foyer.

"Hey Rox," Milly called out, stopping me in my tracks.

She hesitated for a moment. "Erm…she's a good girl, you know? Josie, that is."

"Yeah, Mill, I know." Why did everyone keep telling me that?

I entered the room and found mum asleep. Taking up my usual chair next to her bed, I sat and watched her for a while.

She looked like an angel, so still and peaceful. Her face was fresh in the glimmer of sun that peeked through the blinds. The cancer was barely noticeable while she slept. In her waking moments, though, as she struggled to move, the disease that consumed her was somehow omnipresent. I leaned forward and gave her a small kiss on the head.

"Mum," I said in a whisper, trying not to startle her. I didn't like to wake her when she looked so peaceful, but I also didn't want her to think that I hadn't come to visit. I knew she looked forward to seeing me.

"Mum," I repeated a little louder.

She stirred once and worked to open her eyes. "Hey kid, I didn't hear you come in."

"That's okay, how you feeling?" Mum struggled to move up her pillows.

"Like death warmed up." She rubbed her eyes. "But I suppose that's what I am really, just warmed up death, and if I'm honest, I don't think it'll be long now kiddo." She delivered the words so matter-of-factly they hit me like a punch to the chest. My jaw immediately clenched as I laboured to swallow the lump in my throat. Don't you dare blink, I told my filling eyes, she doesn't want to see your tears. I inhaled through my nose, striving to pull in some of the already limited air. My heart rate increased to an anxious thud, my ears pricked with heat, and my face tingled as though I had been injected with something wrong. I did some slow intakes of breath and exhaled them, while all the time, "please don't faint, please don't faint", repeated in my head like a mantra.

I knew what she said was true, it wasn't news, but still, hearing her say the words stole the breath from my lungs. She was ready. She'd had enough. But *I* wasn't ready, I didn't want to let her go, not yet. It was too much. Mum offered a sympathetic smile. She knew me, and she knew I was doing all I could to keep it together and hold back my tears. She reached out for my hand, and I squeezed hers tight, maybe a little too tight for such fragile bones.

"I'm sorry," I said quietly, "I know you don't like seeing me like this. I can keep it together most of the time, but this..." I gestured between us, "this is too hard."

Mum cleared her throat the best she could. "Listen to me." Her tone was serious. I nodded, unable to speak.

"I want you to do your ol' Mum a favour. I want you to promise me that you will open up and let people in. Don't be like me. Being hard as nails don't really get you anywhere. I know deep down you're not like that. You have a much softer and soulful side than I ever had."

She reached her hand up and stroked my cheek in a display of tenderness that was so unlike her. She continued.

"Let them see the real you, my sweet, caring, kind, intelligent daughter who would write me poems when she was a kid. Show people who you really are. Don't make the same mistake I did, choosing arseholes because you think deep down that's what you're worth, because you're worth so much more."

I squeezed my lips tight and hard and nodded. The weight and wisdom of her words, made my hands tremble.

"So are you Mum, you're worth so much more." My voice shook. "I wish you could've seen that." I leaned forward and laid a kiss on her forehead as one single tear disobeyed me, rolling from my cheek and onto her headscarf.

"Love you, girl, I didn't mean to upset you."

"I love you too, Mum."

~

I HAD SOMEHOW MANAGED NOT to break down in the room, but by the time I got just a few yards down the corridor, I came undone. Every tear I had been holding began to free-fall, all together, all at once, big salty tears, one after the other, drenching my face. I crouched against the wall and put my head between my knees to stop me going light-headed like always. Every part of me convulsed as I tried to get a hold of my breathing. My mum, *my mum*, was dying. Snot streamed from my nose, and as I wiped at my cheeks, smears of mascara streaked my hand. Short gusts of breath repeated on loop, and the tiny whimpering sounds that escaped me were alien. *My mum.* The lump in my throat strangled me, and I struggled for air, gasping with every intake, shaking and out of control. My eyes burned, my throat closed, and my fists clenched tight. I had fallen apart, so absorbed in my pain that even my fundamental senses had become redundant. I guess that's why, in all my anguish, the hand resting on my shoulder had gone unnoticed. I hadn't seen her, I hadn't heard her, and I hadn't felt her, but there she was, consoling me. In my moment of need, there was Josie.

CHAPTER 8

JOSIE CROUCHED BESIDE ME WITH her hand on my shoulder. I hid my face in my arm and didn't look up. "Just let it out," she said softly. "Just let it all out."

As much as the last thing I wanted was for Josie to see me in such a state, her permission to release a proper hearty sob, was the best thing she could have said at that moment. So, I did. I let it all out. All of it. All of me. Everything.

We must have sat for at least fifteen minutes on the hard corridor floor. Me sobbing and Josie saying nothing, just staying close and letting me know she was there. By the time I got a grip on my emotions, I was empty. I wiped at the combination of snot, tears and mascara with the sleeve of my hoody.

"Bet I look attractive." I barely recognised my own voice through the rasp.

Josie smiled a sympathetic smile. "Oh, I don't know, I've seen worse."

I managed a little chortle through my sniffling as I wiped my face some more.

"Want to talk?" I'm a pretty good listener, or so my degree says."

"I don't even know where to start." I wiped at my eyes again before continuing. "I just feel like everything's falling apart, you know?" I leaned back against the wall, tucked my knees into my chest, and wrapped my arms around them. "It's like I have no control over anything that's going on in my life. Like I'm just watching it all happen, and there's nothing I can do." I stopped my whine.

Josie shuffled up beside me. "Go on."

"Oh, I don't know. It's like..." I tried to conjure up a way of describing how I felt. "It's like...you know when it's a warm summer's day, and you're sunbathing, and you feel the breeze on your skin, and even through your closed eyelids, you can see the speckles of light from the sun? And then a cloud passes over, and it's just dark, like ridiculously dark and your skin gets goose pimples from the contrast?"

Josie nodded, hesitating a second, "I think I know what you mean."

"Well, it's like that, only the sun's been gone for a really long fucking time."

Josie remained silent, then said tentatively, "So, you're saying there's no light in your life, and you feel left out in the cold?"

"Yes, that's exactly what I'm saying, and I'm afraid the sun's never going to come back. I'm afraid *I'm* never going to come back." I blew out a breath and turned my head to look at Josie. "I've not always been like this, you know. I used to be so happy and carefree, and now look at me, I'm miserable most of the time, and just this morning I entered into an abusive relationship with Alexa."

Josie's eyebrow rose.

"It's okay, I just found myself yelling at my Echo and threatening a robotic voice."

Josie looked a bit relieved. She nodded and studied me for a moment. "Well, for what it's worth, do you want to know what I see when I look at you?"

I shrugged but felt a tiny bit of hope.

"I see someone who's going through a heartbreaking and traumatic ordeal and is still somehow managing to keep their shit together. Someone with the biggest heart who's holding down two jobs to pay for their mum's care. Someone who's not only gorgeous on the outside but beautiful on the inside as well. Roxy, I see you, and I can tell that you see this…" She waved a general gesture of all of me, "As you being weak, but I can promise you that you are so much stronger than you think and you will get through this." Compassion filled her eyes so fully that I couldn't keep my lower lip from quivering.

"Oh. Come here." She wrapped her arms around me and pulled me in close. I rested my head on her shoulder and closed my eyes. She tightened her grip, and I snuggled further into her neck, basking in the rich warmth of her perfume. Her hands stroked my back, comforting me. A small moan of contentment left my lips.

"How can you be so nice to me? After how I treated you last night?" I asked, through a sniffle.

She paused her stroking. "Well, actually, that's why I came here, to talk to you about last night. I know you're having a terrible time at the moment, and perhaps it's not the best time to be starting something–"

"Wait, I have something to say first…" I took in a breath. "The way I behaved yesterday was unforgivable, and I'm not going to let you excuse it just because of what I'm going through with Mum. If I'm really honest, I probably would have done the same thing three years ago before any of this. The thing is Josie…" I swallowed hard. "The thing is… I'm a pusher."

Josie thought for a moment then her dimples came out to

play. "Ah, you sell drugs? Well, at least that explains the fancy pad." A teasing smile played games around her lips.

I narrowed my eyes and pouted. "No. A people pusher."

Josie's eyes widened. "Like human trafficking?" She was not making it easy for me in the slightest.

"Stop!" I laughed, thumping her on the shoulder. "What I mean is, I have this tendency to push people away. It's like if there's a chance I could get close to someone romantically, I flick a switch and make up lousy excuses to not see them again. It's a self-preservation thing. I've always been the same. I run the moment I think there's a chance I could get hurt."

Josie looked into my tired eyes and tenderly tucked a strand of tear-drenched hair behind my ear. "Well, you're not running now."

My eyes remained locked on to hers. "No, I guess I'm not."

She shook her head ever so slightly. "Why the sudden change?"

I shrugged. "I don't know...something Mum said, believe it or not."

Josie's eyebrow shot up. "Susan dishing out advice? Now *that* I'd like to see."

I laughed briefly. "She has her moments." I laid my head back in the crook of her neck. "Hey, can I ask you something?"

"Uh-huh."

"I'm going to a friend's house party on Saturday. He's celebrating getting his debut book published. He said I can bring whoever I like, and I'm just wondering if you would like to come? As my date?" I sat up again and waited, looking at her hopefully.

Her expression was thoughtful.

"I mean, I understand if you don't want to after last night?"

She chewed on the inside of her cheek, saying nothing, just looking at me.

"Look, if it's that hard a decis–"

She reached out and touched my arm.

"I'll come," she said softly, giving my arm a gentle squeeze.

I momentarily felt all the pain and anguish from just minutes before dissipating.

"But Roxy," Josie added, "No repeats of last night please, if we're doing this, then we're doing it, okay?"

I nodded slowly. "Okay."

And I knew with that one simple word I had just made a promise.

I DIDN'T FEEL LIKE GOING home straight away. I still had three hours before my shift at Chace's, and it was such a lovely evening; I decided to take a stroll to the lakes. I followed the gravel path down to the water's edge and sat on a bench with a plaque that read "Joan Wainwright; Mother, grandmother and loving wife". For a brief moment, I wondered what words I would use if I were ever to dedicate a bench to Mum.

The sun was just thinking about beginning to set, making a combination of burnt oranges and purple haze in the sky and the weeping willows surrounding the water were starting to form silhouettes against the colours. The lake was as still as I had seen it except for two ducks which dipped their heads into the water occasionally creating gentle ripples. Visiting the lake always reminded me why we chose this specific home for Mum in the first place. It really was something special.

A dishevelled looking man sitting on a bench on the opposite side of the lake caught my eye, and he noticed me at the same time. He offered up a sympathetic smile which seemed to say "I know what you're going through, it's hard isn't it?" and I returned his smile with what I hoped said something like: "It's hard but we need to be strong".

I sat for about twenty minutes, just staring at the ripples in the water and waited for the man to leave before pulling a notebook and pen from my bag. I opened to the first blank page and let the pen hover just above the first line. I touched the point to the paper, hesitated for a moment and lifted it back up from the page. I shuffled on the bench and attempted once more. The pen touched the paper but there was still nothing. Where were the words? What had happened to all the words? They certainly weren't flowing through me, that was for sure. A frustrated sigh whooshed out and I slid the pad and pen back into my bag, pulled my phone from my pocket and called Cayden. He answered after the second ring.

"Hey, gorgeous. To what do I owe this pleasure?" He sounded chirpy.

"Hey Cayd, firstly I wanted to ask if I needed to bring anything with me Saturday?"

"Don't you dare bring a thing. We've gone all out, and I mean *all out*. I've got a DJ booked, we have enough alcohol to sink a ship, and I'm testing out my best culinary skills on the food. You won't be disappointed. And secondly?"

"Secondly, I know you said I could bring someone and I invited Clara."

"Oooh, I can't wait to meet that one, she sounds like a hoot."

I rolled my eyes. "Hmm, yeah, we'll see about that. But I wanted to ask if I could perhaps bring someone else too."

Cayden started giggling and shushing whoever was making him laugh.

"You want me to call back?"

"No, no, sorry, it's Dean, he's misbehaving."

"Hi Roxy, I'm looking forward to meeting you." An unfamiliar voice called out in the background.

"You too," I called back, "Anyone who can make Cayd this giddy is cool in my books. So Cayd, can I have a plus two? Or…?"

"Yes, Christ, bring whoever you like, the more, the merrier. Do I know them?"

"No." The word was drawn out.

"Oh my god, is it a date?"

I smiled into the phone. "Yes, it's a date. Her name's Josie, and she's a psychologist and a university lecturer, and she's also a very attractive redhead."

Cayden laughed. "She's a what? Jesus Christ, she's gonna have a field day with you, and we all know how much you love a redhead."

"Right? It's only our second date, and I royally fucked up the first so I'm really hoping it goes well, you know?" My legs frantically swung back and forth beneath the bench.

"Wow, I've not heard you get your knickers in a twist over anyone before. Usually, she just ruins them, then sends them home." The last bit was clearly directed to Dean.

"Hey! I heard that!" Unfortunately I wasn't nearly as shocked as I pretended to be.

"I'm only playing, sweetie. I think it's great you're bringing a date, and I for one cannot wait to meet the person who made it to a second date with *the* Roxanne Mackenzie."

I laughed again before changing direction. "Listen, Cayd."

"Yeah?"

I looked out over the lake and smiled. "I'm really happy for you, you know? For everything, I mean."

"Awww, is Roxy going soft? Could it be the new love interest by any chance?"

I smiled shyly into the phone. "It might have a little something to do with a certain someone, but we'll see, it's very early days. I suppose I better let you get back to what you were doing."

"You mean *who* I was doing?"

"Oh, Christ. Okay, bye-bye, be gone. I'll see you Saturday."

I hung up the phone before I had to hear things I would

really rather not. Now, that was Cayden taken care of, I just needed to break it to Clara that Josie was coming too.

~

BY THE TIME the night of Cayden's party arrived, I had pulled myself together. After my mini-breakdown in the corridor, I felt cleared out and more able to tuck things back into that pocket of my mind labelled "too hard to deal with." The past couple of days had slid by uneventfully. Mum seemed to have perked up, and I had taken a couple of busy shifts at the club and was finally looking forward to a night off. I spent the afternoon clearing up after Clara and getting the flat into a pristine state for when Josie arrived. We had agreed for her to meet Clara and me at our place so we could all travel together. Clara, of course, did nothing to help with the cleaning and stayed in her room right up until the very last minute. She emerged just as I tidied the last of the dishes away.

"Convenient timing," I jibed, whipping her arm with the tea towel.

"Ow, what the hell?" She rubbed her arm and frowned.

"I've been clearing up the aftermath of whatever tornado snuck in here last night, and you decide to appear seconds after I finish because you what? Didn't hear the hoover through your soundproof door?"

Clara looked around the living space and shrugged. "Not my problem you're OCD about having the place clean for the teacher chick. I thought it looked tidy before."

I rolled my eyes, slinging the tea-towel on its hook. "She's not a teacher, she's a lecturer."

Clara shrugged once more, before walking over to the drinks cupboard and removing a bottle of red. "Whatever, same thing, she wore a scarf to a nightclub…at night…in an actual club."

I had no argument, Josie *had* done that but, actually, I kind of liked it. I thought it made her look chic and gave her a sexy, intelligent look. I chose not to share this with Clara.

"Be nice. She'll be here soon and you promised to be on your best behaviour. And, remember what I said, no matter how pissed you get, under no circumstances do you tell her what we do for work."

Clara rolled her eyes wearily. "Yeah, yeah, I get it. Teacher chick must not know about nakedness blah blah blah."

"Clar, I mean it." I glared at her.

She threw her hands up in surrender. "I know, Christ! I said I get it. But if I knew I was going to be third-wheeling it and having to watch every word I say, I wouldn't have bothered swapping my shift to get the night off. And anyway, maybe you should just tell her, see if she's still interested then. At least then you'll know where you stand and can stop shitting yourself that she's going to find out. Which she will, of course, you arse."

I rubbed at my eyes but couldn't get rid of the frustration. "I know, and I will. Just not yet. I need to see how it goes first before I go opening my mouth and ruining it before it's even begun."

"Okay, your funeral."

Clara poured her first drink, oblivious of the effect that word had on me. I shook it from my mind.

"Now, are you going to sort out this mop or what?" I pointed to my hair, which was more than usually unruly and in desperate need of attention.

While Clara fixed my hair, she made a start on the wine. I had made a very firm decision to stay away from alcohol for a while. I knew I had to be on my best behaviour. Josie had made it clear she wouldn't put up with a repeat of the other night, and I didn't want to let her down, or me for that matter. Clara was not so reserved with her drinking, however, and I couldn't help but worry what state she might get into, or specifically, what she might say when in that state. I still hadn't got to the bottom of what was going on with her the other day, but whatever it was appeared to have dwindled, and although I could never describe her as the friendliest of people, she seemed to be okay with me again.

Tina Turner's "Proud Mary" blasted from the speaker, and every time the "rollin'" part kicked in, Clara and I shimmied towards the mirror in sync, making it impossible to style my hair. For the first time that day, I felt relaxed. Until there was a knock at the door, that is. The mix of excitement and apprehension must have shown on my face because Clara looked back at me in the mirror with a raised eyebrow and a curled lip.

"Oh, get a grip," she spat as I walked backwards out of the room with my middle finger raised before quickly changing demeanour as I got to the front door. I self-consciously patted my hair and smoothed my top before opening it.

As the door swung open my jaw dropped at the vision standing there.

"Holy shit!"

Josie pulled at the strap of the snug green dress that hugged every inch of her perfect body. "Erm, hello to you too." She smiled uneasily.

I blinked, taking her in, and then blinked once more because it was all I was capable of. She looked...simply stunning. Her red hair fell long and loose, partly covering one side of her face. Her dress was cut low, dipping in all the right places and showing a flawless cleavage. Her eye-makeup was darker than usual, it had a smokiness to it that gave her eyes a seductive depth and made my mouth suddenly desert dry. I had gawped longingly at her for an inappropriate amount of time.

"You look insane." I managed, shaking my head at how beautiful she really did look, and how much more dopy could my response have been?

She smiled warmly. I continued to gawp.

"So," she elongated the word, "Are you going to invite me in or what?"

"Yeah, sorry. Of course, come in," I mumbled as I pulled myself out of my head and stood back to let her in. She walked past me, leaving a lingering hint of that gorgeous scent I was fast becoming used to and made her way to the living room where Clara had got to work on pouring them both a drink.

"This is for you." Clara handed the glass to Josie. "Take this as an apology for the other night. I'm sorry I was such a dick. I was clearly having too much fun lezzing it up and forgot my manners." I watched the exchange, dumbfounded.

Other than her use of the word "lezzing," I had to admit, I was impressed. In all the time I'd known Clara, I don't think I ever heard her apologise; to anyone.

Josie took the glass from Clara and smiled gratefully. "It's fine. To be fair, I found you kind of amusing." She clinked Clara's glass with her own.

I cleared my throat, "Erm, please do not encourage her. She has it in her to behave a whole lot worse than the other night, believe me."

Josie's eyes widened. "I'm intrigued."

As they made small talk, I took the opportunity to admire the beauty in front of me. I had thought Josie attractive, sure, but right there, in my living room, she looked sexy as hell, and if I'm honest, I couldn't wait to be alone with her, providing we could get through the evening without me stuffing everything up, of course.

"So, how did you two meet?" Josie directed the question towards Clara.

I swallowed, feeling the blood drain from my face.

"At work," Clara said casually.

"Oh, okay, you work at the club too then?"

Clara snapped her head to me, looking all wide-eyed, clearly thinking I had told Josie about our job. I had no choice but to intervene.

"Yes." I nodded at Clara. "We met at Chace's. Clar here taught me everything I needed to know about *bar work*, didn't you?"

Clara relaxed somewhat. "Right, yep, that I did." She turned back to face Josie before continuing. "But she still can't pull a pint for shit, let me tell you."

Josie laughed and arched an amused eyebrow, and I figured she hadn't picked up on Clara's hesitation. Although I was relieved, I didn't like one bit how sketchy that felt. I made up my mind then and there that if the night went well, regardless of how much of a disappointment I felt to myself, and how difficult I would find it to present me as a rock-bottom-failure, I would come clean about what I did for a living and deal with the consequences. But first, we had the small matter of Cayden's book launch.

~

CAYDEN'S TWO BEDROOM HOUSE IN Chelsea actually belonged to his parents. His dad's considerable inheritance from Cayden's grandfather had been enough to buy a villa in the south of France plus a place in one of the most affluent parts of London. Because his parents spent most of the year in France, Cayden had Chelsea rent-free and because of that, he just needed to pick up a few shifts at Manney's, and that was enough to keep him going, which left him a lot of free time to write.

Josie, Clara and I decided to take the train to the party rather than me having to drive across the city. After a short walk to North Greenwich station, we boarded the train, and Josie and I spent the next ten minutes listening to Clara recount tales of her sexual conquests, most of which I had heard before. Josie laughed in the right places and asked all the right questions, making an effort to get to know my friend, but something flashed in her eyes resembling confusion. I suspected; she was wondering how I ever ended up living with someone as brazen as Clara. Clara, however, oblivious to Josie's possible reaction, continued her ramble and went on to finish off the story of how she seduced a police officer after he pulled her for nicking a mascara from Superdrug. Great.

We changed trains at Green Park station and Josie and I sat side-by-side opposite Clara on a four seater booth. The top of my arm touched lightly against Josie's. It was something I had been consciously aware of from the moment we took our seats. The warmth of her skin against mine sent mini shivers down the back of my neck, even though it was just an arm. I wondered if Josie shared in my hyper-awareness: that every time the train shuddered, our arms pressed together. Even though the evening was a muggy one, which of course felt a whole lot worse on a stuffy carriage, I knew the heat that rose in my body was the result of being close to Josie. She had done it on purpose too, made herself look that desirable. I figured it was punishment for how I had behaved the last time we were together, and now she was enjoying making me sweat – literally. Frankly, I would have been happy to skip the party altogether, if it wasn't such a big deal for Cayden.

The train jolted to a stop, which was a relief as Clara was about to share an anecdote about how she got the nickname "Clap" at school and people in the surrounding seats had begun tutting and eyeballing each other. We piled off at South Kensington, and I led the ten minute walk to Cayden's place while Clara continued to overshare her life. I stopped just outside the Georgian townhouse where the music could be heard from the street.

"Is this where your friend lives?" Josie asked, looking up at the towering building with its ivory painted brickwork and striking sash windows.

"Yep. Huge, isn't it? It's not his though, it's his parents' but it makes a pretty good party pad." I pressed the intercom button.

"This place is sweet." Clara shouldered me out of the way and repeatedly buzzed the intercom.

After a minute or so of no one answering, Clara's patience wore thin. She leaned over the railings to one of the windows and began battering at it with her fist, leaving Josie and I standing at the door. I took out my phone to call Cayden. As I scrolled to his name in Favourites, two hands grasped my hips from behind. I inhaled sharply, feeling the skip in my heartbeat. Josie pulled me into her and rested her chin on my shoulder. I leaned back, so her lips brushed lightly against my neck, and I closed my eyes as a small moan of anticipation escaped me. Josie whispered in that low sexy voice, "I'm glad we're doing this."

I looked over to Clara, who was still banging away on the window like a crazy person and smiled. "Yeah, me too."

CHAPTER 9

THE DOOR SWUNG OPEN REVEALING a smiley, wide-eyed Cayden holding a champagne flute in each hand with the party already in full swing behind him.

"Someone said the window was about to be smashed in so I…" His jaw fell open. "Wow! Where on earth have you been hiding these two beauties, Mackenzie?" He ushered us from the hallway and into the party.

The living rooms alone were larger than my entire flat, with the doors between them folded back and Cayden had done an excellent job of reminding people what the party was all about. Against the back wall of the second room were two gigantic banner posters displaying the cover of *Pink Ribbons*. And between the posters was a table stacked with copies of the book and strategically placed pink and black roses. The turnout was good. There were already at least fifty people talking and mingling and it was still relatively early.

"Not just happy to arrive with one stunner on your arm, you had to bring a harem?" Cayden's voice was a few octaves higher than usual to be heard over the music which was coming from the DJ set in a corner of the front room.

Clara held a finger in the air. "Erm, I would just like to point out that I'm not part of anyone's harem."

Cayden flashed his killer smile. "Rox said you were a feisty one, she wasn't kidding. I love it." He turned his attention to Josie. "And my God, Rox, you weren't messing when you said she was a hotty."

Josie raised one eyebrow with a smile as she turned to me. I rolled my eyes. "That's enough of that thanks, Cayd." I poked him in the chest.

"Aww, someone feeling left out?" Cayden lifted me in a bear hug and spun me around, "Roxanne Mackenzie, let it be known that you are still the most beautiful female in this room or any room for that matter." I squealed for him to put me down, aware of a large number of people now staring at us.

Once the introductions were taken care of, and Cayden was done with embarrassing me, he dragged us all through the throng and into the kitchen to where he could introduce us to the new man in his life who was busy slicing lemons and limes.

"Honey, I would like you to meet one of my very best friends, Dean – Roxy; Roxy – Dean." Dean laid down the knife and wiped his hands on a tea-towel before tugging me into an embrace.

"Wow," I said as the brick of a man squeezed me within an inch of my life. The guy was an Adonis. His broad shoulders and solid pecs threatened to bust out of his tight, salmon coloured t-shirt.

I looked at Cayden. "I'd say you have more than one reason to celebrate tonight?"

"Oh, you ain't kidding, honey." He looked Dean up and down with a deliriously happy grin.

Dean smiled warmly at Cayden before turning his attention back on me. "Honestly, Roxy, it's so nice to meet you at last. Cayd has told me so much about you. He's forever going on about how talented you are. You must let me have some of your writing sometime, I would love to read it. If it's half as good as he says it is, I'm sure my mind will be blown."

My eyes went to Josie, who blinked at me in confusion.

"Oh, I'm sure he's just being a good friend and talking me up. He's the one with the publishing deal after all. Anyway, Dean, this is Josie." He let me go and grabbed hold of her to wrap her in the same bear hug he had given me and said how gorgeous her hair looked.

"And this is my housemate Cla…" I turned, expecting to find Clara behind us, but she wasn't there.

"I think she went to get a drink," Josie whispered.

I rolled my eyes, she could be so bloody rude at times. "I'll introduce the two of you later. I think Clara's gone to get a drink, which is probably what we should do and let you get on with your slicing."

"Ladies, help yourself to anything," Cayden gave an airy wave as he groped Dean's tight bum with his free hand. "The DJ's a friend, so he'll play everything you request. The buffet's in the dining room on the left, and the drinks table is next door. I'm gonna go mingle for a bit and catch up with you later." He pecked me on the cheek, before leaving the kitchen.

Josie and I made our way back to the living room where Madonna's "Get Into The Groove" filled the high-ceilinged room and at least thirty people danced. Clara was nowhere to be seen. It would have been easy to spot her too, given that the guests were mostly men. A waiter passed carrying a tray of drinks, and I grabbed a champagne for Josie and orange juice for myself.

"Not drinking tonight?" Josie's expression was one of surprise.

"No. I'm giving it a miss for a bit. I want to show you I can act like a civilised human being. I expect the champagne's good, though?" I nodded to her glass.

She sipped her drink. *"Really good."* Her eyes widened to emphasise her opinion.

"We should try the food too, Cayden's an amazing chef." I took her hand without giving it any thought and froze, looking at her hoping she could see the question in my eyes. She looked down and smiled at our fingers locked together, giving me my answer and my stomach did a small flip.

We made our way to the dining room, weaving between well-dressed guys as best we could, and found a long table groaning under a spread of food fit for Nigella. It was seriously posh grub and looked so colourful and elegant, I was almost afraid to touch it. Almost.

We piled our plates with dainty finger things which were an assortment of canapés, petite bites served on tiny porcelain spoons and luscious sushi pieces and found a spot tucked away beneath the stairs where two chairs and a bookcase made an inviting nook. It felt like we could almost be alone.

"Umm, so good." Josie covered her mouth as she spoke.

I smiled, enjoying the sight of her tucking into a tiny, baked shrimp cup.

"What? Do I have something on my chin?" She self-consciously dabbed at the sides of her mouth.

"No, you don't." I continued to grin at her goofily.

"Then what are you smiling at?"

"Just you. You really do look sensational tonight."

Josie smiled and tilted her head. "You're pretty smooth for a change. But, for what it's worth, I have to agree with Cayden, you most definitely are the most attractive woman not only in this room but any room."

We went on looking at each other like a pair of saps until Cayden interrupted us, wanting to introduce us to a couple of his friends. I watched in awe as Josie comfortably mingled with people she hadn't met before. Regardless of the subject, whether it was art, literature, politics or even celeb gossip, she had something to contribute. Cayden's two friends ran their own tech business and seemed to find her work at the university fascinating. They began to list anyone they had ever known who'd gone to London University to see if she knew them, which of course she didn't as they were obviously much older, in a distinguished silver fox way. She looked so at ease and so comfortable that I took the opportunity to slip away to check where Clara had got to.

I scoped out the living room first, to see if she was harassing the DJ, which she wasn't. Then I passed through the kitchen where Dean was still prepping drink accompaniments and then I investigated other rooms, which were all empty. Finally, I found myself outside in a spacious, high-walled courtyard which had been made magical by strings of fairy lights crisscrossing the roof of a small wooden gazebo. Clara was sitting on a bench with her back to me.

"Oi! Where the hell did you disappear to?" I sneaked up on her.

She almost leapt out of her four-inch heels.

"Shit, you made me jump." She took a drag of her cigarette. "Nowhere. Just mingling."

I sat beside her. "Well, I went to introduce you to Cayden's other half, and you'd vanished."

"I told you, I was mingling. I met him anyway. The hot one with the muscles. They're all bloody hot, and not one of them likes the pussy."

I rolled my eyes. "That's why you're out here, sulking? I did warn you they would mostly be gay."

"Not sulking. Just smoking." She held her cigarette up and widened her eyes. "Where's the teacher?"

I glowered.

Clara sighed, "Fine. Josie, where's Josie?"

"She's chatting to a couple of Cayd's friends." Silence fell between us. "Clar, what do you think of Josie? I mean, she's cool, isn't she?"

Clara mouthed out a smoke ring and shrugged. "Yeah, she seems alright."

I bent to look at her properly, "Oh, come on Clar, the woman's fire."

She scoffed. "Yes Mackenzie, she's a good-looking chick, and she really does seem alright."

I eyed her. It wasn't much, but this was Clara, so I knew to take all I could get in the way of deep and meaningfuls, and if Clara thought Josie was "alright" then I knew that was something.

"I just hope I don't mess it all up, you know?"

Clara jumped up and paced away from me. "Then don't! It's not rocket science, is it? You like her, go for it and don't fuck it up. Simples."

She flicked her cigarette to the floor. Okay, so Clara definitely wasn't one for deep and meaningfuls, but actually, she did have a point, maybe it really could be that simple.

I picked up Clara's fag butt and stubbed it out in a thoughtfully placed ashtray, then I dragged her back to the house. She was reluctant at first, but once inside, a couple of the guys complimented her on how she looked, and she began talking to them until the three of them were dancing their butts off in the living room like reunited besties. And even though she knew they were all off-limits, the way she had sandwiched herself between them, gave me the impression she was starting to enjoy herself. I left her to it while I went to find my date.

Josie was in deep conversation with Cayden when I came upon them in a window seat on the landing. "Ah, there you are. This one here just came up with a genius idea." Cayden's grin was huge as he laid a friendly arm across Josie's shoulders.

"Oh yeah?" I took a sip of my warming juice and waited for Josie to explain.

"Well, I was just saying to Cayden he should get you to market his book for him. Because everything you do is commission-based, it won't cost him anything and seeing as Amazon's your best marketplace and Cayden's book's on Amazon, it's the perfect combo. With your affiliate experience, I'm sure you could definitely push his sales up."

My suddenly lukewarm orange juice got stuck in my throat. I coughed to make it come back up, holding out a finger, silently asking for a minute before I could answer, Josie got up and patted me on the back. I eventually cleared my airway and pulled back from choking to death.

"Good idea. Josie, great idea." I hoped they didn't hear the slight squeak in my voice, or would at least attribute it to tepid OJ. "Cayd, we'll definitely have to meet up and workshop some ideas. In the meantime..." I grabbed Josie's arm, "I think a couple of us need to give Dean a hand or he's going to miss the whole party to chopping citrus."

I dragged Josie through to the kitchen where we did exactly that. After twenty minutes or so, there were enough lemons, limes, mint garnishes and cucumber slivers to last this party and leave a lot over for others. But it was nice because it allowed me to get to know Dean who seemed like a great guy and an amazing fit for Cayden. As we were setting our handywork out on the drinks table with the help of a fussing waiter, the DJ cut the music, and everyone turned to the sound of Dean clinking a spoon on his glass.

He cleared his throat. "Ladies and gents. We all know why we're here tonight, and it's to celebrate my wonderfully talented and not to mention gorgeous hunk of a boyfriend getting his debut novel published by one of the biggest publishers out there."

Whoops and cheers ricocheted around the rooms.

"I'm sure you'll agree that it's a fantastic read and we all wish him the absolute best with the sales of this book and the many more that are sure to come. So, without further ado, put your hands together for the hottest new author in town, Cayden Lawrence!"

The whole house went mental with clapping and cheering before Cayden made his way to the front of the room. He gave Dean a kiss on the cheek and addressed the crowd.

"Guys, guys, stop. You'll make me blush. Listen, I'm going to keep this short and sweet. Firstly, I want to thank you all for coming. I'm overwhelmed by how many friends and family have turned out to celebrate with me tonight. Secondly, I can't believe this is happening. It seems like only yesterday when me and my friend Roxy who, by the way, is here tonight and let me tell you is every bit the writer I am and then some." He gestured towards me, and Josie squeezed my hand tight while a few people clapped and cheered again before Cayd continued:

"It only seems like yesterday that we were in a small café in Greenwich and *Pink Ribbons* was born. If you'd told me then that I would be here, celebrating with you all tonight, I would've said you were batshit crazy. Yet, here we all are, and I've actually fricking done it." He raised his glass to the room and was met by another round of whooping and cheering. "So look, grab a book, grab hold of me to sign it and for the love of god drink, dance, eat and have a blast."

I raised my glass and yelled. "To Cayden!" And everyone followed with the same short, sweet toast.

Josie and I did exactly that. We drank, albeit fresh, chilled orange juice for me. We visited the food spread once more, unable to get enough of the delicious bites of heaven and we mingled with Cayden's friends who were every bit great for the ego, telling us how beautiful we both looked. We saw Clara a few times but she was dipping in and out for most of the night and seemed to be making friends of her own. Then, eventually, Josie and I found our way to the centre of the room where we danced. And Josie could dance. Well: really well. In fact, I was yet to discover something that she couldn't do well. Her moves were understated and graceful, giving just enough sway to her hips to spike my arousal, and the more we moved together, the harder it became to keep my hands off her. I drew her nearer and my hands ran down her back and landed on her bum. She edged in closer still and pressed her thigh between my legs so we could rock together effortlessly like pieces of the same puzzle, the whole time, holding each other's gaze.

Josie's fingers intertwined around my neck as she moved her hips, grinding on me and I couldn't help but picture the scene from *Dirty Dancing* when Baby walks into the room, and they're all making love with their dance moves. The sexual charge between us had my libido going into overdrive and although I was sure the rest of the party people were too drunk to be paying attention to us, we were probably beginning to be borderline inappropriate. I leaned in and planted a small kiss on Josie's neck. She moaned into my ear and it sent a zing through the parts of my body that wanted her the most.

"You're a good dancer." Her words were breathy in my ear. "The way you move is so sexy."

I stopped moving, looked into her eyes and practically purred: "Are you ready to get out of here?"

Josie nodded. It was a slow, deliberate nod, her eyes glistening with promise.

Neither of us had seen Clara for a while, so I assumed she had just been chewing the ear off someone out the back in the smoking gazebo, but when it came to looking for her, she was nowhere to be seen. A few guys said they had seen her earlier but not for at least an hour. I tried calling her mobile. She didn't answer. Then a text pinged on my phone.

Felt ill. Jumped in an Uber. At home. C x

Relieved that Clara was okay, but a bit narked that she hadn't said goodbye, we booked our own Uber. We danced some more until the driver texted his arrival and then said our goodbyes to Cayden, Dean and a few others we had got to talk to during the evening.

When we were finally in the back of the car, I felt the air was thick with sexual tension, and I couldn't wait to cut through it. I stared at Josie, my breath catching as I once again witnessed the promise in her smouldering eyes. She unclicked her seat belt and slid over beside me. We glanced at the driver to make sure we couldn't be seen, but I didn't really care all that much. She took my hand and squeezed it with enough pressure to send my nervous system into overdrive. I squeezed back and watched her eyes darken with the same desire I knew I felt. I rubbed my thumb against her palm, pressing down before interlocking our fingers once more. We both gripped hard on to each other. The sensation of just our hands firmly together sent a charge directly down below. I clenched my leg muscles.

As though picking up on my need, Josie let go of my hand and slid her fingers on to my thigh. My breath hitched, and I looked down at her hand, watching as she applied more pressure. She kneaded my leg, her hand inching its way up in small, firm movements. My eyes flicked to the driver's mirror. He still had his eyes on the road, weaving his way in and out of the night-time traffic. Josie's face was inches from my own, and it took all I had to not pull her into a kiss. We held each other's gaze as she bit down on her bottom lip, letting her hand massage me deeper, moving closer and closer to where I wanted her – no, needed her.

"Fuck," I mouthed, feeling the effects of her fingers as they slid up to my groin.

She pressed her fingers harder against me.

"That's the plan," she mouthed back, with a look that instantly dismantled me.

CHAPTER 10

I TOOK JOSIE BY THE hand and quietly led her past the living room entrance where Clara was out sparko on the sofa. We made our way to my room and I closed the door behind us. Josie sat on the edge of my bed, leaning back on her hands and staring up at me.

"Hey." She smiled shyly.

"Hey." My teeth grazed my bottom lip.

She looked around the room, nervously before reaching over and sliding a book from my cabinet. She arched her eyebrow and held up the book. "Didn't have you pegged as a *Pride and Prejudice* type."

I wasn't about to have a conversation about my reading habits. I took a few steps towards the bed. "Well, there's a lot of things you don't know about me." I came to a stop in front of her.

"Is that right?" She placed the book on the bed beside her and met my eyes.

"Yup." I ran my fingers through her hair, feeling the sexual tension in the room instantly intensifying.

"Like what?" She closed her eyes at the contact.

"Oh, I don't know." My voice was low, and even to me it sounded a bit seductive. "Like from the moment I clapped eyes on you in that dress tonight, I've wanted nothing more than to get you back here to my bedroom. Or maybe how, every time you touch me, my body reacts instantly, making me want to rip your clothes off and take you there and then, or perhaps–"

Josie reached up and pressed two tender fingers to my lips. "Shush, no more talking." She left her fingers there, lingering on my bottom lip. I planted light kisses on the tips, watching as Josie's mouth curled at the corners and her eyes locked on mine. I took her wrist in my hand and held it as I parted my lips slightly, just enough to let my tongue brush against her skin. She moaned, and it sent tingles right through me in a way that nothing had done before. She moved her fingers against the touch of my tongue before pulling down on my bottom lip, giving her a better view. The look of pure seduction in her eyes was arousing on a whole other level. I wanted to please her more. I took both fingers in my mouth and wrapped my lips firmly around them, causing Josie to close her eyes. I responded by closing my lips entirely around her fingers and sucking them slowly from my mouth, grazing them ever so slightly with my teeth. Josie's mouth widened as she opened her eyes and watched hungrily while I repeated the process. The fire in her eyes told me she needed more. I was right. With her free hand, she reached up and gripped a handful of my t-shirt, pulling me in closer to her. My breasts were now at her eye level, inches from her face and my legs pressed against hers as I continued to greedily wrap my lips and tongue around her fingers, drawing them in and out with increased speed.

"How are you so sexy?" Her tone was throaty and drowning in lust.

I smiled into her fingers, fixing my eyes on hers and watching her pupils dilate.

Josie shook her head, giving in to a thought and without

warning, pulled me on top of her. Our lips came crashing together as we collapsed onto my bed. The kiss was frenzied, fueled by primal need. We explored each other roughly with our tongues and gave in to the tension that had built throughout the evening. I parted Josie's legs with my knee and let the pressure of my thigh press against her. She moaned, and it immediately sent pulses firing off in me. In that moment, Josie groaning with wanton need, became my new favourite thing to listen to. Ever.

We moved rhythmically together, me on top of her, propping myself on my forearms and pushing my pelvis into her, desperately searching for more contact – I *needed* to feel more of her. I sat up and drew her into a seated position, which left me straddling her. Her hair had been roughed up in our entanglement and was a wild-red-mess and quite possibly the most alluring thing I had seen; ever. I unzipped the back of Josie's dress and pulled at the strap. She immediately stretched her arms above her head, and I tore the dress off, then paused, taking a moment to look at the exquisiteness under me.

"Your body's gorgeous."

"Well," she rasped before planting a kiss on my chin, "I guess there's a lot of things *you* don't know about *me*."

My right eyebrow rose all by itself, maybe she was right. There was still a hell of a lot I didn't know about this woman, but what I did know meant I wanted to know much more.

"You're so fucking hot." I leaned in and found her mouth again. Josie tugged at my top, wanting me to match her level of nakedness. I drew away from the kiss long enough to slip my top and bra off, remove my jeans, and find my way back to her mouth. Her fingers traced the firm undulation of my abs and she paused to look at me with a perplexed expression. I shrugged, ignoring the question in her eyes and traced her torso and made my way up her small but firm breasts. I landed on her hardened nipple and drew it between two fingers, squeezing it enough to elicit a throaty groan from its owner. I had discovered a sensitive spot. Good. Go me.

She pulled me closer into her, so our breasts were pressing against each other. Her skin was soft and smooth, and the heat radiating off her raged as though it could burn right through me. I drew my lips away from hers and went to work on her neck, sucking carefully, with enough pressure to be pleasurable but not leave a mark. Josie tilted her chin, giving me full access to the part of her I had been admiring from a distance just days before. I traced from her neck to her collar bone, planting firm kisses as I slid further down the bed and her body. I continued until my mouth reached the pink flesh of her nipple. I ran my tongue around the circumference before grazing it with my teeth. My eyes flitted to Josie's face. Her expression was one of wanting. Her lips were parted, and she had a fire burning in her eyes that took me away somewhere else altogether. I sucked her into my mouth, clasping her breast as her pelvis lifted off the bed. I continued to greedily take her nipple in my mouth as my hand worked its way lower, finding the lacy fabric of her knickers. I cupped the soft, warm fabric with my palm, applying enough pressure to feel her, swollen and wet. I dipped a finger just under the elastic. Josie's moans intensified as she continued to thrust into me, willing my fingers to reach her. I pulled back and stroked the inside of her thigh, still taking her nipple in my mouth. Josie's frustrated whimper caused me to smile. I loved how much she wanted me to touch her, I loved teasing her and more than anything else, I loved that look of pure lust in her darkened eyes.

Josie grabbed the back of my head and pulled me away from her boobs and up towards her face. I thought she was going to kiss me. Instead, she pulled my head closer still and breathlessly purred into my ear, "Roxy, if you don't put your fingers inside me now, I swear to god, I'm going to do it myself."

That was it. Her words stirred something deep in me, and I

had to have her. I crashed her mouth ferociously as I grabbed her pants and yanked them down her legs. Josie kicked them free from her foot and parted her legs, giving me all the access I needed. I wasted no time in letting my fingers explore her and slide into her, causing us to simultaneously groan with pleasure. I slipped in only one finger at first but quickly increased it to two. Josie's hands clasped at the headboard as she threw her head back with my every forceful push into her. There was nothing slow and sensual about what we were doing. It was fast. It was rough, and *my god*, it was exciting. I angled my fingers inside her and pounded the quivering wetness. Josie's ragged breath let me know I was finding her most sensitive secret. I quickened the pace again, making sure the palm of my hand had contact with her clit as I thrust my fingers. I kept up the rhythm while our mouths continued to meet in a frantic, almost desperate kiss.

"Fuck!" Josie moaned sharply as I urged a third finger inside her. Each time a guttural moan escaped her throat, a bolt of arousal surged in me, making me quicken the pace and force in which I plunged into her. My whole body moved wildly against her to the rhythm of what my hand was learning from her fevered movements. I had found her rhythm. We were no longer able to kiss, but our foreheads touched as we remained mouth on mouth, panting into each other until…

"Fuuuuuck," Josie let out in a strangled cry as her inner walls gripped around my fingers. She thrust herself onto me, once, twice, three times before loosening her grip and twitching convulsively as the final ripples of her orgasm played out. I relaxed on top of her, leaving my fingers where they were and tried to regain my breath.

"Ummm." Josie let out a satisfied groan through a panting breath before planting a soft kiss on my shoulder.

I grinned up at her, still breathless myself. "You like?"

She nodded. "Oh yes," through a breathy pant, "I think it's safe to say I like, Rox."

I continued to smile up at her as I slid off her still throbbing body and tucked in beside her, my fingers still snug inside.

What?" Her eyes danced playfully, the extra sparkle captivating me.

"I don't know, I guess you just surprise me, that's all."

"Oh yeah? How come?" She shuffled up onto her elbows and lifted the sheet over her naked body.

"I guess, after the other night, I thought you would be a little more…" I paused to come up with the right word, "… subdued?" I frowned as I said the word, not sure quite how Josie would react.

Josie considered for a moment, "Because I asked you to calm down?"

Hearing her say it aloud for a second time didn't sound nearly as bad, and I internally cringed, knowing I had made such a big deal out of it at the time.

"Uh-huh." I nodded, feeling sheepish all over again.

Josie sat up and placed her hands gently on my cheeks.

"Come here." She gestured for me to come up and meet her. I gently slid out of her and climbed up her body until our faces were inches apart. "I shouldn't have used those words. I realised straight away how patronising they must've sounded. I definitely could've worded it better. I was caught up in the moment and lost all ability to articulate. But just so you know, I didn't tell you to calm down because I'm lame or subdued or whatever it is you want to call it. I asked you to calm down because I needed things to *slow* down. I wanted nothing more than to have you there and then and I knew if we continued at that pace we would've slept together and I didn't want to rush things like that." She kept eye contact. "I didn't – don't – want us to be a one-night thing. I'm not into that, and I do really like you, Roxy."

I exhaled, tracing my fingers over her collarbone. "But I just don't get it."

"You don't get what?" She frowned.

"Why you like me. I'm sure a serious academic like you could have your pick of anyone, so why me?" I realised it was a question that had been preying on my mind from the second she showed an interest in me.

Josie sucked in her lips and frowned some more. "You really don't see it, do you? Roxy, you're stunning. From the moment I walked in on you and Susan at the home, I felt an instant attraction to you. I had to be near you and get to know you. There was something about you – there *is* – something about you. Okay, so you clearly have one or two barriers up, but we all have our stuff to deal with. You're funny and smart and–"

"Whoa, whoa, okay, I get it, enough already." I held my hands up in surrender, suspecting the list would go on. "You could've just said I was a good lay, that would have sufficed."

Josie rolled her eyes at my inability to take the compliments and her sigh told me she had decided to let me off the hook.

"Yes, Roxanne Mackenzie, you are a very – no incredibly – good lay," she said, between kisses planted on my neck.

My body's reaction to Josie's mouth on my skin was instantaneous, and within seconds, I had forgotten what we had been talking about and once more drove a wedge between her thighs with my leg. I moved against her in a slow grinding motion while she cupped my bum, pressing me into her and matching my movements. Her mouth close to my ear gave me the full effect of the soft moans and ragged breath escaping her. I throbbed and knew I needed to have her soon, or it would become more painful than pleasurable. As though hearing my thoughts, Josie flipped our positions and lay me out beneath her. She leaned over me, propped herself on both hands and kissed me. We deepened the kiss with our tongues moving against each other as our mouths attempted to become one. It was hurried and passionate. Josie's hair fell over my face and at times encroached on my mouth, but I didn't care, it was like being engulfed in a soft, red-gold jungle. And I only cared about how this woman was kissing me like the world could end any minute. The feel of her tongue against my own made me ache. I couldn't take another minute of not being touched by her. I found her hand and grabbed hold of it, directing it to where I had to have her. She withdrew her hand from mine and shook her head.

"I want to taste you." She was already sliding down the bed. I tilted my head back and blew out a long, tremulous breath at her words. My god, I did want so badly for her to go down on me. She made a trail down my body with her tongue. Perhaps sensing my desperation, she bypassed my boobs and headed straight for my pelvis. She kept eye contact with me as she peeled my pants from my legs and planted light kisses over my shaved area. I thrust against her mouth, unable to wait a second longer. Josie smiled, still looking up at me.

"I'll just get on with it then, shall I? Miss Impatient."

"Please," I begged, in a pathetic whimper.

Josie didn't make me ask twice. She met me with her tongue with the perfect amount of force. No light contact, no brushing up against me achingly slow or dragging anything out, she was going all in. She worked her tongue around every part of me as she explored me thoroughly. The pulses of pleasure her skilled tongue elicited shot through me and had me grabbing fistfuls of sheet with one hand while biting down on my other clenched fist. I moaned from the depths of my diaphragm as she worked the same spot, flicking and licking with the right amount of speed and just the right amount of pressure. She repeated the up-down motions until I couldn't take anymore. My breath caught as the intensity built, and I felt myself sliding towards and then over the edge. A thousand colours filled my vision as one of the most powerful orgasms I have ever experienced crashed through me like a breaking wave as I exploded into Josie's mouth.

"Holy shit." My body relaxed back into a flop.

Josie raised her eyebrows with a small smirk, "*You* like?" She knew damn well what the answer was.

She didn't come up straight away. Instead, she remained down there, tracing my skin with her fingers while she smiled up at me. I hoped it wasn't going to be too long before I felt what it was like to have those fingers inside me, but for the time being, even *I* was done. Josie pulled herself up and lay beside me. I moved so I could look at her face. Her mane of coppery hair was even more dishevelled, and her mouth and chin glistened with me. It was erotic. I kissed her, knowing I was tasting myself. She ran her hand over the sweat that glistened on my stomach.

"That was mind blowing." I meant it. My mind really had been blown.

Josie let out a contented sigh. "*You're* mind blowing."

I smiled, letting the rare sensation of genuine happiness envelop me before an anxious thud started in my chest at how easily it could all be taken away. I froze.

"Roxy, what's wrong?"

I shook my head. "Nothing." I was desperately trying to not ruin this moment.

Compassion filled her eyes. "You thinking about your mum?"

The question caught me off-guard. For once, I actually wasn't thinking about my mother. Instead, I was thinking about how I had lied to Josie about my job and how I knew I couldn't start something with this much potential with a lie. I closed my eyes and took in a deep breath, geeing myself up.

"Josie, I think there's something I need to tell you. I..."

CHAPTER 11

JOSIE INTERRUPTED ME BEFORE I had the chance to complete my sentence. "Wait. Please, wait. Before you say anything else, there's something I need to tell you first." She sat up onto her knees and looked at me seriously.

I shuffled up the bed, lifted the sheet over me protectively and waited. Josie chewed on the inside of her cheek and stared down at her hands for a long moment.

"Okay, go on." I hoped my tone was encouraging and not anxious.

She released a long breath before looking at me steadily. "You know how I said I felt like I knew you when we first met?"

I had no idea where the conversation was heading. "Yes." I drew out the word.

Josie looked down at her fingers some more before staring back into my eyes. "Well, I wasn't making it up." She hesitated, then went on. "I'd heard a lot about you before that first day I met you."

My brow furrowed. "I know. We established that. My mum has a big mouth." I smiled.

Josie shook her head. "Rox, I didn't hear it from your mum like you think I did. Not directly anyway."

I eyed her quizzically. "Okay." It was another drawn-out word, but the thread was becoming difficult to follow.

"The person I heard about you from wasn't *your* mum." Her eyes went back to her hands, and she chewed some more on the inside of her cheek, which I had learned by now meant she was agitated. "It was mine." Her voice was barely a whisper.

I tugged on my earlobe and frowned again, still attempting to make sense of what she was trying to say.

"I don't understand. How could your mum possibly have told you things about me? I haven't even met her – yet anyway."

Josie did something that looked like a sad smile. "You won't be meeting my mum, Roxy." She shook her head, her eyes full of regret.

I leaned forward and stroked her arm. Seeing the pain flash in her eyes was hard.

"Josie, you're going to have to catch me up here, I'm confused."

She rubbed at her shoulder absentmindedly, and I'm sure her eyes were beginning to glisten with tears. She took in a deep breath. "You've actually met my mum. More than once."

"I don't understand."

She continued to knead her shoulder. "It was when your mum first became a resident at Princess Park. The two of them hit it off straight away. I think it was their love of meddling in other people's business that were the foundations for their friendship."

I ran her words over again in my mind, "Wait," I said, as the penny dropped, "Annette is your mum?" I was incredulous.

Josie stayed silent and nodded. My eyes widened, and tears instantaneously filled them.

"Oh, Josie, I am so sorry." I leaned in and traced her cheek with my fingers. "I didn't know."

She shrugged, covering my hand with her own. "Why would you? We always missed each other with you visiting your mum in the morning and me coming in late. Mum talked about you loads though, she had obviously taken a shine to you. I think she had this idea in her head that you and I should get together. You know what they're like, the older gen. They think just because we're both gay and of a similar age we should automatically like each other." She let out a gentle snigger, and I couldn't help but do the same.

"Well, she wasn't wrong." I smiled at her tenderly. "I just can't believe your mum is Annette." I shook my head as I thought back. "It was so difficult when, well, you know. Mum took it hard; we all did. I just never would've known you'd been through that. You seem so," I hesitated and looked for the right word, "together."

Josie sucked in her lips. "Well, what choice did I have? It's not as though I didn't know it was coming, I'd managed to prepare myself to a certain extent, and my spiritual beliefs definitely helped. I used to read to her every day after work. Rumi was her favourite, and I guess, when she died, I found it hard to let go. It'd been my routine for about eight months, so I just carried on reading to other residents, and strangely, it helped me still feel close to her."

I rested my head in my hands as the things Mum had said came flooding back. I got it then why Mum told me to keep my distance. She wasn't getting at me; she was protecting Josie. She knew what she had been through and didn't want me dicking her about when she was so vulnerable. And Milly too, she knew, of course. *Everyone* had known Annette, she was a lovely lady, who kept her humour and niceness right till the end. By the time Mum became a resident there, Annette was in a bad way, but she and Mum managed to strike up a real friendship in the short time they spent together. I remember Mum wanting so much to go to the funeral, but she wasn't up to it, so instead a couple of the nurses arranged a small memorial at the home while the funeral took place. I just couldn't believe that had been Josie's Mum. I rubbed at my wet eyes.

"Josie, honestly, I just don't know what to say. How are you still functioning? It's been what? Four months?" I slipped my arm around her and pulled her head onto my shoulder, squeezing her into me, suddenly feeling very protective of her. She nuzzled against me.

"Well, to be fair, if you'd met me just a month ago, it might have been a different story. Mum was everything to me. She was my best friend, and when she finally gave up and let go, she took a big part of me with her. For the first three months, the part of me that was capable of smiling, laughing and even loving just wasn't there. I was numb. My ability to see the world in a good light was nowhere to be found and I genuinely thought her death had changed me forever, and not in a good way. When I visited your mum that day – the day we met – I'd decided I wasn't going to come to the home anymore. It seemed unhealthy almost, and I needed to do what I could to get back to *me*, but then I saw you, and I guess in a strange kind of way, I took it as a sign from Mum or the cosmos or whatever that maybe I should stick around a while longer." She stopped speaking and pressed the back of her hand over her mouth, masking a yawn. "That night at the club, that was the first time I'd been out in fourteen months. I only went because my friend insisted on it as she was doing a DJ set, and there you were again, and I just can't ignore signs like that." Her voice trailed off into a slow murmur, and I could sense that she had closed her eyes. I ran my fingers through her hair and smiled.

"You think we were supposed to come together?" I whispered close to her ear. Josie shrugged and yawned once more.

"I just think there's something about you that I'm drawn to, and I love how it feels when we're together, that's all." Her voice took on a distant sleepy tone as she snuggled into me. I planted a light kiss on her head and hugged her gently.

"Me too, I feel the exact same way."

"Rox?" she asked sleepily into my chest, the word barely audible.

"Yeah?"

"What was it you were going to tell me?"

"Huh?"

"Before I told you about Mum. You said there was something you needed to tell me?"

I kissed her head once more and stroked her arm with my thumb. "It doesn't matter now; you just get some sleep."

I SQUINTED OPEN AN EYE and looked at the alarm clock; it was 6:03am. Once Josie had fallen asleep in my arms, I stayed awake thinking about what she had shared. I couldn't believe I had missed it. She had been so positive, so together, so *normal*. I don't think anyone would have guessed. I was also pissed at Mum, she should have told me. It's not as if I didn't give her the opportunity. There was solace in hearing that Annette was Josie's mum though, and that was the hope it gave me. If Josie could come through it the way she had, maybe I would be able to do the same. I looked down at Josie, still nestled into my collar bone and sighed contentedly. What was it about her that made me do that? If she had been anyone else, I would be planning my escape, *from my own bed*, but with her, it was different. I kissed the top of her head. I seemed to be doing that a lot lately.

"Your hair smells like cinnamon." I wasn't quite sure whether she was awake. Her body wriggled against my side.

"Good morning to you too," she said sleepily.

"It's six, and I'm happy to be awake."

Josie let out a small sultry laugh. "What?"

I smiled. "I said, it's six a.m., and *I'm* happy to be awake. Seriously, you don't understand, I hate mornings, they are my nemesis."

Josie looked up from beneath heavy eyelids and pulled me tight against her. "And may I ask why the sudden turnaround?"

"You may, but I suspect you are fully aware of the answer."

A smile made its way from her lips to her sleepy eyes. "Nope, no idea."

Okay, she was making me say it. "Well, I think it has a lot to do with the gorgeous naked redhead who happens to be wrapped around me."

"Yeah, that's what I thought." She scrunched up her nose and reached up to kiss my chin. "Hey, Rox." She paused then went on. "Did I bum you out last night?"

I punched a pillow up behind my head and pulled her up with me.

"No, not at all. I mean, don't get me wrong, it was devastating to hear, but I'm glad you told me. I just can't believe it."

Josie continued to look up at me with those gorgeous brown eyes. "I'm sorry I didn't tell you sooner. It's just, although losing Mum broke me in two and it's still so raw, the last thing I wanted was for you to be consoling me and worrying about what you can and can't say around me. What you need more than anything is someone to be strong for you and help you through what you're going through, and I would like to be able to do that."

"God, Josie, you don't have to apologise." I swallowed down my guilt at my own kept secret.

"I do. I felt shitty keeping it from you. I hate secrets. I even asked your mum not to say anything until I was ready. Seriously Rox, I am sorry."

I fidgeted, wriggling against the propped pillows.

"Please, stop apologising; honestly, you've nothing to be

sorry about. I don't want to hear you say you're sorry again, okay?"

The guilt I felt for what I was keeping from her was intensifying with every apology she gave.

She nodded into my chest, and I ran my fingers through her luxurious tangle of bed-hair.

"So, what about your dad? Or siblings? I haven't even asked if you have any brothers or sisters, anyone that's been there for you through all of this."

Josie's smile was uneasy and she inhaled a deep, shaky breath.

"Hmm, siblings is a difficult one to answer. Technically yes but I don't see them. As far as I'm concerned, I'm an only child. And as for my dad..." she blew out her cheeks, "let's just say that's a story for another day. I think I've brought the mood down enough."

"That good, huh?"

"Well, as you quite rightly pointed out before; there's a reason people decide to study psychology and more often than not it's because on some known or unknown level, they have a deep desire to understand their own demons and the messed up actions of others. But, like I said, that's a story for another day. Right now, I'm more interested in rehashing last night." Josie pushed out of my arms and came up to kiss me. I whipped my head back before her lips landed on mine. The panic that flashed through her eyes was not lost on me. She frowned, still centimetres from my face.

"Erm...What was that? We're not having a repeat of the other night, are we? I thought we were past that?"

I smiled. We *were* past that, weren't we? "No, no repeat of the other night. I told you, we're doing this. I just don't do kissing in the morning, that's all."

She eyed me suspiciously, "Because?" She drew out the word.

"Because it's not the movies. You can't just wake up and kiss someone without brushing your teeth first. So, unless you have a real desire to get all up in my morning breath, I'm gonna go brush my teeth, fix us breakfast and then we'll see about the action replay." I gave Josie a quick peck on the nose before leaning over to grab a pair of jogging bottoms from the floor, I tugged them on and walked over to rummage in my chest of drawers, sensing Josie's eyes following me as I pulled on a vest top.

"Roxy?" She looked up at me from the bed with lustful eyes.

"Yeah?"

"Don't be too long."

ONCE I HAD BRUSHED MY teeth, possibly removing a layer of enamel, I went to the living room and stopped in the doorway. Clara was still sprawled on the sofa where I left her the previous night. Sensing my presence, she opened one eye.

"Slut," she deadpanned.

Ordinarily, I would have been embarrassed by the thought that she had heard last night's shenanigans, but this was Clara, and it's not as though I hadn't heard her go at it more times than I could count. I think I even recall her asking if I had enjoyed the show on one particular morning like she had done it for my benefit.

"Yup." I nodded slowly as I walked to the kitchen with a goofball grin and turned on the coffee machine.

"You look like you need coffee," I called out. Clara replied with a low grunt, which I took as a "yes." I made Clara's drink first, not wanting Josie's to get cold while I fixed breakfast. I passed Clara a tall latte just how she liked it, with two sugars and a dusting of cocoa powder.

"Ta." She sat and cupped the drink in both hands.

"Pancakes?"

Clara's look of disgust gave me my answer, so I set to work on making breakfast for two. As I cracked four eggs into a bowl and added the milk, flour and a pinch of salt, I remembered how pissed off I was with her for leaving the party.

"So, ready to share why you disappeared last night?" I asked, through the serving hatch.

Clara rubbed her eyes and blew out her lips. "I told you. I felt ill. I left because it was either that or vom on your friend's carpet. That okay with you, Jessica Fletcher?" She took her first sip of coffee.

"Well, you could've had the decency to say goodbye. We would have come back with you."

"You were having too much fun. I didn't want to ruin your night, so I just left."

"Hmm...Why do I feel there's more to the story?" I tried to keep the tone casual as I whisked the pancake ingredients into a smooth batter.

"Oh, I don't know, because you're delusional." I heard her murmur over my whisking even though it was obviously supposed to be under her breath.

I rolled my eyes while I added a splash of oil to the frying pan and set the hob to medium.

"Well, I don't care what you say, you're being shady. What's with you lately, anyway? I barely saw you all night. Are you seeing someone? Is that why you're always sneaking off? To call him? You can tell me. As long as you haven't got involved with that dickhead ex of yours again." I took out the chopping board and sliced a lemon into quarters while I waited for the oil to heat.

I peeked through the hatch to catch Clara rolling her eyes.

"I'm not being shady. I just don't have to share every aspect of my life with you, do I?" Her tone was about as sour as the lemon I had just cut, and I tried not to show it, but I was taken aback. Don't get me wrong, Clara was known to be snappish, but there was a sting to the way she said it that was sharper than normal. We remained quiet while I added the first ladle of batter to the frying pan, immediately satisfied with the sizzling sound the oil gave off. As I rolled the pan and waited for the pancake to set and brown, I wondered if perhaps Clara had found out about my mum and was upset I hadn't shared that part of my life with her. Maybe Josie had spoken to her at the party, or perhaps she was a friend of a friend who had spilt the beans…or maybe…Just maybe, I was being paranoid.

After carrying out a perfect flip of the first pancake, I set the coffee machine going and lined up two coffee cups, adding two sugars to mine. Then, once the first pancake was deliciously done, I made a start on the next, the whole time Clara and I didn't speak. Eventually, I finished up in the kitchen by popping the lemon slices onto the perfectly cooked pancakes and setting two coffee cups and two plates onto a tray and stuck my head back into the front room where Clara cut me an unreadable look.

"What?" My tone was in direct acid proportion to the shitty glare and attitude.

"Nothing."

I sighed.

"Okay, well you're obviously in a good mood this morning, and as much as I'd love to stop and continue this riveting conversation, I have a seriously hot chick waiting for me in my bed, who, by the way, has the body of a goddess.

Against her will, Clara's mouth curled up at one side. She wasn't mad at me, so maybe it was just the side effects of a hangover.

"Just go, you perv, go do your duty for lesbidom." She found herself hilarious as she shooed me from the room.

CHAPTER 12

I PUSHED OPEN THE BEDROOM DOOR with my foot while balancing the tray. Josie was sat up in my bed with the sheet mostly covering her but letting a little cleavage show. I smiled, appreciating the sight. Her hair fell in loose waves and was obviously freshly brushed, and she had a twinkle in her eye, which told me we were not about to continue our tough discussion from earlier, but something else. I set the tray on the dresser and passed her the coffee and plate. She didn't take her eyes from me.

"What?" I self-consciously tucked my hair behind my ear.

She smiled an easy smile. "I don't know." She hesitated and squinted and wiggled her nose before continuing, "I guess, doing what I do for a living, it's easy to fall into the trap of thinking I have everyone figured out." She took a sip of her coffee, made an appreciative noise and studied me over the mug. I sat beside her.

"You're surprised I can make pancakes?"

She let out a low chuckle, "No, well, actually, maybe a little, but I'm surprised you've allowed me to stay long enough for you to make me pancakes, that's what I'm getting at." She watched me intently then. Her words had mirrored my thoughts from earlier, and I wanted to at least be upfront about this.

"Well." I reached over and laid a hand on the sheet that covered her leg. "I have to admit, there's something to that. This…" I gestured between us, "is not something I'm used to, but don't get it confused. I'm not, nor have I ever been some fuck-girl who makes false promises and messes people around. I've always been upfront with any past…" I took a moment to consider the most appropriate word, "relations. But I guess I've just never found someone who made me want to see how it goes. And go with it."

Josie smiled. "Until now?" She took her first forkful of pancake.

I nodded. "Until now."

I took my own plate from the dresser, and we ate in comfortable silence. Every so often, I couldn't help a smile as I thought back to the previous night and how natural we had been together. Every time I thought about the effect Josie's touch had on me, I felt my toes curl, which is exactly what I was doing when she eventually spoke.

"What are those?"

I jumped. "What?" I looked around to where Josie pointed, and at the piles of notebooks stacked below my window. "Oh, that's just my writing."

Josie's eyes widened. "*Just* your writing? There are more books there than the British Library."

She set her empty plate carefully on the bedside table. "Would you mind if I had a look?" Her tone was hopeful. "I heard how Cayden talked about your writing last night, so I'm thinking it must be pretty special."

I let go an annoyed sigh at Cayden, having bigged me up so much.

"Crap. Sorry, have I crossed a line? Is that one of those questions you should never ask a writer?"

I laughed at her worried expression. "No, I'm not particularly precious about people reading my stuff. It's just Cayden has a tendency to be a little too over-enthusiastic."

Josie smiled. "So...?"

"Yeah, you can take a look. But you have to promise not to laugh."

I pretty much regretted the words the second they left my lips. I knew what my writing could be like, every now and then I would write something special, but for the most part, I could fill an entire book with utter crap. Josie lifted the sheet higher against her chest and began to attempt to get out of bed.

"Wait!" I jumped up and dashed over to the stacks to select the notebook, spilling a little of my coffee down my t-shirt as I did. "I'd like to take a look first."

I picked a notebook out at random and flicked through the pages as fast as I could, scanning and making sure Josie wouldn't be reading any of my deepest darkest secrets. It quickly became apparent the notebook was written just before I moved to London. Filled with my hopes and dreams, all written in a mixture of poetry and prose and I figured I would rather Josie read that than some of my darker times. I reluctantly passed the notebook to her. She took it from me and sat up against the headboard with her knees hitched up as she began to turn the pages. I fiddled around with the bottles and crap on my dresser, lining them up in height order. Then I arranged them the other way around. Then I did it again. Every now and then I glanced at Josie who seemed to be engrossed in the pages and reading with what looked to me like a perplexed expression. I wondered if maybe she was struggling to make out my handwriting. Eventually, after what felt like an hour, only I'm sure it was a few long minutes, she spoke.

"Are you serious?"

Her voice was a hell of a lot higher than I had heard before, surprising me so much that I jumped and knocked over a large can of hairspray.

"You wrote this? *You*?" Josie didn't wait for me to answer, she went on, "Rox, this stuff is amazing. You're a fantastic writer. Everything you've said in here about your vision for your future, and how you're going to get there, it's all put so beautifully. Why didn't you tell me you were so good?" Her gaze was intense.

I looked away, feeling my cheeks flush.

"Well, firstly, I would like to point out I take complete offence at your inability to believe *I* wrote that." I widened my eyes in deep shock. "And secondly, I didn't tell you because funnily enough, I don't usually start conversations with "Hi, I'm Roxy, and I'm a fantastic writer", besides, I have Cayden to do that for me." I pulled a silly face.

Josie didn't laugh. Instead, she shook her head. "No, I'm not surprised you wrote this." She shook her head again, correcting herself, "Well, actually, if I'm honest, I am a bit surprised. You don't talk anything like how you write. Not that there's anything wrong with the way you talk because there's not, but just meeting you, you would never know there's a hidden Whitman in there. Seriously, Roxy, why didn't you go to uni?"

She had clearly worked herself up, and it reminded me a little of how she spoke when she talked about Rumi or her work. But it was the first time I had really seen the full-on enthusiast come out in her, and if I hadn't been so annoyed by the question, I would have found it arousing.

"I just didn't want to go." I turned my back on her and began to pick up the clothes that were strewn over the floor.

"Hmmm, I'm not sure that's the truth."

I stopped gathering, and said nothing, wondering how she knew that.

"Roxy, look at me." She had adopted a gentler tone.

I let out a deep breath and turned to find her regarding me with an almost pained expression.

"Roxy, I *really* would like to get to know you. The real you. I don't want you to tell me the same bullshit story you've been telling everyone else, including yourself. I need you to let me in." She paused and then asked me again, "Why didn't you go to uni?"

I leaned my back against the chest of drawers and clutched the bundle of clothes to my chest.

"You know, when I was eight, I had this teacher, Mr Henshaw. He would bring his guitar into class once a week and have us all gather around, crossed-legged on the carpet. I remember him playing songs like "He Ain't Heavy" by The Hollies and "Baker Street" by Gerry Rafferty. He would ask us all what we thought the lyrics were about, and I was blown away by how, in just a few minutes, the words could tell such an emotional story."

"And that's when you fell in love with poetry?" There was a hint of something that resembled excitement in her voice. Her enthusiasm made me smile.

"I guess so, yeah. I began writing every day. Just silly snippets really, trying to make sense of the world around me." My attention was drawn to Josie's bra on the floor. I hooked it with my toe, held it up and wiggled my foot.

"Stop deflecting." She whipped the bra from my foot. "Carry on."

"Well, one day, Mr Henshaw gave each of us an assignment, to come up with an original poem based on the subject of the sea, and mine turned out pretty good."

"Oh yeah? Do you remember it?"

I rolled my eyes. "Would you believe me if I said I didn't?"

She shook her head. "Nope."

I closed my eyes. "Okay, but you're going to have to promise not to take the piss. I was eight, remember?" Josie drew a little cross over her heart with her finger.

"I promise."

I quickly replayed the poem in my mind to see if I really could still remember it, and when I could, thought – what the hell. I let out a breath and cleared my throat, "Okay, it went something like...

Under the sea where the creatures lie,
Beautiful mermaids floating by,
Colourful anemones open in blooms,
Dolphins swimming in the bluest lagoons,
Fishermen fishing in the sea,
Lighthouses flashing in emergency."

Josie's eyes widened. "You wrote that when you were eight? You were a child prodigy."

I shrugged. "That's what he said. He called my mum into school especially, to tell her she had to develop my talents, and if I remember correctly, I think that was the first time she ever used the line "I don't know where you get your brains from, certainly not your ol' mum that's for sure"," I mimicked Mum's voice and Josie smiled.

"I can hear her saying that."

"Yeah, well, anyway, after that, writing kinda became my thing; poetry, prose, songs, letters, scripts, even short stories. It was just nice to be good at something, you know? And this continued on through school and even college until I was offered a scholarship into Warwick."

Josie sat up straighter, and her eyes widened. "Whoa, what? That's huge. So, why didn't you go?"

I shrugged again. "I wanted to. It was *Warwick* for Christ's sake, and believe me, I had longed for that ticket out of the housing estate for years, but by the time the college year was finishing up, Mum was given her first diagnosis. I couldn't bear the thought of living halfway across the country when she needed me most. I would never have been able to concentrate on my studies when I knew she was at home ill. So, I chose to be a devoted daughter rather than carrying on with my education. It's a decision I don't regret and would still make today."

Josie's smile was sympathetic.

"Please don't look at me like that" I was already beginning to wish I hadn't said anything.

Josie shook her head. "I'm sorry, it's just so sad. So, what made you move to London in the end?"

"Well, once Mum had gone into remission, she pushed me to move out. She knew how much I hated living there. It wasn't a very nice place, and I always felt as though I didn't belong. I'd drifted away from my friends who, if I'm completely frank, had made some piss-poor life choices, either having kids way too young or getting into drugs. So, I convinced myself it would be a good move to come to the city. I needed a fresh start and I figured being in the mix of it all would inspire me, and it did for a while. I was even starting to get some of my work published." I thought back wistfully to that happier time in my life.

"Then your mum got her second diagnosis?"

"Yup. I spent most of my time to-ing and fro-ing between here and Southend, making it impossible to concentrate on writing while holding down a couple of jobs. Obviously, the past six months she's been at the home, and any time I've gone to write, I just freeze. It's writer's block at its finest, I think, and each time I attempt to write and can't it just ends up making me feel worse. So, I've pretty much stopped trying."

"I guess that makes sense given the amount of stress you're under. But it will pass, you do know that, don't you?"

I nodded. "I know. I just hope it's soon. I miss it, you know? That feeling I get when something comes out of me that I didn't even know was in there. I don't think there's anything that compares. I know it sounds silly because anyone can write at any time, but I just always had this idea of going to uni and really developing my skill. I wanted to learn how to be the best I can be."

Josie's sympathetic expression had now been replaced by the same excitable little glint from earlier.

"Well, you're young, there's still time. Writing's not something that comes with a shelf life, you can succeed at any age. Your talent's really something, and I don't know if it's intuition or what, but I don't think you're someone who's destined to pull pints their whole life. I could feel that before I even read your work."

My eyes dropped to the patterns on the quilt as I swallowed her comment about pulling pints. When was I going to tell her the truth?

"I know what you're saying, but as much as I know I would love the work and the learning side of things, I guess I just couldn't imagine myself at uni now, I would be so much older than the other students, it would be weird."

Josie held her hand out, and I reached and took it. "Come here." She pulled me on to the bed. "Did you know that if you live until you're eighty, that's only four-thousand weeks?"

I laughed at the randomness of her question. "No, I can't say I'd figured that one out."

She ran her hand through my hair. "Well, it's no time at all, is it? Think how quickly a week flies by. If losing my mum has taught me one thing, it's that life really is short Rox, too short to not take something on if it means a lot to you."

I looked her in the eyes, and my lips curled into a small grin. "How do you do that?" I asked quietly.

"Do what?"

"Just make everything seem so simple."

She shrugged. "I don't know. Maybe because at their core things really are simple. In my experience, people tend to over-analyse and complicate situations."

"People? Or me?"

Josie placed a hand on my cheek and smiled.

"I think you're scared. I think deep down, you're afraid of not measuring up, but baby, you can't go through life afraid of not being good enough, regardless of your background. It would just be such a waste."

My insides jolted at the term of endearment. I didn't know what this woman was doing to me, but I knew for damn sure that she could ignite things that I didn't even know existed. I couldn't even say why, but for the first time in a long time, I sensed a small sliver of hope.

"WHAT IS YOUR FACE?" THOSE were the four words I was greeted with as I entered Mum's room.

I closed my eyes and opened them again. "Mum, that question makes absolutely no sense."

With a shaky hand, she slid her reading glasses slightly down her nose and squinted up at me. "You look different." She continued to study me. "Wait a minute, I think I can just about make it out now." She drew in a sharp breath, "You've had sex!"

Oh, for fuck's sake. I laid a hand on my cheek and shook my head, incredulous.

"Mum, I did not have sex."

She stared at me some more while I did everything within me to not let the smile that was tugging at my lips spread across my face.

"Oooh, you did! You wait 'til I see Julia next door, I was just saying to her the other day that I thought you needed to have a good–"

"Mum! Stop!" I stuck my fingers in my ears.

Mum let out a low rattly chuckle. "Okay, I'll shut up but as long as you know that not a lot gets past your ol' mum. I've known you since you were smearing poo up the walls, and I know that face."

I ignored her comment and went to put the kettle on, then I let the smile escape and thought that maybe a good cup of tea would keep her quiet for a bit. While I waited for the kettle to boil, I thought about telling Mum about Josie and me. I really wanted to have it out with her about not telling me that Josie's mum was Annette, but it was still very early days, and I wasn't sure I was prepared for her opinion, not just yet anyway. Besides, Josie and I had both agreed that morning it was for the best that we keep it hush-hush for a while.

Once the kettle boiled, I made tea for Mum with lots of milk, how she liked it, and took it back over to her bed.

"You seem spritely today." I handed her the tea. She took the cup from me and looked down into it with a hitched nostril.

"What? We on rations? I need a bloody ladder to get down into this thing."

I didn't have the heart to tell her I wouldn't fill it because of the shake in her hands.

"No, sorry, I just didn't add enough water to the kettle, I'll make you another one after if you want."

Mum rolled her eyes, dismissively.

"Anyway, I said you seem good today."

She nodded. "I am actually darlin'. You know how it is, some days better than others."

I became distracted by my phone vibrating in my pocket. With excitement stirring in my insides, I slid it out and smiled when I saw it was a text from Josie.

What are your plans this weekend? x

I smiled like an idiot as I typed out my reply.

Working Saturday night. Free Friday and Sunday x

I placed the phone on my lap and turned my attention to Mum, who was looking rather proud of herself.

"What?" I asked, not bothering to wait for her response before there was a ping, and I read the next text.

Can you get out of work Saturday? x

"Sorry, two secs." I had to respond even though I knew it was rude.

"Oh, don't mind me." Mum's tone was deliberately sarcastic. She sipped her tea and continued to eye me suspiciously.

I could maybe ask Clara to swap shifts. What are you thinking? X

The next text came through immediately.

A weekend away xx

I read the words and then re-read them, unable to help the grin that was making its way over my face. Mum cleared her throat, and I looked at her, feeling the excitement leave me immediately.

Lovely idea, but there's my mum. Xxx

You need a break, Rox. You need a couple of days away from it all. Xx

I placed the phone back in my pocket and let out a breath.

"Spill." Mum knew there was something on my mind.

I looked at my fingernails, trying to find a way to articulate what I was about to ask.

"Mum," I hesitated and tried it out three different ways before I just opened my mouth. "How would you feel if I was to miss a couple of days this weekend? I could ask Em to come and visit you while I'm gone."

Mum narrowed her gaze triumphantly. "I bloody knew it. You're going off to have sex."

I rubbed at my pink cheeks, and before I could protest, she added. "I don't mind. You go, have fun. You deserve a break. Will be nice to see your sister anyway."

"Are you sure? And you would get someone to call if you needed me?"

"I'm not going anywhere yet kiddo. Go. Have fun."

I smiled and gave Mum a kiss before taking my phone from my pocket again.

What would I need to bring? xx

Hiking shoes and wellies. I have all the camping equipment. xx

CAMPING? HIKING? I think you have the wrong person. xx

Haha. Maybe, but I hear in psychological circles Nature and the outdoors have a healing effect. Don't knock it until you've tried it. xx

I don't own wellies or hiking shoes! xx

You don't own wellies? Maybe I do have the wrong person. xx

I can buy them?! xx

So, that's a yes? xxx

It's a yes, providing I can get someone to cover my shift. Where are we going? xx

It's a surprise xxxx

CHAPTER 13

"PULL THAT A BIT TIGHTER," Josie yelled from the opposite side of the tent.

I tugged at the stretched rope, "Like this?"

She craned her neck to see if I was doing it right and shook her head, "No, it needs to be taut. You're going to have to stretch it at least another foot, then hit the peg in while I hold this up to stop the frame collapsing."

I did as she asked and hooked the rope over the metal peg while hammering it into the hard ground. When the stake was fully buried, I stood, and grinned over at Josie, pleased at my achievements.

"What's next boss?" I wiped a trickle of sweat from my forehead before resting a hand on each hip. Josie got up from her kneeling position in one graceful, strong movement, clasping onto the tent as she rose. The tent remained upright for approximately five seconds before the structure slowly began to tilt to one side before collapsing into itself in a crumpled heap.

"Oh, come on. You have got to be kidding me," I whined, "I did everything you told me to." My rather pleased-with-myself grin had rapidly turned into a petulant pout.

Josie chuckled. "Maybe I should take it from here."

She walked around the pile of canvas toward me and held out her hand for the mallet. Reluctantly I handed it over, rolling my eyes.

"It's not that easy you know, having to pull on that while positioning the hammer in just the right place, so I don't hit my fingers, and not to mention that the ground is rock hard."

Okay, so I knew I was throwing out a barrage of excuses and felt ridiculous for doing so, but I had just messed up most pathetically and felt as though some justification was most definitely in order. Josie let out another laugh, taking the mallet from me. She effortlessly removed the peg from the ground and repositioned it, hitting it into place with a few thumps. She looked up at me and smiled smugly with a hint of playfulness. Cocky. I crossed my arms over my chest.

"Oh, whatever, Calhoun, you've done this before."

Josie smiled, moving to the next peg and rope thingy that she insisted was a guy.

"If you want to make yourself useful, why don't you go and grab the rest of the stuff from the car, and I'll get this thing up."

I studied her for a moment. The idea that I had just been demoted from tent constructor to bag carrier in the space of a minute didn't exactly fill me with pride, but I knew that the sooner the tent was up, the sooner we would get to relax and do whatever you do in tents.

"Fine," I said, stretching out the word, "I know my place, I'll go fetch the bags and leave you to do the real work."

I heard Josie laugh as I headed in the direction of the car park. I went at a leisurely stroll, taking in our surroundings. The camping ground belonged to the National Trust and was set on a working farm in Snowdonia. It nestled in a small valley and had panoramic views of pine forests and mountains as far as I could see, and to someone more accustomed to the sights of Southend and Greenwich, it was simply breathtaking.

Josie had picked me up super early that morning. She hadn't come in, but texted when she arrived, letting me know she was outside. My eyes had nearly popped out of my head when I saw what she was driving. She had rocked up in a twenty-year-old sapphire blue VW Beetle, which is quite possibly the coolest-looking car I had ever driven in and literally nothing at all like I imagined Josie would drive. We'd got out of London and headed west and had spent the journey getting to know one another a little better. Then, after a couple of hours on the motorway, I made the link that we were going to be spending the weekend in Wales, which was exciting as it's not somewhere I'd been before. When we arrived at the camp site, I was pleased to see it had basic facilities including toilets, two showers, somewhere to wash dishes and a log shed. I had half imagined a field with nothing or no one around for miles, but there were at least thirty pitches each distinguished by a tinned fire bowl surrounded by four large logs for sitting on. Because the site didn't take advance bookings it worked on a first come first serve basis and Josie had been keen to arrive in good time and wasted no time in claiming the perfect pitch for the tent. She chose one next to the stream on the high side, making a joke that it might drown out any noise that could come from the tent later that evening, and after working out where the sun would rise the next morning she made sure the tent would fall within the shade footprint of a sheltering tree. She certainly had the whole extreme camper thing going on, I had to give her that, and I was happy to let her take the lead, given I had only camped once with school when I was fifteen and hated every second of it. Something in the back of my mind, though, told me this weekend was going to be different, and I was relieved to have finally made it to a tent and a proper weekend away.

It had been a pain trying to find someone to cover my shift because Clara had plans for Saturday night. They were plans she wasn't prepared to go into with me and plans she wasn't prepared to reschedule either; two facts she'd made clear in no uncertain terms. Thankfully though, Stacy needed the Thursday off for a family get-together, so she was more than happy to swap, meaning the only thing I had left to tackle was the guilt over leaving Mum. Even though she had made it brutally clear I should get away, mirroring what Josie said about me needing a break, and even though my sister Emma had agreed to visit on both days. I still couldn't seem to shift the feeling of general crapness at buggering off with Mum the way she was.

I passed the communal toilet block and headed out into the small car park, where two cars were now parked alongside the Beetle. I took my phone from my pocket and checked to see if any signal bars had miraculously appeared since the last time I looked, but of course, they hadn't. I sighed heavily, turned off the gadget and opened the Beetle's front boot. After staring dumbfounded at the mountain of gear stuffed into the small space, I hitched what I could over my shoulders and staggered back to camp.

"How long did you say we were staying again?" I puffed as I dropped the bags on the grass. I knew the answer, I was just trying to make a point. Josie smacked the final peg into the ground and came over to me, resting an arm over my shoulders.

"At some point over the next two days, I promise you'll be thanking me for each and every item I packed, you'll see." She smiled a carefree smile, and I smiled back, letting any feelings of guilt I had at being there evaporate into a summer's day in Wales. I was going to enjoy it, damn it. I was going to enjoy Josie, and I guess the truth was that a break away from everything I had going on *was* well overdue.

Once we'd finished unloading the rest of the car's contents, which took three trips in total, Josie busied herself organising everything into mysterious rightful places, and I sat in one of the camping chairs, already grateful for that surprisingly comfortable item. I watched her with admiration from behind my shades as she emptied out a bag of miniature saucepans that sat one in the other. Then came cutlery and a small, shiny kettle which she held up proudly and said made a cute whistle when the water was boiling. She looked every bit the outdoorsy type in a faded grey baseball cap, which she had pulled down her forehead to shield her eyes from the sun, and sometime between arriving at the site and assembling the tent she had tied a blue and green check shirt around her waist, revealing a loose-fitting vest top with the words "good vibes" below a rainbow. She wasn't wearing a scarf which I thought was strange, and I decided then and there I liked the way Josie Calhoun dressed when she wasn't being an academic just as much as when she was.

Satisfied that everything was where she needed it, Josie sat in the second chair I'd placed next to mine and handed me a bottle of Thatchers. I lifted it to my mouth, enjoying the feel of the cold needles of liquid hitting my throat. It made me let out a contented sigh. Josie turned to face me, lifting the peak of her cap slightly to meet my eyes.

"You happy?" Her eyes were warm and hopeful. I nodded once, immediately, and leaned over, taking her hand and resting it on my leg. I gave it a gentle squeeze, looked around at the mountain scenery and said quietly, "Yeah, I'm happy."

I nodded as I said those words and it wasn't lost on me that at that moment, in that place and with Josie's hand in mine, I actually believed it.

Other than the occasional contented sigh, we sat together in comfortable silence as a lark sang us a song somewhere high above. I peeled my socks off and let my bare feet enjoy the grass as I gripped the blades between my toes and searched my mind for the last time I'd spent any real time outdoors. This then got me to thinking about Josie and if this was something she made a habit of.

"You bring all your women here?" My fingers lazily traced

small circles over the back of her hand. She slowly turned her attention to me, and I could just make out a raised brow under the peak of her cap.

"*All* my women?" Her tone was one of amusement.

I shrugged. "I was just wondering if you make a habit of meeting someone and whisking them off into the wilderness." The sheepishness in my voice was unfamiliar.

Josie's lip curled into a grin. "Ah, I see. You want to know if you're special?" It was more of a statement than a question, but I answered anyway.

"Maybe." I looked down at my toes, which were still grasping at blades of grass.

Josie turned away from me, staring straight out to the mountains and lifted her bottle to her mouth before answering.

"There's not really been too many to speak of in all honesty. In total, I've had three partners, two barely count seeing as I was in my teens and they lasted no longer than a few months." She noticed a tiny money spider making its way across her arm and laid a finger in front of it. When it climbed on she bent and released it into the grass.

"And then there was Kaz." Her voice was clearly tinged with regret as she said the name and I felt an unreasonable tug of jealousy pull at the pit of my stomach.

"Who's Kaz?"

Josie lifted the bottle to her mouth again, took a long swig, dropped it back to her lap, and let out a heavy sigh.

I squeezed her hand, "You don't have to talk about it." I was sensing that whoever Kaz was, it didn't end well. She nodded slowly and then rolled her shoulders as though shifting into a different gear, one that didn't involve thoughts of her ex.

"You know what? Let's not go there just yet. But I want you to know that you are special, and I wouldn't bring just anyone away with me." She reached over and squeezed my knee before bouncing up from her seat and heading towards the woodshed.

And I happily watched the way her bum looked in her tight jean shorts.

The pain on her face had been evident at the mention of the Kaz person, and I hoped that eventually she would open up about it and trust me enough to let me into her world. There was still a lot about this woman I was yet to find out. And, I reminded myself, still a lot I needed to reveal about me, but for the time being, ogling her against the mountainous backdrop was going to have to do.

IT HAD TAKEN ONLY A matter of minutes for Josie to get the fire going. After kicking herself for forgetting the firelighters, she improvised, scouting around the campsite for dried grass and shredding the cardboard from our four-pack of Thatchers into strips. She managed to get the makeshift kindling and twigs alight, and it wasn't long before the logs from the shed were burning too. There were at least five other couples sat around their fires, and I had to give it Josie, ours was burning the brightest in our beautiful setting with the stream burbling close by. I left the camping chair then, moved to the fire pit and parked my bum on one of the strategically placed logs. After some fine-tuning and extra prodding of the fire-bowl, Josie joined me, positioning herself between my legs on the grass. I wrapped my arms around her shoulders and leaned my chin on her head as we both sat hypnotised by the flickering flames.

"This is nice." My voice was low and in keeping with the mellow atmosphere. I was already feeling the cleansing effect of the fresh air and scented wood smoke on my skin. Josie tilted her head up to look at me.

"I told you it was what you needed. I read a study the other day that said people who get out in Nature are on average three times happier than those who never leave the city."

I smiled, thinking she sure did like her studies. "I can see why." I lowered my hands and cupped a breast in each hand.

Josie's eyes crinkled at the corners. "I'm not sure that's quite what they're getting at, but hey, whatever works for you." She grinned.

I let out a low chuckle and kissed her head again, knowing precisely what she meant. Being away from it all, hearing nothing but the crackling of the burning wood, the birds and the splash and gurgle from the stream while breathing the cool, clean air into my lungs, really did feel like the perfect recipe for happy. I withdrew my hands to her shoulders and began to gently press my thumbs into the muscles.

"So, if I'd been unable to make this trip, you would have come alone?"

Josie relaxed back against me and let out a moan, "Umm, that feels good." Her voice was low and hoarse, causing me to momentarily forget what I had asked through my instant arousal. "That was the plan. I try to get away at least once every year, preferably twice. It helps me get some perspective and gives me time to clear my head."

I stayed quiet and continued massaging her. She seemed at ease, and I figured it would be a good opportunity to ask her about her dad.

"So, did your dad take you camping?" I continued to rhythmically press my thumbs into her, but instantly her shoulders tensed, and after a few moments she leaned forward and picked up a stick from the pile she'd gathered. She sat back between my legs and vacantly prodded at the edges of the fire, causing the embers to spit and flicker in all directions. After what felt like a really long time, she answered with a simple, "Yeah." Her voice was small and hesitant, and honestly, nothing like I had heard from her before. I wondered if I had pushed too soon.

"You don't have to talk about it, I'm sorry." I rushed my words out, thinking the last thing I wanted in this peaceful place was to make her feel uncomfortable and retreat.

She let out a heavy sigh. "It's okay. It's just…" I couldn't see her face, but I suspected she was frowning, "I guess I just get frustrated with myself. I've talked it over a million times and analysed it to death. But regardless of whether or not I know how and why it affected me, it's still something that, even after all these years, I've been unable to shake."

I laid my hands on her shoulders and resumed massaging the tightened muscles. "Did something bad happen to him?" I wasn't sure I wanted to know the answer.

She shook her head, "No, nothing like that. Last I heard he had a villa in Spain with family 2.0, but that was six years ago now, so who knows."

"You haven't spoken to your dad in six years?" I pressed down into a firm knot in her neck.

She snorted sardonically, "I haven't spoken to my dad since I was thirteen. The last I saw of him was twenty years ago, the day he packed his bags and left Mum and me, but not before telling me if he ever laid eyes on me again, he would kill me."

My hands froze on her shoulders, and I was pleased she couldn't see my face and the extent of my wide-eyed shock. "He did what? Christ, what happened?"

I felt her shoulders lift and then drop back under my hands as she took a long deep breath.

"Well," she started before pausing. Again, I wondered whether she might be questioning how much she wanted to let me into this part of her life.

"Go on." I tried to sound encouraging, wanting for her to open up and let me in.

"Well, for the most part, he was the perfect father. He worked as an IT consultant which took him away a lot, but whenever he came home, he would always make an effort to spend time with me. Each time he returned, he would pick me up and spin me around, smothering me with kisses before getting a gift from his suitcase, and it was always extravagant. I honestly thought he was the best dad in the world."

"Thought?" I knew the story was inevitably going to take a turn.

Josie leaned further into me and tilted her head back so I could see her face. I moved my hands from her shoulders and wrapped my arms around her, resting just above her breast line.

"It was my thirteenth birthday and Mum, Dad and I had planned to spend the day together. We weren't going to do anything too special, just some shopping and maybe grab lunch. Early that morning, after I'd opened my presents, dad took a phone call, which was an urgent call-out for him to attend a job in the Netherlands. He said he needed to be on the first flight out and was really apologetic, promising that as soon as he returned, he would make it up to me. I understood the importance of his work and, to be honest, was at the age where I just wanted to hang out with my friends anyway.

"He'd been gone two nights when a few of my friends invited me to go bowling. I felt terrible leaving Mum, but she said she'd be okay, and she trusted me enough to know I would be home when I said I would and not get up to any trouble."

Josie looked into the fire and prodded it again with the stick. I waited.

"So, I met my friends outside the bowling alley and we all decided to go and get a milkshake first from Nelson's Diner which is just a short walk from where we were. We were all laughing and joking together, probably talking about boys and stuff when I froze. We were outside the diner, and through the window, I saw my dad with two people. One was a young red-headed boy of about four and the other a tall brunette woman." The end of the stick Josie had been prodding the fire with caught aflame. She twisted it on the side of the fire bowl to extinguish it.

"Did you confront him about not being in the Netherlands?" Although I felt like shrieking, I dropped my voice to just above a whisper to keep the conversation private from the other campers.

Josie shook her head. "No. I just watched him. I watched him wipe sauce from the boy's face before squeezing him on the cheek and giving him the same smile I thought he saved only for me. And then I watched him lean in and kiss the woman lovingly on the lips, it was only a peck, but the affection on both their faces said everything."

"Shit, That's brutal." I tried to imagine how it must have felt for a thirteen-year-old to see that.

Josie nodded. "Yup, but that's not the worst part. So, I wasn't sure what to do at first. I told my friends I felt ill and needed to go home and all the way back all I could think about was how the hell I was going to tell Mum what I'd seen. I knew it would break her heart, and I guess there was a part of me that worried she wouldn't believe it. I could barely believe it myself. When I arrived home though and saw her sitting alone on the sofa, I broke down crying before I'd said a word. Eventually, I managed to let her know what I'd seen, and without any hesitation, she believed me straight away. I think on some level she'd suspected it but just didn't want to admit it."

"He was cheating on her?"

"He was having an affair. Well, not really an affair, it was a relationship that'd been going on seven years, during which time he'd had a son; my half-brother."

"Fuck." I said the word under my breath so as not to draw attention from the other campers, although I'm sure they were all just as much in their bubbles as we were.

"Yup. When he got back from his 'Netherlands trip' Mum was ready for him. She had done some digging around and found out everything she needed to know. That night, it felt like the roller-coaster of screaming and crying went on for hours while I stayed in my room wondering what the hell I'd done to my family." Her voice was tinged with regret as she pulled her knees to her chest. I kissed her tenderly all the while inhaling the scent of her hair.

"But it wasn't your fault."

She nodded and shrugged, "I know that now, but try telling thirteen-year-old me. I was a mess. Once the yelling finally stopped, my dad came into my room. I thought he'd come to say goodbye, but instead, he grabbed me by the neck and told me I'd torn our family apart and if he ever saw me again, he would kill me. I know he didn't mean it, and it was the shock and anger speaking, but I was petrified. I saw a side to him I'd never known, and at that moment all the illusions I had of the perfect father went up in smoke."

I shook my head, feeling a sudden rush of anger. "Josie, I'm so sorry." I didn't really know what else to say.

She shrugged again. "Hey, look, it was a long time ago, but it did leave me with some deep-rooted trust issues. After that, it was impossible to let anyone in. Any time I got close to someone, I became possessive and paranoid and ruined things before they even took off. It was the lies that got me the most. If Dad had cheated and it was just a mistake, I could have lived with that, but he spent seven years pretending to both me and Mum, it made me question everyone's motives." Josie stopped talking, giving me time to take it all in.

I let out a long, angry breath. "What is it with men, not being able to keep it in their fucking pants?" My mouth was full of a bitterness as I thought about both Josie's father and my own.

Josie looked up at me, "Shit, that's right. I remember now. My mum told me, your dad left when you were a baby, right? Ran off with your mum's best friend? You must think I'm a brat going on and on about my dad when you didn't even get to know yours."

I shrugged. "You can't miss what you never had, right?" I tried for nonchalance.

Josie studied me with sympathy. "I'm not sure that's entirely true. You may feel like that consciously, but on a subconscious level, I expect there's probably more going on than you think."

I grimaced and shrugged again. "I don't know, maybe. Mum thinks it's made me emotionally unavailable, which I guess would explain a lot." I realised then that I had never spoken to anyone about this stuff. Not knowing my dad and the reasons for me not knowing him was something I kept in that part of my mind labelled "too difficult to deal with" and I barely ventured in there myself, let alone talk about it with someone else. I wriggled about uncomfortably on the log.

"I get it," Josie said, "I somehow managed to cut myself off from anyone I thought stood a chance of hurting me too, until Kaz, that was."

"Your ex?" I was surprised she was going there so soon after closing off about it.

She nodded. "Uh-huh, that's the one. When I met Kaz, I finally found someone who I could open up to. Who understood me. Who knew my past and loved me with it, not just in spite of it. Kaz always said she loved what happened with my dad because it turned me into the wonderful person I'd become." There was a wistful, almost longing tone in her voice, and I had to admit I felt another pang of jealousy at hearing her talk about a woman so fondly. I squished it down.

"So, what happened to you two? It sounds like you were made for each other." I tried to ask the question as casually as possible, without any hint of snarkiness, but Josie's quirked brow let me know I hadn't hidden it well. I bit down on my bottom lip and squinted, "Sorry."

She let out a small laugh, "It's fine, and if it's any consolation, we were far from made for each other. She made that abundantly clear the day I walked in on her snogging the face off her best friend one New Year's Eve, just two weeks after Mum had been diagnosed with cancer. After six years together, when I'd finally learned to trust again, Kaz did that, and all my initial fears that people are lying, cheating arseholes resurfaced, and I was right back to square one."

"Fuck," I hissed, drawing Josie into me and hugging her as tight as I could manage without hurting her. I shook my head and tried, by my hug and kisses, to let her know how sorry I was that she'd had to go through that. It was then I knew that no matter how strong and confident she seemed, the remains of that broken-hearted thirteen-year-old, would probably never fully trust again.

Josie turned around, so she was kneeling between my legs and facing me. "Sorry for being such a downer, I invited you here to cheer you up, not bombard you with my sob story." She smiled apologetically and I ran my thumb across her cheek.

"You're far from a downer Josie, you're one of the most positive people I know. I'm glad you feel like you can talk to me. It's good to get to know you, childhood traumas and all. And for what it's worth, and as much as it pains me to say it, I have to agree with that arsehole ex of yours. Everything you've been through really has turned you into a pretty wonderful person."

I smiled at her with fondness, wanting her to know I really meant what I said. Somehow, she had turned a painful period in her life into a thirst for knowledge of human behaviour. Instead of using her crap childhood as an excuse to go off the rails, she had set out to understand not only the people around her but herself too, and that really impressed me.

Josie got up on her knees and pulled her shoulders back, "Right," she said firmly, "I'm snapping out of this now. We're here to have a good time. Not to dredge up old childhood crap." She rested a hand on each of my knees, and bounced a little, seemingly changing up her physiology to better reflect how she wanted to feel, as though it was a technique she used regularly.

"So, any idea what we might be doing tomorrow?" She was now smiling.

I reached up and stretched, feeling some of the weight from the previous conversation dissipate.

"Go on, enlighten me."

She laughed. "You really don't know?"

I shrugged dramatically, "No idea."

Josie studied me, seemingly bewildered by my lack of understanding. "We're in the middle of Snowdonia, I asked you to bring hiking boots, and we passed at least three signs naming the biggest attraction around here and you still have no idea?" She was losing patience but still a little amused. I pursed my lips and lifted my shoulders to my ears before letting them fall. Josie shook her head, exasperated, but at least now she was smiling.

"Snowdon, Roxy. Tomorrow we are hiking up Snowdon."

"Oh, Fuck, no!"

CHAPTER 14

"WAIT! WAIT! PLEASE WAIT!" I groaned between breaths, leaning against a stack of slate tiles. The beginning of the walk had been fine, more than fine actually; it was beautiful. For the first hour, our attention had been solely focussed on the small cascading waterfalls and turquoise rock pools to our right. The sun illuminated the scene, its glow splashed the greenery around us in gold light, and we could hear rushing water all around. All of these things had lured me into a false sense of security. So captivated by the scenery, I hadn't noticed the gradual incline of the path until I looked back to where we had started. We were high. Eventually, though, as we moved away from the stream, and the gradual incline gave way to a far more no-joke series of rock steps, my tranquillity and sense of wonder from before was soon replaced by apprehension. Spotting each new peak in the distance, I would ask: "Is that it?" and every time Josie answered, "No, that's not it."

There was only one thing I knew about Mount Snowdon: that it was the highest peak in England and Wales. Therefore, I knew that every time Josie said: "No, that's not it," it would be higher than the one I was currently looking at and this petrified me.

I wouldn't say I was full-on acrophobic, I could look out over my balcony without any qualms and obviously swing around a pole, but when faced with an extreme height – like mountain high – to say my heart rate took on the choof of a runaway train would be an understatement.

Josie came down a few steps towards me after realising I had stopped. She took a swig of water and smiled. "You know, Miss Mackenzie, for someone who lives a somewhat sedentary life, you're a spritely one. I was expecting you to be flagging by now, but instead you're giving me a run for my money." She quirked a brow.

I looked up. "I have no idea what that means."

Her eyes widened. "Sedentary?"

"Uh-huh." I was actually more concerned about the peaks off in the distance than whatever it was she was accusing me of.

Josie folded her arms over her chest. "Honestly, how's anyone supposed to believe you're a writer?"

Now she had my attention. I grinned up at her. "I don't know really because half the time I don't even English." I made sure my reply was playful after the penny finally dropped she was making a dig about my lack of vocabulary.

Josie rolled her eyes and smiled.

"Seriously though, I just don't know if I can do this." I looked out at the mountainous backdrop and winced.

She took a couple of steps towards me and closed the gap between us. She gently rubbed her thumb across my forehead to remove a bead of sweat which was caused by fear and not the exercise before she brought her lips to mine and kissed me softly, pulling back only to speak. "Listen to me." She paused to kiss me. "You most definitely." Another kiss. "Can do this." One final kiss.

I blew out a breath, wondering if she had any idea at all of the effects her kiss had on me before my mind swiftly returned to the peak.

"I don't know if I can."

Josie held both my arms, so she was looking directly into my eyes.

"Listen, you can take as long as you need, we don't have to rush. Why don't you walk in front of me and set the pace? I'm happy to take it slow, but I think you should challenge yourself and step outside your comfort zone. I think it will be worth it." She held my gaze with nothing but hope.

I squinted at her curiously. Christ, this woman could literally ask me to roll down the mountain naked, and I would probably do it. What the hell was it with her that had me not just leaving my comfort zone but *wanting* to. Her energy definitely had an infectious quality to it and after spending the morning watching her bouncing around in her element as she happily took in all her surroundings, pointing out this peak and that slate ruin where the miners used to stay, and saying a cheery "hello" to other walkers. I had to admit, a little bit of that enthusiasm was beginning to rub off.

I exhaled loudly and slumped into submission. Besides the fact that my survival instinct was screaming at me not to do it, I managed to convince myself that I would do it, I was going to do it for the beautiful woman who'd invited me here to share the experience with her.

Taking the lead had been a good idea. There was less pressure to keep up with Josie's stride, meaning I could set out the pace and keep a hold on my unruly breathing. I refused to look down though, and mostly looked straight ahead of me until eventually, when looking up at a rugged summit off in the middle distance, I chanced my luck once more. "Please tell me that's Snowdon?" I wanted it done and out the way.

Josie halted and looked up to where I pointed, shielding her eyes from the now dazzling midday sun. She nodded a slow nod, "Yes, that's it. You can just make out the people on top."

I squinted, struggling to make out anything. "That cluster of ants?"

Josie nodded. "Uh-huh, that's them."

I groaned, feeling the confidence from before about getting up there falter. It was bloody daunting. I could just make out where the track gave way to precarious scree, and it was steep. Like, really steep. Practically vertical. If I was going to attempt that, then I needed time to get my head around it. "I think this is probably a good time to stop for lunch," I said with a shaky voice.

~

"THINK OF IT AS A reference point." Josie laid out our lunch of cheese sandwiches, grapes and Texas BBQ flavoured Pringles.

"What do you mean?" I took a sip of water and poured a little over my forehead, immediately relishing the cooling effects.

"The challenge of this walk. You would never expect to do a walk like this. If I'd told you about it before we came here, you probably would've Googled it, saw how high it is and decided it wasn't for you and you couldn't do it."

"True." I grabbed a triangle of sandwich.

"So, now, once you reach the top–"

"*If* I reach the top," I interrupted through a mouthful of bread and cheese.

"*When* you reach the top," Josie countered, "You will always have it in your bank as something to refer to whenever you think you can't do something. You can be like 'I think I can't do this, but I thought I couldn't climb Snowdon and despite my fear of heights, I did, and I didn't even take the easy route, I conquered Watkins'. And plus, doesn't the view alone just make it worthwhile?"

I turned from the rolling, spectacular landscape and looked at Josie, really taking in the shimmer of her deep brown eyes, the faint freckles scattered over her nose and the perfection of her smile.

"It sure does." My tone was dreamy and barely above a whisper.

An enormous grin broke across her face. "You're quite soppy when no one's watching, aren't you?" She looked at me all kitten-like.

I ignored her tease and dropped my eyes, picking up a loose stone and rolling it down the hill.

"So, what's your reference point?" I wasn't even bothering to be subtle with the change of subject.

She sat up straighter and crossed her legs on the grass. "That's easy. Getting my PhD so young. You wouldn't believe the battle that went on inside my head while I studied for it. I told myself over and over I would never be able to do it, that I wasn't good enough, that I didn't have it in me and then I aced it with honours. I figure now if I could do that, I can do anything."

I smiled and leaned over to her, returning her kiss from earlier. Being close to Josie and kissing her whenever I wanted was beginning to feel surprisingly natural.

"What was that for?" she asked, once we parted.

I shook my head. "I don't know. You're just so…" I searched for the right words to describe what I felt when I was around her, but nothing my mind presented me with seemed to capture what I felt.

"So what?" Her dimples emerged, and it made me draw in a breath.

I cocked my head, peered at her through slits and blew out

the breath, "Just so…different." I offered lamely, shaking my head, not knowing what I meant myself.

Josie let out a low chuckle. "Good. Different's good," she said simply and took a bite of her sandwich.

REACHING THE PEAK OF SNOWDON was more challenging than I could have bargained for. On at least three occasions I froze and had to stop. Each time this happened, Josie comforted me and gave me words of encouragement. Her words were reassuring and finally, my need to want to impress her and maybe even impress myself a little, actually won out, and by the time we did reach the top, I saw how completely right she was. The satisfaction at having pushed through and faced my fears, felt amazing. And Josie was right, I would now always have this experience in my bank as a "reference point". All this, along with the sensational views, really did make it worth it. By the time we got back to the campsite, we were both in need of a shower and, after striking up a conversation with a couple who assured us the water was hot, we decided to give it a go.

The campers had been right, and the water was indeed hot, what they failed to mention, however, was that it piddled out of the faucet so slowly it would take fifteen minutes just to rinse the shampoo from my hair.

After our really long showers we had each changed into pyjama bottoms and thin hoodies and dried our hair using electricity from a plug socket in the shower block and the hairdryer – that, of course, Josie had remembered to pack.

Once we were back at the tent pitch, the sun had set fully, taking some of the heat from the day with it and I was more than grateful to be tucking into a chicken flavoured Pot Noodle from the camping chair while Josie got the fire going to a steady roar.

"I'm proud of you, you know?" Josie tossed a handful of twigs on the fire.

"Thank you." There was something really warming about hearing her say those words. "You know, I'm kind of proud of myself." I laid down my empty Pot Noodle tub and wandered over to the sitting log with a blanket wrapped around my shoulders.

She grinned, her eyes following me as I carefully sat.

"Come here." Josie beckoned me over to where she was sat on the opposite side of the fire.

I eyed her curiously and made my way over to her.

"Lie down here." She shook her blanket out onto the grass.

I playfully wiggled my eyebrows at her.

"Just do it."

"Why?"

"Because I'm going to massage you. You must be aching after today."

Actually not too bad, but I wasn't about to tell Josie that. I did as I was told and laid down, face-first and full length, and it felt good. Josie positioned herself at my ankles and rubbed her palm up the back of my calf with enough pressure to let me know I had been on a hike.

She carried on carefully kneading my muscles and after spending an attentive ten minutes on each leg, Josie insisted she take care of the other side too and I wasn't complaining. I turned over and sat with my back against the log while my foot rested on her lap as she continued working her magic. I tilted my head back to the twinkling night sky.

It was the perfect evening. The fire was gently spitting and crackling in the background, the temperature was still warm, and the company, well, the company was exceptional. I watched Josie intently as she continued to relieve my legs of their phantom strains and I became mesmerised by how gorgeous she really was. I loved how the firelight danced in her eyes while the muscles in her toned arms tensed as she rubbed me. It was hard to believe, I thought, that just a few weeks ago, I had never even met this woman, and now, here I was, in the middle of nowhere, feeling completely and utterly at one with her.

"You know, this is probably one of my favourite ever trips away," I mumbled sleepily as physical exhaustion began to settle in, "It's just so...peaceful."

Josie stilled her hands on my legs and inclined her head. "Peaceful is the one who's not concerned with having more or less. Unbound by name or fame, he is free from sorrow, from the world and mostly from himself."

I stared at her, grinning goofily. "I like that."

Josie resumed her rubbing and shrugged, "I can't take credit. It's all Rumi."

I nodded a slow nod, "Well, I think you were right before, I really should check this Rumi guy out. Although there's always the possibility that I like it only because I like hearing it from you in that sexy voice of yours. You got any more stored away in that exceptional brain?"

She smiled. "Hundreds."

I wriggled, sitting up straighter against the log, "Go on then. Recite your favourite."

Josie stopped massaging me and laid her hands into her lap. "Oooh, that's a hard one." She looked up at the stars as she thought. "Okay, I'm going to go with the poem that speaks to me the most about who I am. So, if you can make sense of this, you'll make sense of me."

I raised an eyebrow and leaned back on my hands. "I'm intrigued."

Josie cleared her throat. "Yesterday I was clever, so I wanted to change the world. Today I am wise, so I am changing myself." She stopped speaking, and her expression was expectant.

"Is that it?" I was somewhat underwhelmed.

"*Is that it*? That is one of the most profound statements I've ever heard, and you're asking me, '*Is that it*?'"

I held my hands up and laughed. "Okay, I'm sorry. Maybe I didn't listen properly. Try me again."

Josie eyed me suspiciously.

"Honestly, I would like to hear it again. I will really try to get the message this time, I promise."

She did as I asked and repeated the poem once more, this time a little slower so I could really take it in, which is what I attempted to do. "So, he's basically saying that since he has become wise, he realises the only way to change the world is to change himself?"

"In a nutshell, yes. But to add to that, I think he's alluding to the fact that we have no control over what goes on in the world. Realistically, all we can control is our reaction and attitude to it. So, if each of us took the time to work on ourselves, we would remain calm and rooted in our inner world regardless of what went on externally, and consequently, the world would be a far happier place."

I leaned forward and planted one small kiss on her nose. "I love how passionate you become when you talk about this stuff."

Josie moved her lips to just millimetres from mine, "Yeah? Well, I love how passionate you become when I do this." She sucked in my lower lip, taking it gently between her teeth. I moaned in agreement as her fingers edged up my thigh and into my shorts ever closer to my pants line. I pulled back from her mouth and watched as a mischievous grin overtook her face.

"What are you up to?" I propped up onto my elbows and scanned the campsite to make sure we were alone, which we now were.

"What? I have no idea what you mean." She traced my neck with her lips and sucked at my skin.

"Uhmm," I moaned, my breathing becoming raspy, "I think

you know what. One minute you're reciting poetry and getting all philosophical and the next minute you're...Uhmm," I moaned again, unable to resist the gentle tug in my pants that Josie's kiss was provoking in me, and unable to finish my sentence.

Josie moved her mouth to my ear and nibbled at my lobe, her teeth applying enough pressure to make me hiss in a breath.

"I mean," she began to whisper into my ear, "if you would rather stay up and have a philosophical debate, I'm all for that too. It's your decision."

That tone she used sent my body spiralling out of control and tiredness or no tiredness, there was only one reply I felt capable of giving.

"Get in that tent, now."

I WOKE TO THE COMICAL MIX of sounds of zips being pulled and the tweeting of birds I'm sure Josie could name. I pulled my sleeping bag over my head, trying to hide from the sunlight that had risen above our tree and now illuminated the tent's interior with slightly weird green light. The air was too stuffy inside the sleeping bag to stay that way for long. I got up onto my knees, reminded by the pleasurable ache down below that somehow, I *had* managed to find some energy the night before and unzipped the inner liner to see Josie packing up our gear. She stopped what she was doing and smiled a broad smile.

"Good morning, gorgeous."

I pointed at my hair, which I could feel was a bird's nest on top of my head.

"I very much doubt I look gorgeous right now." My morning voice was groggy.

Josie shuffled her way over to me. "Your hair is a visual reminder of last night, and believe me, it's sexy as hell." She leaned in to kiss me. I turned my face suddenly, offering her my cheek.

"Sorry, I forgot about the no-morning-kisses rule." She held her hands up in submission. I let out a small laugh.

I looked at the packed bags, "Do we really have to leave today?"

She nodded. "Unfortunately, we do. We both have that little thing called work tomorrow, and if we don't leave soon, we'll hit the Birmingham traffic."

I let out a grumpy huff before catching sight of something out of the corner of my eye. "And are they staying here?" I nodded to our wellies which were affectionately placed toe to toe alongside each other by the fire pit log.

Josie's pale cheeks reddened. "No, I just wanted to look at them a while longer." She looked away and cleared her throat.

I didn't know if my mind was foggy because it was so early and I was missing something about wellies, or whether she had lost the plot and preferred to stare at wellies rather than the views surrounding us, I was afraid to ask.

"And that's because?"

I crawled from the tent and Josie sat beside me. She pulled my hand onto her lap. "Okay, promise you won't laugh?"

"I promise I will try not to." It was the best I could commit to.

"Well, I've just always found the image of two sets of wellies sitting together kind of romantic. There's something about them that depicts togetherness and coupling. I know it's silly, but when I woke up this morning and saw our wellies side by side, it filled me with a kind of warmth that's hard to describe, and I felt happy."

I lifted Josie's hand to my lips and kissed it gently before inclining my head and looking at the wellies once more. It wasn't silly, it was cute, and actually, I could see exactly what she meant, it *was* kind of romantic.

I LET OUT A GUSTY SIGH, unable to hide my disappointment as the last of the bags were loaded into the boot, and we climbed into our seats about to depart. The sound of Josie clicking her seatbelt into place made me unconsciously release another heavy breath.

She raised a questioning eyebrow. "You okay, Rox?"

"I guess," I said, with what I'm sure was a forced smile. She unfastened her belt and twisted to face me, giving me her undivided attention. "What's up?"

I mirrored her movements, turning to face her too.

"I don't know. I've just had such a great time here with you and, for the first time in as long as I can remember, I've actually allowed myself some happiness. Spending time with you has been the only thing that's been able to distract me from everything going on with Mum, and I'm punishing myself for that; but it's just so good to feel like me again."

Josie squinted one eye. "Sooo, your moody face is because you're happy? Okay, well, remind me never to piss you off then."

I laughed and poked her shoulder. She knew exactly what I meant.

"I think what I'm trying to say is, I know as soon as we leave here and you drop me home, I have to go back to facing reality and dealing with what's going on in my life, and let me tell you, that sucks." Part of me was talking about Mum, but there was also another part of me that was thinking about my job, which was beginning to feel like more of a burden and a big dark cloud than ever before.

She took one of my hands and placed it between hers. "Are you not coping?" There was an overwhelming sincerity in the way she asked that question.

I rubbed at my forehead with my free hand. "Oh, I don't

know. I thought I was. But maybe not. The doctor reckons I'm so stressed it's making me pass out."

"Psychogenic blackouts?" Her question was immediate. Of course, she would know what it was.

"That's the one." I nodded. "It's only happened a few times, but it's pretty scary that I have no control over my body, you know?"

Josie nodded. "I do know. Stress can do funny things to the body. It's your mind's way of protecting you. Fight-or-flight and all that jazz."

"You're so clever." I scrunched up my nose and rubbed it against hers in an attempt to lighten the mood. Josie put her hand to my chest and creased her forehead into a deep frown.

"If I were clever, I would know how to make you feel better. I would know all the right things to say to help you through this shitty time and keep you smiling." Her expression was one of regret as she looked down at our clasped hands.

"Hey," I said, "Josie, look at me." Her eyes slowly edged their way up to mine. "You're doing a pretty good job at making me smile, believe me. Look around, I'm here for Christ's sake, climbing mountains and sleeping under the stars. Before I met you, I could barely get my arse out of bed before eleven. It's just..." I hesitated while I attempted to articulate what I wanted to say, "I guess spending this time with you and getting to know you has highlighted the contrast between how I feel when I'm around you and how I feel when I'm not." I felt like that pretty much covered it because really, that's what it was. Josie made me feel so good that the lows felt even lower because it was such a distance between the two extremes. Josie nodded slowly, seemingly understanding the point I was trying to make. She thought for a long moment and then spoke.

"Look, I know there's nothing I can say to take away the pain of what you're going through. But my advice, for what it's worth, is just to try and be as present as you can possibly be in the moment. In this moment and the next moment and the one after that. Because right now, you're worrying about how you're going to feel when you get home, and we haven't even left here yet." She ran her fingers through my hair. "We're still here, you and I, with stunning countryside all around us. We still have a five-hour journey home where we can continue to discover more about each other, and when I drop you back, I expect a long drawn out kiss goodbye before I go. We still have all of that. So, can we not worry about how you might feel when we're not together and just be in the moment, together?"

I took in a deep breath and released it slowly, feeling my face break into what felt like a joyful smile. Josie had done it again. Once more, she had held up a mirror to me and made me see another way, a better way. I let her gaze enfold me.

"You're one in a million, you know that, right?" And I realised then and there she could quite possibly be the one in a million for me.

CHAPTER 15

I RUBBED AT THE BRIGHT red lipstick smear on my front tooth and checked the mirror once more to see if it had done the trick. I kept staring at my reflection for a while, which seemed to be my new thing, just staring at myself and wondering how it all went so wrong. My face looked solemn and unimpressed, and I worried I might be developing a resting-bitch-face. I certainly looked nothing like the person I had been just that morning when I had nothing but UV-cream on my cheeks, the sun on my face and the fresh Welsh air in my lungs. I was free and, more importantly, *me*. Now, I was dressed like a slut, wearing caked-on makeup and looking a lot like someone I despised. Unable to look at my face any longer, I drew in a long breath and closed my eyes.

"Rox, any idea where your crazy bitch of a flatmate might be?" Stacy called across the dressing room, snapping me out of my reverie.

My eyes sprung open. "What am I? Her minder?"

Stacy held her palms out as she sauntered over to me.

"Whoa, chill there, little one. I was only asking." She came up behind me and joined my reflection in the mirror. "Everything okay with you two?"

I watched in the mirror as my facial expression softened. "Yeah, sorry, Stace. I didn't mean to go off. We're cool, I just haven't seen her for a bit that's all." It was the truth.

After Josie had dropped me home, I'd jumped in the shower, threw on fresh clothes and headed straight out to visit Mum. The flat had been empty, so I just assumed I would see Clara once I arrived at the club – wrong. It was unlike her to just go AWOL. Actually, that's not true, it was unlike Clara to go AWOL without asking me to cover for her first.

"Has she not texted in?" I asked, softening my scratchy tone while working on getting my hair to stay in place with yet another grip digging into my head.

Stace took the grip from my hand and placed it perfectly into the bun without any scalp digging.

"Nope. Paul's not heard a thing, and Nicky's off sick, so we're going to have to go double rounds tonight, and if I'm late out and miss my date with Andy that hopeless little shit's gonna know about it."

I laughed despite myself. Stacy was the longest-lasting member of staff at Chace's, and as the eldest, she naturally slipped into the role of head "dancer". Her sets were full of life like she really meant it, and her tall stature and blonde hair that reached halfway down her back gave her an Amazonian presence. Because of that, she and Clara clashed. Their fight for alpha-female position had them locking horns on more than a few occasions, and I know for sure that I would never want to be the one to get between them both if it ever really kicked off. I took out my phone and typed out a text to Clara.

Clar, where are you? Stacy is losing her shit!

I laid the phone on the dresser and zipped up the front of my black PVC dress. Just as I went to slip a stocking on over my foot, my phone vibrated. I reached for it expecting a reply from Clara. Instead, Josie's name appeared on my home screen. I smiled, sat back and opened the text.

Hey you, I know it's only been a day, but I miss you. Just found myself at a loss and thought I might pop in and keep you company at work tonight? Xx

I blinked at the screen and my heart leapt into my throat while my pulse played out its own internal drum and bass set. Fuck! I tried to come up with a reason for Josie not to come. My clammy hands shook as I desperately thought of what to say. I could just ignore the text, I thought, pretend I hadn't seen it. But what if she turned up anyway? Quick Roxy, think! Think! I thought about telling her I hadn't gone in to work, but she would probably want to come around. My pulse continued to batter at my throat. I took a deep breath, knowing I mustn't get into a state. Blacking out right now would not be helpful. I began to type.

Miss me already, eh? Good to hear. Me too. Probably best you don't come to my work, it will be heaving tonight because it's 2 for 1 and my boss doesn't like it if we have friends loitering at the bar. Could meet tomorrow though? xx

I hit send, thinking that my response was believable enough but not feeling happy about it in the slightest. I hated lying to Josie. Especially after everything she had shared with me over the weekend. I stared at the phone, waiting for her response.

"Rox, you're up," Paul called out from the holding area as he always did. Those three words were becoming my nemesis.

"Shit." I grabbed the stocking and yanked it over my foot. It caught on a toenail, and a ladder stretched right the way up my leg. "Oh, for fuck's sake." I dragged it back off and decided to leave it. I looked at my phone: no reply. I slipped into a pair of stilettos and picked up my phone, willing the text to come through.

"Rox, ge' a move on." Paul's cockney accent whined out again.

"Okay. Jesus. I'm coming!" I left my phone on the dresser, looking back at it as I dragged my feet to the holding area, but the screen didn't light up.

Paul was pinching the bridge of his nose when I arrived.

"You can't be this last minute, kid." His tone was terse. "You *know* what arseholes they become if they're made to wait."

"Paul, chill. Stace isn't even off the stage yet." Just as I said those words, Stacy came sauntering off, holding her underwear against her chest. Paul pushed me out from the small of my back, making me glare back at him. I plastered my face with a forced smile in time for my entrance and began my routine.

The weight of lying to Josie laid heavy on me as I fumbled at the pole. I elevated myself from the platform, not sure if I was even pretending to smile any more. As I climbed the pole, one of the guys near the front caught my eye. His slimy leer along with the bead of perspiration on his forehead made me shudder, and I couldn't help but make the comparison between what I was doing now and what I had been doing that morning. I spun around the pole and copped an eyeful of another punter. His top lip was curled in an almost menacing sneer which evoked visions in my mind of him rubbing his palms against his crotch. My stomach churned unpleasantly at that thought and, for the first time since starting at Chace's, my true distaste for what I was doing became very real and rose in my throat like bile. I slid from the pole and turned my back on the blokes, no longer able to look at their faces. I was behind on my routine and still fully clothed, and apparently, this hadn't gone unnoticed as one of the customers shouted out: "Get it off!" I winced at the command and struggled to remember my next step. I took a few steps forward and nearly fell as one of my stilettos buckled beneath me. This too, did not go unnoticed.

"What's up with her? Is she drunk?" A voice bellowed.

I straightened myself out and closed my eyes tight shut then I opened them again, determined to continue. Knowing I couldn't stay with my back to the punters for much longer, I turned around and clasped the pole, looking past the men's heads and out to the empty bar in the hope it would help me keep focus.

"We're down here, sweetheart." One of the men called out.

"You gonna do what they're paying you for or what?"

I drew in a steadying breath and clenched my teeth together, trying to hide how uncomfortable their heckling was making me.

"Come on, sweetheart, hurry it up!" A voice shouted.

"Yeah, fucking 'ell luv, you gonna get 'em off or what?"

I slowly brought my hand to the zip of my dress which run all the way down the front of my torso and held it there for what I hoped looked like a tantalising moment as my heart beat fiercely in my chest.

"Just can't get the sluts these days." The guy with the gleaming, beaded forehead sniggered. My eyes locked onto him and his sweaty smirk, and suddenly, the routine I had committed to muscle memory was nowhere to be found.

"Seriously, what's up with this bitch?" Another voice shouted out.

"Yeah, come on luv, show us your tits." Another joined in. My eyes darted from one voice to the other and all I could focus on was the darkness of their eyes and how within them, there was a complete indifference to me as a person. They just saw me as a thing there for their sexual amusement. I was just a nobody, a nothing, a no-body without feelings. Their shouts and jeers continued to vibrate in my ears and I shook my head trying to make them stop. Out the corner of my eye, I caught one of the bouncers making his way over to the stage, but it was too late. I couldn't do it. I dropped clear of the pole and darted from the stage, running back out to the holding area where Stacy and Paul were watching open-mouthed. As I barged past them scrubbing at the tears running down my cheeks, Stacy automatically raced out onto the stage to replace me. I slumped at my dresser and dropped my head in my hands.

"What the fuck was that?" Paul asked in a voice I hadn't heard him use before.

I ignored him.

"Rox, outside, now!"

I followed Paul out through the fire doors. We stood in the alleyway, and I shivered already, having forgotten my dressing gown. Paul ignored my discomfort, lit his cigarette and took a drag.

"I'll ask you again. What the fuck was that?" He was staring at me, coolly.

I slumped against the wall, trying to fight back more tears. Paul continued to stare.

"Rox, I don't wanna be an arsehole here. You know I respect all you girls, and I'm willing to overlook your fainting thing the other week because I'm assuming it couldn't be helped, but what just happened in there could. I can't have you going out looking like someone's holding a gun to your head. It's bad for business."

I covered my face with my hands. "I'm sorry." My voice was small and full of regret.

Paul let out a loud, long sigh.

"If you don't want the job, Roxy, if it's not for you, all you have to do is tell me. I've got girls lining up to take your gig. Leave or get your shit together. It's up to you." He threw his fag butt to the concrete, ground it hard with the toe of his shoe and stomped off back inside. I slid down the wall into a crouch and let my mind drift back to when I had made the decision to sell my soul.

My sister Emma had called a family meeting at our mum's house. Em, her husband Jake and my brother Ben, were all sitting around the dining table when I arrived. I knew it was not going to be good. Em spoke first.

"She can't stay here any longer."

We all remained silent.

"She's deteriorating by the day and needs more care than she's getting here," Emma continued. Again, silence. All eyes fell on me.

I shrugged. "So, I'll look after her. I'll leave London and move in. I've been thinking about it for a while now anyway. Mum will hate it if we tear her away from everything she knows."

I looked at them all expectantly, not exactly receiving the response I anticipated. Emma and Jake shook their heads before I had finished my sentence. Ben said nothing, no surprise there. He had barely said a thing about Mum's illness since the day she got her diagnosis, and I guess, working out on the oil rigs, he could easily bury his head in the sand – or the North Sea at any rate.

"Rox, you can't do that." Emma's tone was stern. "She needs twenty-four-hour care. You'd go out of your mind. Not to mention you would be giving up a life of your own for goodness knows how long."

"I can do it. I know I can. I don't want Mum to be with a load of strangers in some hole of a home where no one knows her."

Em expelled an exasperated sigh. "It wouldn't be a hole. We would find Mum somewhere lovely, near the water maybe, where we can all visit her. We all agree this is for the best, Rox."

I looked at Ben, who still hadn't said a word. He caught my eye, then looked away.

"Well, if everyone's agreed, why the fuck have you bothered dragging me here? Why not just call me and tell me you've all voted rather than go through the motions of pretending I have any say in this at all?" I slouched back in the chair and folded my arms. Emma's eyes filled with tears. Jake moved next to her and placed a reassuring hand on her shoulder as her lip quivered. I softened at that. I loved how much of a support Jake was to Emma and I would always be grateful that Em had met him so young and he was able to set her on the right track and show her a better life. I blew out a puff of air. I wasn't used to seeing Emma show that kind of emotion. I tried a different tack.

"I'm sorry, alright. We're all upset. I shouldn't have taken it out on you, Em. It's just a lot. You know? You've obviously all had a bit of time to get your heads around this. Just give me a moment to think it through and to talk things over with Mum before you make any decisions, okay?"

Emma nodded, too upset to talk. I should have known that Mum had been in on the discussion that had taken place behind my back. When she woke, and I finally managed to speak to her, she made her position clear. I was met with, "No, you bloody won't be doing anything of the sort. You moved to London to get away from this place and make something of yourself, and there's no way I'm coming between you and a better life. You're not a nurse, and it's not going to be too much longer now before I need one. You'll want me to be with professionals who know how to take care of me. You really think I'd want you wiping my arse?"

I knew Mum well enough to know when she meant business. That woman knew how to deliver the final word so no one would even dream of challenging her. I could tell this was one of those times, and no amount of arguing would change that. When I went back downstairs, my slumped shoulders told Emma all she needed to know, and she burst into action.

"Right, that's decided then. We'll find her the best home there is. Jake and I have discussed it, and we'll put in half the money with Ben. I know you barely have enough to get by, so you don't have to worry about that."

I shook my head, "No! I'll find the money. I'll get a new job, I'll do whatever it takes." I was the eldest, and there was no way I was going to be the only one not contributing to Mum's care.

"But–" Em tried to interrupt.

"But nothing, I'll find it!" My sister could tell from my glare that it wasn't up for discussion.

Later that night, I searched the internet for jobs that would pay enough for my share of Mum's care. I typed into Google "Highest paid jobs in London without a degree." And winced at number one – chicken sexer. Picking up one-thousand chicks an hour and peering at their bums, for twelve hours straight, to determine their sex? No, thank you very much. Number two on the list suggested the oil rigs, which my brother did, but being detached from society in that way, I knew I would hate it. Number three recommended becoming a prison guard, something told me I was way too corruptible for that one, I'd be smuggling in drugs and taking bribes within my first week. Out of the question. I stopped short at number four, which read "Anything within the sex industry – sex sells." I let the cursor hover over that one for a while before slamming my laptop shut, wondering how I could be so ridiculous as to even consider it.

Overnight though, I guess my moral compass did a bit of a twirl, and in the cold light of day, I found myself thinking I could at least consider it. Prostitution was not an option, having some bloke pump away on me for money was not a notion I was prepared to entertain. But stripping? That could work. I had never been particularly shy about my body and had enough people compliment me in the past to know I wouldn't be laughed off a stage. How hard could it be? I did a bit of research on the best-paid clubs and without much more thought than that, dialled the number for Chace's. The following week, I met Paul, and to my surprise he came across as genuine and down to earth, sort of talking me into it in his thick cockney accent.

"Girl, give i' a go. You go' a pretty face and a good bod. Worst case scenario you 'ate it, you can leave any time." He made it sound so simple I thought it would at least be worth a shot. Stacy trained me out of hours, meticulous in everything she showed me. The twists and turns and various techniques were overwhelming, and at first, I thought there would be no way I could pull it off. But for whatever reason, when I mounted the pole, I took to it so easily it sent Stacy into a squealing mess shouting out to Paul that I was a natural and, I guess, the rest was history.

My first night at Chace's ended with me going home and crying for an hour in the bath. I knew I had broken some fundamental moral code that I hadn't even really been aware of. It's not that I'm anything like a prude or even that I gave a shit about the guys. I didn't fancy men, so it was just acting, but I guess, for me, my first night of taking my clothes off for money, sat heavy on me as confirmation of how miserably I had failed. You can take the girl out of the council estate, but I guess you can't take the council estate out of the girl. Or something like that. At the time, I thought I would feel ashamed forever. That after every shift I would be in tears, holding onto my knees in the bath and trying to scrub and soak it all away, but by the third or fourth shift, I can't remember which, it had become second nature. And I managed to push my shame to the back of my mind. The amount of money I earned allowed me to not only pay my share of Mum's care, but I was able to rent my own place instead of sharing and still have enough left to put some aside. I convinced myself that it wasn't that bad.

I snapped back to the present, knowing if I didn't get out there and finish my sets, Paul would have me out on my arse, and I hadn't yet figured out the repercussions of that. I reluctantly pushed myself up off the wall with a groan and went back inside. Before heading out to the stage again, I had a quick glance at my phone and found a reply from Josie.

Your boss sounds like an arse. Tomorrow sounds good. I may have a little plan for the evening. I'll pick you up at 7pm xx

A peculiar mixture of guilt, relief and excitement bubbled up as I read the text and typed back.

As long as it's not another bloody mountain! Reference point or no reference point I'm done with heights. But yes, tomorrow sounds good. I'm looking forward to it xx

I laid the phone down and went back out to the holding area where Paul gave me a nod and a tight-lipped smile as I walked past. After digging deep for resolve, I somehow managed to finish my shift and even get some cheers and wolf whistles, even though the entire time Josie played on my mind. What on earth was I going to do about the situation? Was I in too deep to come clean? Or was I in too deep not to come clean? The pole wasn't offering any answers as I spun around it.

CHAPTER 16

THE FIRST WORDS TO LEAVE my lips when I found Clara on the sofa clutching a pillow to her chest were: "What the fuck?"

She groaned when she saw me, pulled the pillow over her face and told me to "Shush."

I was not in the mood for her bullshit. "No, I won't shush." I whipped the pillow away, but she rapidly replaced it with her arm and covered her eyes.

"What is *with* you? You didn't turn up for work, making me go double rounds and then you couldn't even be arsed to reply to my text and let me know you're okay, and now what? You're not even going to bother to apologise?" My voice was raised to a level I would usually deem unacceptable, but she had really pissed me off.

"Drop it, Rox." Although the words came through a muffled sniff, she still managed to make them sound like a warning.

I perched on the arm of the sofa and dipped to get a better look of her face. Shit. Was Clara *crying*? My anger slowly began to dissipate at the thought of Clara being genuinely upset. I reached out and touched her arm, she immediately tensed up.

"Clar…" I hesitated. "What's going on with you?"

She stayed silent, and I could have sworn I saw her chin quiver. I sat for a moment, searching my brain for some words, any words that might let her know that it was safe to tell me. Eventually, I spoke.

"Listen, you're clearly going through something, and I understand if you don't want to talk about it, but I just want you to know I'm here, okay?"

I watched as her stomach jittered with what I thought was a contained sob. I paused, then added, "I care about you, Clar. You're a complete arsehole most of the time, but I would do anything for you, and I want you to know you can trust me, if you ever want to talk that is." It sort of sounded better in my head and saying it aloud it came out a bit lame, but I hoped she got the gist of what I was trying to get across.

Instead of speaking, Clara simply held out her fist to fist-bump me, and I couldn't help but smile at her detached gesture as I bumped her fist back.

~

"I KNOW I'VE ONLY MET her a few times, but it's hard to imagine Clara crying," Josie said as she squeezed her way on to the crowded tube beside me. "She seems pretty guarded, like she's been through some stuff."

I clasped the grab bar with one hand. "You're not wrong there. She hasn't told me much but lets out snippets here and there about her ex, who treated her like shit. When I met her, she was living in a complete shithole, even though she could afford better. But other than that, she really doesn't talk much. It's crap. I've no clue what to say or do. She's awkward when it comes to affection, so I don't even feel like I could hug her, you know?"

Josie held her position next to me, and we both waited while the tube emptied and filled.

"Maybe just give her space. She'll be more likely to open up when she's less emotional." I gripped tighter to the bar as the train jolted but was unable to keep my balance. Josie instinctively reached out and grabbed at my hips to steady me. We shared a knowing smile at our close proximity in a carriage full of strangers.

"Are you really not going to tell me where we're going?" I tried to ignore the thought that all I wanted to do was recreate the kiss she had given me when she had turned up at my door to pick me up.

She shook her head, "Nope. I told you. It's a surprise." She had a mischievous expression and twinkling in her eyes, and it took all I had not to grab her to me and kiss her. I was curious where we would be spending the evening, but if I was honest, after such a shitty night at work and an even worse morning, I was just happy to be in Josie's company. She really was becoming my happy place.

Josie led me off the tube at Monument, and we hurried to the Northern Line, where we got on yet another tube. "This mission better be worth it," I teased as we both squeezed on to yet another crowded carriage. From behind, Josie met my ear with her mouth, "Oh, it will be." The whisper against my skin caused the small hairs on the back of my neck to ping to attention.

WE GOT OFF THE TRAIN at Angel station, where Josie took me by the hand and led the way through the throngs of north Londoners. I couldn't help but smile at her enthusiasm as she dragged me through a series of streets following a route she either knew or must have memorised. Eventually, after a ten minute walk down Goswell Road, we stood opposite Northampton Square Garden, staring up at a red-brick building I didn't recognise. Josie turned to smile at me in a way that suggested I should know where we were. A confused frown and quick shake of my head let her know I hadn't the foggiest.

"Come." She dragged me along once more before stopping in front of a large steel gate. "There." She nodded at a sign which read, "University of London," then studied me eagerly for my reaction.

"Oh, your work?" I said it flatly, not hiding my disappointment well at all. Josie rolled her eyes.

"Just wait, there's method in my madness, you'll see." She grabbed my hand again and pulled me through the gate and up to the main entrance. She was excited, and when Josie was excited, regardless of whether I was attending a "bring a friend to work day" or whatever, I couldn't help but be affected by it. I laughed inwardly as she led me into the building and through a maze of corridors before we finally settled in an empty hall with a tiered semi-circular seating arrangement.

"Okay, you take a seat there, and I'll just be at the front." Josie gestured for me to sit.

"Okay." I did as I was told.

Josie hurried to the front of the room to what looked like a projector and began to fiddle with it.

"Wait, are you going to lecture me?" I called out, shuffling to get comfortable in the upright chair that had one arm made into a sort of mini-desk thing.

Ignoring my question, Josie picked up a remote control and pressed it, which caused a large screen to light up.

My eyes widened. "Oh my god. You *are* going to lecture me, aren't you?" I clapped my hands together like an excited schoolgirl. Josie grinned and scolded me with her eyes.

"I'll give you a lecture in a minute if you don't stop playing up and let me show you what I've spent the entire day planning for you."

I raised an eyebrow. "More of a turn-on than a threat but please, continue…" I sat back against the plastic chair's uncomfortably low back with my arms folded, intrigued by whatever the hell this was going to be. Whatever it was, the chair was obviously designed to keep me awake.

"Okay." She passed the remote from one hand to the other. "The other day, when we talked about you attending uni, you said you couldn't imagine yourself doing it now." She tucked a loose strand of hair behind her ear before continuing. "So, I've set up this evening for you to take a good look around and get a feel for what it could be like. Obviously, once the night's over, if you still think it's not for you, I'll drop it, and we never have to mention it again. I just thought it would be good for you to at least entertain the possibility." She looked expectant as though trying to judge my reaction.

I bit my lip, "Okay" I said, drawing out the word in my habitual way that meant anything but "okay."

Josie visibly relaxed, and I realised she had been nervous about how I might react. Her shoulders relaxed and she stood straighter, pressing at the remote and revealing the title page of what looked like a PowerPoint presentation. The title read; "Roxy's Induction to University," I swallowed an embarrassed grin. Shit, she really had put some effort into whatever this was.

"So, as you've probably figured out, I will personally be carrying out your induction, and as I am still aware this is supposed to be a date, there may be one or two small surprises along the way. How does that sound?" Her voice was no longer hesitant, she was assured and confident, and frankly, it was arousing. I crossed the room and settled both hands on her hips.

"Well…" I said, leaning in for a kiss. "I'm certainly not complaining about the hot lecturer."

Josie pushed at my chest. "Nuh-uh." She drew her head

back. "Fraternising with the Faculty is strictly against university policy, and we can't have you being excluded on your first day, can we?" A cheeky glint sparkled in her eye that told me she was enjoying this a little more than she should be.

I held my hands up in submission. "Fine. So, what's the plan?" Admittedly, I was enjoying the odd light-heartedness of it all myself.

"Well, your first introduction to student life will take place in the sports hall." She reached under the table, pulled out a JD Sports bag and handed it to me. I eyed her suspiciously before I looked inside and took out the contents. A full set of activewear all in my size was revealed. Shorts, trainers and a vest top which all still wore their tags. She had bought them especially.

"I could have brought my own clothes, you know?" I held the top against me, impressed that she had picked the correct size.

"I know, but something told me if I'd asked you to bring trainers along, you would've automatically jumped to the conclusion we were going hiking, and I worried you might've bailed."

"Hmmm, you may have a point." I knew deep down that, in fact, nothing she could have told me would make me bail on a date with her. I chose to keep that to myself.

Josie nodded to the garments in my hands. "So, are you going to just fondle the clothes? Or are you going to try them on?"

"Here?" I looked around.

"Yup." She grinned.

"But, aren't there people around? Like other students?"

Josie shook her head, "Nope. Not this time of night. There's never anyone here. Even the caretaker goes off at six. Just you and me, baby." She wiggled her eyebrows, and I laughed, trying to disguise the visceral reaction I felt at her use of the jokey endearment. Just another thing that fell naturally from her lips and penetrated straight through to my core.

"Well, in that case..." I slowly inched my top up my torso. If Josie was to insist on this "no fraternising with the Faculty" rule, I planned on making it as difficult as possible for her. I kept my eyes fixed on hers as I slid the top over my head, revealing a black push up bra. Josie's lips parted as she took in the sight of me. I lowered my hand to the zip on my jeans, and with a cheeky wink, slowly unzipped it. Josie's eyes flitted from my chest to my abdomen as I peeled the jeans sensually down my legs, leaving me in my pants and bra. Her nostrils flared, and her breathing slowed to a deep, heaving excitement as she came to me. I let her get close enough that she could feel my body heat before I repeated her own words back to her. "Nuh-uh. No fraternising with the Faculty remember? Your rules, not mine."

Josie spluttered and grinned. "Touché."

~

AFTER CHANGING INTO THE NEW gear and being guided through another maze of corridors, we entered the sports hall. The room was vast and echoey with six large cages against the back wall housing every item of sporting equipment imaginable. Josie walked over to one of them as I re-tied the laces to my brand-new Nike Airs.

"You should probably know..." I started, without looking up, "if you're trying to scare me off this place, this is not the room to do it in. You saw for yourself at the weekend that me and gyms sort of go together."

Josie took a basketball from its cage. "And you should probably know this part of the curriculum tour was more for my benefit than yours because I get to see you looking all hot and sweaty in a pair of shorts, so just humour me." She threw the ball at me, which I caught in both hands against my chest, taking her by surprise.

"Oh, is that right?" Josie raised a surprised eyebrow before charging towards me with determination. I dribbled the ball from side to side, making my way to the basket end of the court. I occasionally looked up at the target as Josie attempted to block me with her long limbs. She reached in, trying to swipe the ball from me, but I jinked and side-stepped her, and after a few more bounces of the ball, I was close enough to the target to take my shot. Without looking up, I launched the ball in the direction of the basket. We both drew in a breath as we watched it lazily circle the hoop three times before dropping through the basket.

Josie threw her hands up in the air, "Oh, come on! You've got to be kidding me?"

I widened my eyes at her and made my mouth into an "O", pretending to be shocked by the accuracy of my shot. Okay, so, maybe I had forgotten to mention the estate I grew up on had a basketball court within a multi-use games area, and when I wasn't at home writing, it was where I spent most of the early '90s – hanging out with my friends and kicking their arses at basketball. But, she didn't need to know that, right? Josie ran to retrieve the ball.

"Right, that's it." She grabbed the ball and dribbled it to a spot where she could take her shot. I attempted to block her in the same way she had done to me, but actually, her moves were pretty impressive. She bounced the ball between her legs effortlessly, and she wrinkled her nose at me as she did it, which I took as her thinking my first shot was just a fluke. In that instant I took advantage of her smugness and lack of concentration and swiped the ball, turning towards the basket and looping it towards the ring. We watched as it sailed right through, barely flicking the basket.

"Oh, I think that's another score? Or is it points I get or a goal or something?" I didn't bother to hide my own smug grin.

Josie shook her head. "You jammy git…" Our laughter echoed in the vast space.

"Next?" I stretched out my arms and pretended to crack my knuckles. I was ready to prove myself in whatever other tasks she had planned. Josie looked at her watch and squinted. "Okay, well, it's not on our itinerary, but we have a bit of time. See that rope over there, hotshot?"

I looked over at the nice thick gym rope attached to the ceiling, which must have been thirty foot above us. "Uh-huh. What about it?"

"Climb it." Her shit-eating smile told me everything I needed to know: she didn't think for one minute I could do it. I squinted at the dangling woven white cord and assessed its length. How different could it be from the pole at work? All it required was upper body strength, right? I reached my first hand onto the rope and looked at Josie who stood close by with her arms folded, still looking insufferable. This competitive streak in her had been duly noted, I told myself.

"So, what's the bet?" I asked innocently.

"The bet?"

"If I make it to the top, what's riding on it?"

Josie squinted as she thought. "Okay, if you make it to the top, all the way to the top, I'll lift the rule on student-lecturer relations, how about that?"

I looked up at how far I had to climb, thought about Chace's pole and smiled.

"Oh, you have so got yourself a deal." I took the rope in both hands and pretended to struggle to lift myself from the floor. Josie tried to stifle a laugh. I had another go at pretending it was too tricky, letting out a groan as I put no strength at all into lifting my body weight.

"Give it up, Mackenzie," Josie commented happily, and that's all I needed. I took a deep breath and exhaled. Right. I grabbed at the nicely nubbly rope with all the determination I could manage and hoisted myself up. Okay, so it wasn't quite like working the pole. The bloody thing moved in every direction beneath me for one thing, and admittedly it was a lot harder to keep a grip on it than I imagined. But I managed to steady it a little between my feet and found I could get a decent grip with them, and I gripped hard with my bare skin, which made it easier. Looking up, it felt like a long way to go, and I wondered momentarily how I would ever do it. Reference point, Roxy, reference point. The words rang in my ears. I'd hiked bloody Snowdon for Christ's sake; this was nothing in comparison. I engaged my biceps and upper body and pulled with all my might; I was not going to let Josie see me fail. One hand after the other, I grabbed the rope and clamped my feet like a monkey and lifted, and after an amazingly short period of time, with the rope still swinging out beneath me, I found myself at the top with my fingertips touching the ceiling. I crowed down to an open-mouthed Josie. "See this? Touched the ceiling!"

As I descended the rope, I looked down at Josie who continued to stare, wide-eyed and evidently stunned into silence. I gave a cheeky, bordering-on-cocky wink as I jumped off the last few feet.

"What are you? Even I can't do that." She leaned in and squeezed my bicep, which, now pumped, actually looked quite impressive. "First the six-pack, then flying up Snowdon and now this? I thought you didn't work out?" She eyed me doubtfully.

I shrugged. "I don't. I have no idea how I just did that."

Josie slanted her eyes and gave me the amused and disbelieving expression, which I had grown to associate with her trying to figure me out.

"Well, you continue to impress me."

I smiled, knowing I owed what just happened to her. "Hmm, it was the reference point," I said reluctantly.

"What?"

I blew out a breath. "I used the reference point."

"You didn't?" Her expression was one of excitement.

I nodded. "Yup. I looked up, thought 'there's no way in hell I can do this' and remembered that's exactly what I thought when I saw that bloody peak towering above me, and I just went for it."

"I love that." Josie's dimples showed as she smiled.

"Yeah, well, I think I kinda…" I swallowed, feeling my entire face turn serious, "…love that too."

CHAPTER 17

"SO, ABOUT THIS BAN OF yours." I stepped into Josie's space. "I mean, I wouldn't want to force you to do anything you don't want." I made sure each breath was felt on her lips.

"Nice distraction technique. Do you always use sex as a way of avoiding what you want to say?"

"Do *you* always use psychoanalysis to distract from letting your body feel what you want it to?" I stepped in closer.

"Umm, you're getting good at this." Josie pulled her bottom lip between her teeth.

My eyes fell to her teeth, grazing her lip. "I'm learning from the best." Our mouths were almost touching.

"We're going to be off schedule." Josie's voice was a low rasp, making the word "schedule" sound like the sexiest thing on earth. I closed the gap between us and pressed my lips lightly against hers before pulling back to speak.

"Maybe next time you create a schedule for us, you should factor in how irresistible you find me."

She laughed uproariously and pushed at my shoulder. "Oh, get over yourself monkey girl, I could resist you if I wanted to."

"Oh yeah?" I grabbed her hands, taking her by surprise, and

guided her back until I had her pressed against the wall. I raised her arms above her head with enough pressure to prevent her wriggling free. "I don't feel much resisting going on." I separated her legs with my knee. She moaned and parted her lips in anticipation. I kept her hands locked in place with one hand and tilted her head with the other. Then I roughly kissed her neck and sucked on her skin, releasing it only to touch her with my tongue. Josie moaned again.

"God. That feels good."

"How long have we got?" I asked into the nape of her neck.

She closed her eyes. "Long enough."

The heat that flared between my legs was instantaneous. I reached inside the leg of her shorts and tugged her pants aside, grateful for the easy access. She was ready for me. My fingers easily slipped up into her, and I plunged two fingers deep inside as her muscles clenched around me at my unexpected and quick entrance. But Josie's gasping groan let me know she approved. I continued to lock her hands in place above her head as I moved in and out of her urgently while her guttural moans echoed throughout the hall. The idea we could get caught any time only intensified the ravenous yearning. I took my mouth from her neck and found her lips. Our tongues crashed together, battling for first place. The movements were hurried, and we searched each other greedily, both wanting so much more. Josie's back arched, thrusting against me as much as her restriction would allow, and I quickened the pace of my fingers moving in her.

"Make me come." The hot air of her breath was like silk on my mouth. My spine tingled at her words and I could feel my own arousal on my inside thigh. I pulled my fingers from inside her and immediately found her swollen parts. I pressed against her, instinctively knowing the perfect speed to move at and Josie's strangled pant filled my ear as my fingers moved wildly against her clit. She hissed in a breath and held it before finally letting out a shuddering groan from deep in her throat as her orgasm tore through her.

"Fuck." I released the tight grip on her hands.

Josie's hands dropped to my shoulders and she stroked them. "Fuck, indeed." She was still breathless and smiling

I smiled back. "So, how long have we got exactly?"

Josie looked at her watch. Her eyes widened when she saw the time. "Crap." She ran her hands quickly through her hair. "We've got to go."

She straightened her shorts, grabbed my hand and nonchalantly led us out of the sports hall and into the corridor.

"Oh, I see how it is, enough time in the schedule for you to get your kicks but not for me?" I teased as she pulled me behind her.

"Believe me, we're going to need a lot longer than a ten-minute slot for the things I want to do to you, but it's going to have to wait until later. We don't even have time to change now." Her tone was unusually flustered, and as she led us from one hallway to another, I wondered what could possibly be so time-dependent on a tour around the building.

Eventually, we entered through a double door and into a dimly lit canteen. A canteen that smelled unusually *really* good. My stomach reacted with a gurgling sound. Josie had asked me to hold out on eating before our date, and as we walked further into the canteen, I could see why.

"Hope you're hungry." She led me over to a small table in the far corner of the room. As we neared it, the magnitude of her effort became clear. It looked like it had been taken straight from a French Michelin starred restaurant. There was a cream damask tablecloth with intricate gold embroidery, silver cutlery, tall, glittering wine glasses and a single rose in a small vase. It was enough to make me catch my breath and stop dead. Josie pulled out a chair that had a delicately embroidered cushion on the base to match the cloth.

I sat and smiled up at her. "I can't believe you've done all this."

She settled opposite me, took her phone from her bag and tapped away on it until Adele's "Make You Feel My Love" filled the room.

I laughed, and it sounded nervous. Josie lifted an elegant-looking bottle of wine and filled her glass.

"I wasn't sure if you're still swearing off the drink, so I brought a non-alcoholic brand."

I smiled, both grateful and amazed she had even thought to do that. She continued.

"I hope it's not too corny. I wanted to make this special for you. Admittedly, I hadn't imagined we'd be wearing shorts and vest tops, but I guess it's a small price to pay for getting...held up." She smiled with the kind of warmth in her eyes that caused my skin to tingle.

I sipped the alcohol-free vino, which surprisingly tasted quite good, and marvelled at how Josie had organised this whole thing, for me. I couldn't remember a time when anyone had done anything as romantic as this. *Was* it slightly corny? Maybe. *Is* it something Clara and I might have ripped the piss out of if we had seen it on some reality TV show? Probably. But *did* it make me feel like the most special person on earth who wanted nothing more than to jump up and down on the spot shouting "I've met the most amazing woman on the planet."? Definitely.

I smiled back at Josie, about to tell her how amazing she was. Not just for the meal but the whole evening, when a woman wearing a toque and white chef's jacket appeared from behind kitchen swing doors and placed a plate in front of each of us. "Good evening. Your starters; breaded mozzarella with a marinara sauce."

I was so stunned I didn't know whether or not I had thanked her before she disappeared back the way she came. I looked at the plate of beautifully presented food and at the swinging doors before turning and settling on Josie.

"You hired a private chef?" I was unable to keep the surprise from my voice.

Josie picked up her fork and shrugged on a small satisfied grin.

"Are you for real?"

She shrugged once more. "I told you, I wanted to make tonight special."

I blew out a breath of disbelief and amazement. "This another one of those things you do for all your women?" I took a bite of the warm stringy mozzarella stick.

"Just the ones who have incredible talents."

I wiggled my eyebrows. "You think I have talents?"

Josie smiled and cocked her head. "You're one-track-minded Roxanne Mackenzie. You know that, right?"

I nodded. "I do."

"And do you also know you use humour as well as sex to get out of serious conversations that may involve you opening up? A little bit like someone else I know?" She held my gaze.

I knew damn well who she meant. Mum used humour to hide behind when anything came up that she felt was too challenging to deal with. My eyes widened. "My mum uses sex to get out of conversations with you?"

Josie pursed her lips, suppressing a grin. "And do you realise you're doing it now to avoid the comparison I just made between you and your mum?"

I held up my finger and thumb, showing a small space between them. "A little bit." And I gave her what I hoped was an endearing grin.

Josie watched me closely, and I got the impression that maybe she wanted a little more. She wanted me to open up. She wanted personal, and I figured, with the soft music, candlelight, and stunning company, if there were ever going to be a good time to talk from the heart, this would be it.

I laid down my fork and sat up straighter. I could do this, right? "Okay." I started, drawing in a breath. "I can be serious." The second the word serious left my lips, my mouth twitched.

"Really?" Josie raised an eyebrow.

"I can…" I cleared my throat. "Wait…" My mouth twitched again, and I could feel the slight widening of my nostrils. I swallowed."Wait…I can…I promise." I breathed in another breath and let it out, feeling my need to laugh dissipate.

"I guess…" I began. "I guess, if I'm honest, I don't like being compared to my mum. I love her more than anything, I do, but I don't want to end up like her. She's a good person with a lot of love in her heart, but she's spent her entire life miserable and full of regret. I don't want that for myself. I want to be happy and have a purpose. I want to feel like I'm progressing in life and working towards something. I want to be someone who enjoys every day, who takes every opportunity handed to them and who's not afraid to try." The words sort of tumbled out of me in one long rush.

Josie smiled. "There, that wasn't so hard, was it?"

"I suppose."

"And for what it's worth, you are different from your mum. You're softer. Well, with me you are anyway."

"Thanks. That means a lot." I took a moment, thinking I had started so I may as well continue. "And I suppose, while I'm at it, there's also a part of me that can't help but wonder if I'm as special as all this implies." I gestured to the table. "And, I guess, it got me thinking about your past relationship and how you were with Kaz. There, how's that for opening up?"

Josie studied me for a short while, doing that cute thing she did where she chewed on the inside of her mouth. And I knowingly pushed to the back of my mind that I was using this excuse and this secret of Josie's to still avoid talking about the one I so badly needed to share with her if I wanted her to trust me. I shivered and looked across the table at her.

"Okay. Well, yes, you are as special to me as all this is making out. More so even. I don't know where you ever got the idea that you're not special, Roxy, whoever planted that seed in your younger years, has a lot to answer for, and no, I've never done this or even anything like this for anyone in the past, not even Kaz. And as I've said, other than that there's not a lot to tell in terms of my past relationships."

"So, you've really not seen anyone since her?"

"Nope."

"Is that because between her and your dad you've been put off relationships?" I didn't know where this newfound ability to ask every question on my mind had sprung from, but I was going with it.

"You're quite insightful, do you know that? If you didn't have your heart so set on writing, you would probably make a great therapist." She lifted her wine glass in a toast and then took a sip.

"Is this conversation making you uncomfortable, is that why you changed the subject?" Jeez, I was really on form tonight.

Josie stopped the glass mid-sip and smiled. "Not in the slightest. I've told you before, I like conversations that mean something." Her eyes locked onto mine as I thought about how every conversation I'd ever had with her meant something to me.

"So, do you think your dad doing what he did, and Kaz cheating on you has put you off relationships?"

"I guess it's made me more cautious, if that's what you mean? I would like to think I'm self-aware enough now not to drag my past traumas into a new relationship."

"So, you don't have trust issues?"

She cleared her throat. "I'm not saying that exactly. I'm fully aware that the role of the subconscious mind is to keep me safe and protect me from any perceived danger. I've been burned, and I suppose the fear of being hurt again might seep out in small ways, but I'd try to not let it impact anything. I know there are no guarantees in any relationship, and you can't predict what might happen, but naturally, because of what I've experienced, it's important to me that I'm able to trust the person I'm with. Why? You got some deep dark secret you need to get off your chest?"

She'd asked the question light-heartedly with a playful smile, but that did nothing to prevent the panicked lump that formed in my throat and the scramble of questions that barged their way to the front of my mind. Should I tell her? Now would be a perfect opportunity, wouldn't it? If not now, when? But hadn't I left it too late? I had lied. She had just stressed the importance of trust and I've lied to her and not just once but repeatedly. My mind continued to speed on at a hundred miles an hour as I tried to settle on a decision. I knew the right thing to do, of course, I did. Everything inside me screamed to just tell her, get it out in the open and deal with the consequences, but at the same time, I'd never had anyone look at me the way she was. Like I was something more, something special, destined to go on to bigger and better things. I didn't want to risk losing that, not yet anyway, just because I'd been daft enough to lie about nothing much in the first place. The lies were the thing now, I realised, not the bloody stripping.

I shook my head slowly. "Nothing springs to mind." I tried to sound as natural as possible.

Josie nodded. "Good. Well, let's start as we mean to go on then." She held her glass in the air between us. "To trust."

I lifted my glass and met hers with a clink. "To trust."

I struggled to swallow.

THE REST OF THE DINNER was delicious. Admittedly, I might have enjoyed it more if I hadn't spent the majority of the time berating myself for not taking the opportunity to come clean, but that aside, both the food and the company really were sensational. Following the mozzarella, we devoured a main course of sirloin steak which had been cooked to melt-in-the-mouth-perfection with all the trimmings, and to finish, we shared a gooey chocolate brownie topped with vanilla ice-cream. I steered the conversation on to light-hearted subjects, through fear of digging myself another hole, and it worked. By the time we finished, I had somehow managed to shake off the sinking feeling from earlier or at least push it again to the back of my mind, and I had found a way to work up some excitement for the rest of the tour.

Throughout the evening, we dipped in and out of the main lecture hall where Josie presented me with a new cute title for the next stage. Her itinerary, as she referred to it, included a soft drink at the campus bar where she kicked my arse at two games of pool, a play around in the science lab, which she quickly re-thought due to my inability to pass any apparatus without fingering the buttons, and a quick trip to the rec rooms. Finally, I once again found myself in the main lecture hall, staring up at the projector and waiting for the final slide.

I closed my arms around Josie's waist from behind and locked my fingers against her now nicely rounded stomach. "Remind me why we're doing this again?" I was still bewildered by the immense effort she'd put into the evening.

Josie dropped her head against my shoulder, and laid a tender kiss on my cheek.

"Because, Miss Mackenzie, I know regret when I see it. I know it's a cliché, but it's truly better to regret the things you did do rather than the things you didn't. Also, I wanted you to know I believe in you and really feel you could be and do anything you want, and I want to support you and be there to witness your success."

I smiled so wide my face almost dropped off. "You want to be there?" I knew what she'd said contained so much more I could've focused on, but that part stood out most.

She nodded against my shoulder. "Yes. I really do."

I clutched her tight against me. "I think I would like for you to be there too."

The last slide on the projector read, 'Amongst the Greats.' Josie had planned a walk through the English department, where she pointed out rooms where talented writers had both studied and taught. The most famous of them had been recognised by the university in framed photographs on the walls of the corridors and included names I knew and, to my surprise and delight, Wilfred Owen.

"Feeling inspired yet?" Josie sported a knowing grin.

I mindlessly traced my finger over the frame of a writer's portrait I didn't recognise. "Of course. It's hard not to. I don't think I'd realised how much I'd suppressed wanting to go to uni. I suppose I'd managed to convince myself it was no longer a dream of mine, but being here now, it doesn't seem so impossible."

Josie walked over to me and laid a soft kiss on my lips. "Then, my work here is done."

CHAPTER 18

JOSIE'S HEAD RESTED ON MY chest while her silky, muscled legs wrapped around me. A cute whistling sound came from her nose each time she exhaled, and a sweet after-sex scent filled the air, taking my mind back to the previous evening and the electricity between us when we got back from the university and ended up in a sweaty, rampant entanglement on my bed. I traced Josie's side with my fingers and she remained perfectly still, wrapped up in the bedsheet while I stayed wrapped up in the warm and fuzzies that started at my toes and made their way to the grin on my face. My god I could get used to this, I thought as I planted a small kiss on her ear.

The effort Josie had put into the previous evening, told me everything I needed to know. It was one of – no *the* – most thoughtful thing anyone had ever done for me. It wasn't just the romance of it all either, although that was mind-blowing in itself, it had actually captured my imagination and stirred up feelings I thought were dead and buried. For the first time in as long as Mum had been ill, I felt inspired again. I mulled it over, thinking about the logistics of it all. If I went to uni, how would I afford it? Would I have to move and give up the lease on the flat? Would I still see Clara? And what about Josie? Would it work if I had to move and put distance between us?

"Shush." Josie pulled her nakedness tighter against me.

"I didn't say anything." I wondered if she could be sleep talking.

"I can hear your mind running overtime." Her morning voice was adorable.

"I'm just thinking about how it would all work, that's all."

"We'll make it work." She looked at me from beneath heavy lids and smiled.

"We?" I liked how the word felt on my lips.

"Yes, we." Josie stretched to give me a small peck on the chin before continuing. "I've been thinking, and I can't make any promises, but there may be something I can do to help. I won't go into details, in case it doesn't amount to anything, but I have an idea. Just leave it with me, okay?"

I rolled my eyes. "What are you? My guardian angel? Sent to guide me in a new life direction?"

Josie shrugged. "Maybe."

I laughed. "I was joking."

"I know, and so am I, but I do believe everything happens for a reason, that fate has brought us together at the perfect time. I honestly believe we were meant to meet. I felt it the second I laid eyes on you in your mum's room."

"You think we were destined to meet?" My voice was tinged with scepticism.

"Destiny, fate, the universe conspiring, whatever you want to call it, I believe there's a greater force at play that's brought us together, yes."

I thought for a moment about her words and the ramifications of what she was saying.

She searched my face. "You disagree?"

I shrugged. "I guess I've not really given it much thought."

Josie rolled onto her side. "I have. I think about it every

time I'm with you. It's an intense feeling I get that overwhelms me. It's like I've known you before, in a distant past and now we're back together. I know it sounds a bit out there, but it's the only way to explain what I experience when I'm with you. I just can't shake this feeling we were meant to meet."

I looked over Josie's shoulder and at a framed photo I had of Mum on my bedside table. "And my mum?" I was wondering how she fitted into this whole "universe conspiring" theory of Josie's.

"And your mum's the one who brought us together, like the catalyst. Think about it. If it hadn't been for your mum being in the home, we would never have met."

I fell quiet for a moment. "We would have met at the club," I said finally, thinking back to our second encounter.

"We may have seen each other, yes, but we wouldn't have talked. I assumed you were with Clara, remember?"

She had a point, but I didn't quite know how I felt about Mum having a terminal illness being the thing to bring Josie and me together. It felt warped, and as much as I didn't want to say it out loud, and as much as I was developing feelings for Josie – feelings I didn't know I was still capable of – if it meant Mum not having that awful disease, I would have accepted having never met Josie, that much I did know.

"What are you thinking?" Josie ran her hand gently over my cheek, and I felt myself turn my head from it.

"I'm just wondering why Mum had to get cancer for us to meet, that's all. Whichever God lined that one up must be pretty twisted." My tone had more bite to it than I'd intended.

Josie's eyes widened. "No, shit. Baby. That's not what I meant." She leaned onto her elbow and looked into my eyes. "Your mum's path is your mum's path, and for whatever reason, I believe that would've happened regardless. I just think the universe has taken pity on you and provided a way for it to not be all bad, that's all I'm saying."

I nodded, still not convinced. It must have shown on my face.

"I really didn't mean it how you've taken it. Christ. I know if you could do anything to take it away, including not meeting me, you would. I know that." She clutched my hand. "I didn't mean it how it came out, Rox. I was just trying, in my messed-up way, to say I think fate has brought us together because that's the only explanation for how I feel when I'm with you."

Her worried look melted something in me. I could tell she was beating herself up for her choice of words, and the last thing I wanted was to be responsible for making Josie feel bad. I guided her hand to my mouth.

"Shush, it's okay." I kissed her palm, letting her know we were fine. It wasn't that I disagreed with her. I did feel things when in her company that I couldn't quite explain, and just because I hadn't yet labelled it as fate, it didn't mean that somewhere, deep down in the depths of my soul, I didn't know the most significant pain I will ever know had been lessened by what was shaping up to be one of the most wonderful things ever to happen to me. I let go of Josie's hand and kissed her forehead.

"Then, yes, I do." My voice was soft and tender.

"Yes, you do what?"

"Believe in fate. Anything that's brought me to you is something worth believing in."

~

AFTER FRESHENING UP IN THE bathroom, I returned to find Josie propped against my headboard, reading from the same notebook I had shown her before. She laid it on its open pages and looked up at me with a bewildered expression.

"You're a genius, that's all there is to it."

"Hmm...I'm not so sure about that." I threw myself on the

bed belly-first and grabbed the book to see which part of my soul I had bared. It was open on one of the back pages and had obviously been written at a later date than the stuff she had read before. It was about my mum.

She was here, but now she's not.

Never will be again, but still is.

Still in that bed. Still in my heart, yet slipping between the space. No-man's land.

Leaving me slowly, painfully, like the sun fading on a summer's day only never to rise again.

Just the moon.

Maybe there's something in the moon?

She will be the moon.

The sun will be no longer, but her reflection will live on eternally in the moon.

I cringed. It wasn't exactly my best work. It was clearly just an attempt at making sense of the pain.

"Pretty deep, huh?" I closed the book and tried to hide my pink cheeks behind it.

"Yes, it's deep and in places quite dark, but there's something so raw about how you capture your feelings. You really are something, you know that?"

I rolled my eyes, still not entirely comfortable with the compliments Josie insisted on piling my way. My self-esteem had taken a battering since working at the club, and as much as she said all the right things, it didn't make it any less awkward to hear.

I looked at my watch. "You know, I'm going to have to make a move in a minute?"

Josie pulled me on top of her and kissed me. I laughed into the kiss before deepening it with my tongue and forgetting myself momentarily, completely guided by the pull in my pants that had other ideas about what I should be doing with my afternoon.

"Okay." Josie withdrew breathlessly. "You're right, we need to stop this, or neither of us will go anywhere, and I've got a pile of work building up."

"Uh-huh." I lowered my lips to her neck and grazed it with my teeth.

"Ummm, that's not helping."

"But it's nice, right?" I smiled into her lips.

"You, Miss Mackenzie, are a huge distraction."

Our mouths met again in a delicious entanglement for what seemed like the hundredth time that day. Kissing Josie felt like a cure-all prescription. The second her lips touched mine, everything faded into oblivion, leaving just us. Two people who couldn't keep their hands off each other. We got lost in each other, and as clichéd as it sounds, it felt like time stood still. Only, time didn't stand still; it ticked away, tut, tut, tutting at us in judgement because we both really did have things to do. Josie pulled away first, leaning her forehead against my own.

"Behave," she said, panting and grinning into the word.

~

WE LEFT THE BUILDING TOGETHER and gave each other a lingering kiss goodbye before getting into our separate cars. I watched in my wing mirror as Josie's Beetle trundled away before I turned on the car radio and started out to Chislehurst. Throughout the journey, every song that played took on a new meaning. The chipper songs I usually turned off were now the ones I scrunched my nose up to and bopped my head to as I sang along.

It was another scorching day, and something about the sun, the music and the excitement building in my stomach had me smiling goofily, not only to myself but at complete strangers as they pulled up in their cars next to mine. The colours around me were sharper. The sky was bluer. The sunbeams on the windshield were luminous, and the sporadic patches of grass looked as green as I had ever seen. Somehow, I had managed to find a spark of happiness in all my pain and worries, and for me, that was worth celebrating.

I thought back to the last time I'd felt that good. It was when I first arrived in London, filled with the optimism of all the good things to come. I'd walked as though I was destined to be someone, like everything around me could be acted upon, and like I actually believed I was good enough. I was proud of who I was back then, of who I would become and now because of Josie, I was beginning to sense that glimmer of hope once more. She really had given me back my happy.

~

WHEN I REACHED RECEPTION, MILLY was chomping on a Ginster's pasty. "Someone's cheery today." Her comment came through a mouthful of food.

I laughed. "And you got all that from the way I walked through the door?"

"Uh-huh, you have happy feet today. People walk slower when they're sad. It's a fact."

I thought for a moment then nodded. "Well, it's an interesting theory and appears to have some validity."

"Huh?" Her forehead crinkled up.

I laughed again. "I think you're probably right. That's what I'm saying. I am happy." I scribbled my name in the visitors' book.

"Good. It's nice to see. Wouldn't have anything to do with a Miss Josie Calhoun would it?" Her grin was mischievous.

"What are you? Some sort of Oracle?"

"Well, let's just say, I hear things." She flicked the page of her magazine, letting me know our conversation was done.

I shook my head. Bloody mother and her big mouth. I made

a beeline for Mum's room, noticing maybe Milly was right, I did have a certain swagger today. When I entered, I was ready to give Mum grief for talking about my business to the staff when I came to an abrupt halt. Mum was sitting up in bed, clutching onto her chest. The wheezing sound turned me to ice. Her face was colourless and her eyes flashed with fear. I rushed to her bedside as the walls closed in on me.

"Mum, it's okay, I'm here."

Unable to speak through rapid gasps for breath, Mum signalled to the box of tissues on her cabinet. I swiped at the tissues and handed her one. She coughed and spluttered into it until it was covered in speckles of red.

"Mum, how long have you been coughing up blood?" It was my best I'm-not-shitting-myself-at-all voice. She attempted to answer but couldn't get her words out through the rattly choke of a second coughing fit.

"It's okay, you don't have to answer. I'm just going to speak to the nurse, I'll be right back." I walked out of the room slowly, closing the door lightly behind me and once out of view, bolted down the corridor to the nurses' office. When I burst into the room, I found three nurses sitting around reading magazines and drinking coffee. Breathless words left my mouth in a stream of panic.

"She's coughing up blood and struggling to breathe."

My frenzied tone caused the nurses to spring into action. They threw their half-eaten sandwiches onto the coffee table and flew from their seats. I followed behind as they sped down the corridor, immediately slipping back into their roles and pulling their apparatus from their pockets.

When we reached the room, Mum was still hunched over the tissue, coughing into it. The nurses fussed around her, taking swabs and blood pressure and peering into her eyes with a flashlight while I just stood, watching, frozen, saying and doing nothing, more scared and helpless than I have ever been.

Was she leaving me? The commotion continued until the morphine took effect and Mum finally fell into a comfortable state. The nurses said they'd checked everything they needed to and felt happy she would be okay and reassured me they would each take turns to monitor her throughout the night. I collapsed into my usual chair beside Mum and stroked her emaciated hand. A familiar wave of guilt hit me. How dare I allow myself to feel so happy? I should be giving her my full attention, not off in the clouds, getting swept away by the prospects of my future when she...

I cut off my wretched internal dialogue, realising that the self-flagellation needed to stop. Feeling happy was okay. I deserved to at least try to live my best life. Mum would want that, and I shouldn't punish myself for it. I knew pain and heart-break were on the horizon, and it made no sense to not spend time with someone who could lessen that. I squeezed Mum's hand and whispered into the low-lit room.

"Mum, I know you know about Josie." Unsurprisingly she didn't respond. "I know you think I'm going to mess it up and hurt her and, if I'm honest, I'm shit scared I might. But I don't want to, and I'm going to do everything I can to make it work. Mum, she's not like anyone I've ever met. She makes me happy and I hate myself for that because I shouldn't be feeling happy when you're like this, it's not right. But I have to take a chance, don't I? I have to know."

Mum was so deeply drugged even if she had heard me, she couldn't have responded, but in saying it out loud, I had answered my own question. I took the phone from my pocket and made the call.

"Hey, you." It sounded like Josie was smiling into the phone.

"Hey."

There was a short silence. "Is everything okay?"

I didn't answer straight away as I fought back the tears.

"Rox? Are you there, baby? Has something happened?"

I squeezed my eyes shut. "I'm here. What are you doing right now?"

"Just looking over some notes for work. You want to come over?"

I nodded, even though I couldn't be seen. "I need you."

"Come to mine straight away. I'll text you my address, and you can tell me about it when you get here."

"Okay." My voice cracked with the final word.

I slipped my phone back in my pocket, kissed Mum's hand and set off.

CHAPTER 19

AS I PULLED INTO JOSIE'S road, just off Bromley Common, a peculiar mix of butterflies and moths fluttered about inside me. The butterflies were for Josie. Although I had only seen her a few hours earlier, I couldn't help feeling excited about being in her company again. The moths were for Mum. What happened at the home was a sharp reminder that the last day was imminent. My eyes stung at the thought. I wiped at them and looked in the wing mirror, trying to get rid of the mascara smears but knowing it was pointless, the moment Josie laid eyes on me she'd see I'd been crying.

With red eyes and flushed cheeks, I walked up to Josie's front door, taking in the street she lived on. The quiet cul-de-sac felt like the type of place the milkman still dropped off glass-bottles of milk. I expected kids played curby in the street during the day and if Josie ever forgot to take the bins out, a neighbour would kindly do it for her. There was something very grown-up about it all. The road could have been plucked from any small town or village, which made it hard to believe it was still London. The door opened, and Josie greeted me with concern written all over her face. I managed a tight smile and a small shrug before she held her arms out to me. I fell into her and let her squeeze me tight.

After a minute or so, I pulled away from Josie's shoulder, wanting to say a proper hello. I looked her up and down, noticing "at home Josie" for the first time. She wore beige harem pants and a thin cotton lime-green hoody, and her cheeks were flushed in a healthy glow. She looked as gorgeous as ever.

"Hey," I said once I met her eyes.

She cocked her head. "Hey. You want to talk about it?"

I nodded and let her pull me from the front hall through to her living room where immediately I was hit by a soothing scent of sandalwood and lavender. Josie gestured at her sofa.

"I'll make us a cuppa, and you can tell me what's happened."

I did as she directed and watched Josie leave the room before taking in her living space. It wasn't anything like my place. In fact, it wasn't anything like any place I'd seen. There were brightly coloured side lamps, glass candle holders hanging from the ceiling, multi-coloured cushions, figurines I recognised from various religions, fairy lights, and a huge Indian style rug. It was an overwhelming assortment of colours and furnishings. Incense smoke wafted through the room from a stick burning in a small brass holder, which explained the earthy scents from earlier. And the soft, chantlike repetition of an instrument I didn't recognise played in the background. I had to give it to her, the room felt cosy and comforting, and serene. I relaxed back into the world's most welcoming sofa and closed my eyes for a few seconds.

When Josie returned with a tray of chintz-patterned matching teapot and cup set. My face must have asked the question for me.

"What?" Josie laid the tray onto the low circular table.

"This place?"

"You like it?" Her tone was hopeful.

"It's like I've just arrived at a spiritual retreat."

"You think it's a bit much?" She poured tea into the cup and added milk and sugar before she handed it to me. "It was nothing like this when I was growing up. Mum's taste was a lot more modern, but since she left it to me, I've spent the past few months making it my own."

"God, no. I love it. It's exactly what I needed. In the time it took you to make the tea I've pretty much chilled out completely. I guess I just didn't know you were…" I hesitated, searching for the right word.

"A raging hippy?" She offered.

I laughed. "That's not quite the word I was going for, but now you've said it. I mean, I knew you were a little bit "out there" but this is a whole other level." I hoped Josie sensed the playfulness in my voice.

"You've not seen anything yet. Sometime I'll show you a few pictures of how I used to dress. You'd definitely have called me a hippy back then."

"That I've got to see." I sipped my tea. "So, what changed?"

Suddenly, learning more about Josie had taken priority over crying on her shoulder. She finished pouring her tea and came to join me on the sofa.

"When I landed the job at the university, I had to rein it in. I didn't want the students treating me like one of them – you know – offering me weed and whatnot. It's easy for the boundaries to blur. And I suppose I felt like I had to dress a bit more professionally to be taken seriously. Deans are less likely to employ people who look like they've rocked straight up from Glastonbury. I love my job, so it's worth the sacrifice and it's easy enough to pull off a swotty look just by wrapping a scarf around your neck."

I couldn't help but laugh at that.

"What are you laughing at?" Josie smiled and squinted.

"You, wearing scarves all the time. I really didn't get it but now it makes perfect sense."

"I know, it's a bit of an odd thing but I've got used to doing it. I wear them everywhere now."

"Not camping."

"You noticed that? Impressive. I didn't need to wear one in Wales because there was no chance of bumping into any students or work colleagues. So, I took a wild risk."

I widened my eyes. "Ooh, you rebel."

"Right?" She widened her eyes back. "Anyway, I don't mind smartening up and laying it on thick but this is my home, and I suppose I like to create a certain atmosphere to live in. It works for me."

I nodded and appraised the room some more, thinking the mellow ambience of her house, surprisingly, worked for me too.

"Hey." The word took me out of my thoughts. "You want to scoot over?" Josie held her arm out, and I shuffled across the sofa and snuggled into her. It was nice to be held and we stayed like that for ten minutes before either of us spoke.

"Mum's rapidly deteriorating, you know?" My was voice small and fragile.

"I know, baby." Josie ran her fingers through my hair. "Are you going to tell me what happened?"

I blew out a breath. "She was coughing up blood and struggling to breathe. I was terrified and completely fucking useless."

"Hey. I'm sure you did everything you could. You didn't pass out, did you?"

"No, thank god. It's random when it does and doesn't happen, you know? You would think panicking that my own mum was about to die in front of me would've sent me into shock or something?"

Josie's fingers continued to run through my hair, soothing me.

"The mind is a minefield for sure. Just when we think we've

got it all figured out, it shakes things up and wanders off in a different direction." She planted a gentle kiss on my cheek. "I'm so sorry you're going through this. I wish I could've been there for you."

I smiled. "You're here for me now."

I don't know if it was the exhaustion from the day, the late-night, or the gentle journey of the soft music, but the last thing I remembered was Josie laying a blanket over me and softly stroking my cheek.

~

MY EYES FLEW OPEN AS a piercing sound woke me from my dreams.

"What the…?" I shot up and took a moment to get my bearings. I was in Josie's living room. A strong waft of smoke filled the room. Josie was nowhere in sight. I called out to her, panicked that the house might be on fire. No answer. I called again. Nothing. Kicking into action, my eyes frantically darted around the room. As I fumbled in my pocket for my phone, ready to call emergency services, Josie ran into the room, flustered and wafting a tea-towel back and forth under the fire alarm.

"What's going on?" I shouted just as the alarm noise subsided.

"I'm sorry. I didn't want to wake you like this. I tried to make dinner. I knew you wouldn't have eaten earlier, so I thought you'd be hungry, but…" She threw her hands in the air.

I tucked in my lips to stifle a laugh as I connected the dots. "Hey, don't worry. I'm sure whatever you've made will be lovely." Josie's flustered state amused me and not to mention my relief that the house wasn't burning down.

"Hmmm…I don't think you quite understand." She looked in the direction of what I assumed was the kitchen.

I took her hand. "It can't be that bad. Come on, let me look."

Josie led me through to her kitchen, and after a short coughing fit from the fumes, Josie, with her bottom lip protruding, held out an oven tray. It took me a moment to work out what it was, but it eventually dawned that I was looking at a large, black nubbly disc of total inedibility. My jaw clenched as I attempted to stifle laughter. Pizza. She had burnt the living shit out of a pizza which was recognisable only by the empty Goodfellow's box on the kitchen island.

I lifted my fist to my mouth and bit my knuckle, trying to hold it together. The sight of Josie in a pair of oven gloves, holding the charcoal relic out to me, was too much. Something about her deflated expression told me Josie Calhoun did not like to make mistakes, and the more downcast she looked, the more a bubble of laughter threatened to burst out. Josie frowned, making me want to lose it even more. My shoulders jiggled, and without warning, I snorted through no longer suppressed laughter.

"It's not funny." Her eyes narrowed, but I could detect a glimmer of amusement in them.

I attempted my best serious face. "Nope, it's not funny baby, not funny in the slightest." My bottom lip quivered. My eyes landed back on the charcoal and then up to meet Josie's. She was now biting her lip.

"I'm sorry." I gave in to the laughter again. "I'm sorry...It's just...What the hell is that?" I struggled to speak through my laughter. "Is it a new topping I've never heard of?"

Against her will, Josie's eyes crinkled, and she pursed her lips, trying not to smile.

"You are horrible." She tried to glower and failed. "So, I probably should've told you I can't cook?" She laid the tray on the cooker top and removed the oven gloves one by one. She threw them to the floor and hitched herself up onto the bench top.

"Ah, c'mon, I think it's sweet you tried." I walked over to her, wedged my hips between her legs and wrapped my hands around the back of her neck. "I'm sure it will be completely delicious. And anyway, you made me laugh, didn't you? I can't remember the last time I laughed like that."

Josie sighed, clearly still not quite wanting to see the funny side.

"Hey, what's wrong?"

She looked deflated, and in my experience, a deflated Josie was out of character. Her shoulders slumped.

"I just feel so useless, you know? I know what you're going through and believe me, I know how it feels to wake up every day not knowing if it's going to be the day you get the call. I know what it's like to have to mentally prepare yourself every time you step into that room because you're not sure if you're going to be strong enough to keep it together. I get it. And when I look into your eyes, the pain I see is so familiar, I feel it as my own. I didn't have anyone there for me when Mum died, and I really needed someone. I really could have done with someone sticking a pizza in the oven for me at times, you know? I can't believe I screwed it up."

I shook my head and placed two fingers below her chin. I lifted her face to look at me. She blinked with gut-wrenching sadness in her eyes.

"Listen to me." My tone was stern. "You've not screwed anything up. You have no idea how much you've already done for me. Fuck, Josie, before I met you, I was so unhappy, every single day was a struggle. My heart was just something that pumped blood around my body and nothing more. I thought it'd forgotten how to work. And then you showed up."

I stroked her cheek with my thumb and held her gaze.

"Since you've come into my life..." I paused as the words caught in my throat. "Since you've come into my life, Josie, it's like

I've been given a second chance. It's like I can finally see a glimmer of light. And although it's all kinds of wrong to feel like this with Mum the way she is, I just can't help it. You really have no idea how happy you make me. Just knowing you has made me a better person, just breathing in the same air as you makes me feel like I can do anything I set my mind to. For the first time in forever, I'm actually allowing myself to feel optimistic about the future. And it's a future I want more than anything to include you in."

Josie smiled. "Really?" She held my gaze.

"Really. And no amount of burnt pizza will change any of that." We shared a smile, and I went on. "Please don't ever feel as though you're not helping me through this because you are, more than you'll ever know. You're the best thing to happen to me in a long time, and." I stopped, swallowed hard and went on, "I see this thing between us as the real deal."

Josie nodded and sat up straighter and, like magic, her demeanour settled back to its usual confidence.

"I think this could be the real deal too." She swallowed. "My heart was just as fragile when I met you, and I thought it would be a long time before I let anyone in again, but then I met you and I just...I just knew."

Our eyes locked, both blurry with tears that lingered but were not quite ready to fall. The look we gave each other said everything there was to say, there was no need for any more words. I closed the gap between us and kissed her. Just small pecks at first leading to soft, closed-mouth kisses, slow and sensual. My hand slid back up to her neck and through her hair where my fingers gently caressed her head. Josie cupped my cheek in her hand, and our lips moved against each other to a gentle, tentative rhythm. The kiss was sweet and loving and everything I never thought I would want from a kiss, and yet, there it was. The type of kiss that wasn't leading anywhere. It wasn't the starter before the main course. It wasn't the supporting act before the main event, it was…everything. The perfect kiss.

"Wow." Josie slowly pulled away. "I've not been there before."

I shook my head against hers.

"Me either and now I don't ever want to leave."

CHAPTER 20

"LISTEN, I'M NOT SAYING I don't like LP or Lucy Spraggan, I'm just saying it's predictable, that's all. I bet there's a hundred-thousand other people out there who peg "Lost on you" and "Tea and Toast" as their favourite songs. They're lesbian clichés." Josie smiled, looking rather proud of herself.

"Okay then, Miss Originality. What's yours?" I interrupted before she had a chance to answer. "No wait, let me guess." I narrowed my eyes. "I've got it. Bob Dylan "Blowin' in the wind"?"

Josie laughed. "Very close, I do love that song, but for me, hands down, it's Dory Previn and "Lady with a Braid".

I rolled my eyes. "Oh, now who's being predictable?"

"You've never heard that song in your life, have you?"

I screwed my nose up, "Nope."

We had spent the morning lying on Josie's low, Japanese-style-bed asking each other a barrage of questions with the idea of getting to know one another better. We knew the big stuff: our family histories, our biggest fears, deepest regrets, that kind of thing, but we had barely touched on the simpler things in life like music, films, and food. So, we decided that's what the day would be about, getting to know each other's small day-to-day likes and dislikes. With every answer, Josie revealed herself to be quirkier than I had imagined, and with every response she gave, I found myself liking her just that little bit more.

"Wait, I'll put it on." Josie scrambled around under the covers to find the pants she had misplaced the night before. After locating them, she slipped them on and crawled out of bed in a way that had me wanting to do less talking and more using our tongues in other ways. As she fumbled around her CD collection, I took the chance to check my phone and see if I had any missed calls from the home. The screen was clear, and I laid the phone back down, knowing no news had to be good news. Josie found the CD and loaded it into the player, just another reminder of how old-school this chick could be. I don't think I had known anyone to use a CD player for at least five years. Josie came back to bed and snuggled into my chest as we both lay back to listen to her favourite song. I had to give it to her, although it wouldn't be my usual taste in music, it was pretty special. The lyrics had a beautiful simplicity to them and told a story of two people spending the night together for the first time. We lay in silence and paid attention to each word as I felt the folk melody somehow strengthening the bond between us. As the track ran into another, I found the courage to ask a question that had been on the edge of my mind from the moment I arrived at hers.

I rolled onto my side to face her. "Hey, can I ask you something?"

"Sure." She mirrored my movements and rested her head on her hand.

"Does it worry you how different we are?"

Josie frowned. "What do you mean?"

I squeezed her side for reassurance. "I don't know, I guess I just mean who we are as people, we're quite different you know?"

Josie remained quiet for a moment as she digested what I'd said. "Are you asking this because I like folk music?" Her lips curled. "I mean, I can turn it off if it's bothering you?"

"No, I'm serious. You like mountain climbing and camping in the wilderness, I barely leave London. Your house is a bloody spiritual retreat, and I know nothing about spirituality. You've got a real job and love delving into people's minds, and I just kind of, I don't know, just don't really seem to have a lot going on." And what I have got going on, I can't seem to tell you about, I thought and felt a bit sick.

Josie shook her head. "Are you serious? You have it all going on. You like reading and writing and pretending you don't like going up mountains when you do. You're deep, funny and talented as hell. They're the things that matter. Who says we have to be into all of the same things? Compatibility doesn't have to equal similarity, does it? I expect there are loads of studies out there that show how differences in relationships can be utterly enriching."

I smiled, enjoying how animated she had become. "You're going to check, aren't you? As soon as you get near a computer, you're going to start downloading studies that prove your point, I can tell."

She nodded. "Damn right, I will, and then I'll present them to you with a smug grin." She smiled before turning serious. "So, where's all this coming from?"

I blew out a breath, laid back on the bed, and covered my eyes with my arm. "Oh, I don't know, I'm sorry, I'm an arse. I suppose I just feel that it's all too good to be true, that there must be a catch and I'm trying to figure it out before I'm in too deep. I know that us being different's not a bad thing. I need to just be present with you like you said and enjoy your company and stop worrying about what might or might not happen, and over time I guess we'll end up sharing each other's interests anyway."

Josie's eyes softened, and she smiled, making her dimples pop in the way I found irresistible. "Yeah? I kind of love that you're using words like "over time" when you talk about us."

I nodded. "Yeah, well, I'm so ridiculously into you." I kissed her nose before continuing. "Which is why I was thinking, how would you feel about visiting Mum today?"

"I was planning on visiting her tomorrow, I have a new book that I think she'll love, not that she'll admit it, of course."

I shuffled and cleared my throat. "Erm…I was kind of meaning with me. How would you feel about visiting Mum today…with me…as my…" I left the sentence hanging, hoping I hadn't misjudged the situation.

"As your…?" Josie repeated, dragging out the words. The woman never bloody let me off the hook.

I blew out a breath. "As my…" I hesitated, cringing internally and squinting my eyes, I felt weird saying what I was about to say. "My…girlfriend?"

Josie tilted her head and smiled, looking pleased with herself for coaxing it out of me.

"As your girlfriend, I would like that very much."

CHAPTER 21

"BOTH VISITING AT THE SAME time today then?" Milly's cheeky grin and a quick twerk of the brows made her accusation glaringly evident.

"Yes, Mill, we're both visiting on the same day." There was a hint of annoyance in Josie's voice as she scribbled her name in the book.

"And did you arrive together?" Milly craned her neck and looked towards the car park as though trying to see which of our cars were outside.

Josie passed me the pen and straightened, addressing Milly directly.

"Yes, we arrived together. We arrived together because we spent the night making love in my bed and now we're off to tell Susan we're an item, and I'm totally shitting myself as you can probably imagine. Anything else you want to know?"

Milly's eyes widened and I smiled at the exchange from which I'd learned one thing: it was official, Josie was nervous.

As I signed in, Milly decided that life would go on and she picked up her phone and got back to the episode of *Loose Women* she had been watching before we arrived. We made our way to Mum's room, but not before Milly piped up with: "Good luck, you're gonna need it." Which got a laugh from me.

Josie hesitated outside Mum's door.

"I'm not too sure this is the best idea now we're here. Especially after the day she had yesterday. Don't you think we should maybe give her a little more time?" There was a hint of frantic nervousness in her voice.

I shook my head and took her hand.

"We don't know how much time we have, and I *really* want her to know about us – properly. It's important she knows I'm going to be okay and I'm capable of this..." I stroked her cheek while she chewed on the inside of it. Josie nodded and let out a breath that sounded resigned and less fearful. She opened the door and gestured for me to enter.

"I'll do it for you," she said quietly as I walked past her.

Mum was sitting up and looking relatively alert, almost like she'd been expecting us.

"About bloody time." Her expression was inscrutable as she looked between us.

"What are you on about?" I immediately figured she was in one of her cantankerous moods.

"You two. About bloody time you got it together and made an appearance, you know, the two of you together, I mean. Is she treating you okay?" Mum shot Josie a pointed look.

"Erm..." Josie looked at me and then back at Mum before her shocked expression turned into an easy smile. She reached out, took my hand, and nodded.

"Yes, she's...perfect." We smiled at each other.

Mum's eyes set on me. "Good, keep it that way."

Christ! I rolled my eyes, trying not to take it too personally. She could be such an arse sometimes, but there was always a tiny glint in her eye that told me she loved me and didn't really mean it. I sat, expecting Josie to take the seat opposite me, but instead, she perched on my knee and draped an arm around my shoulder. I let my hands settle on her hips.

"How are you feeling after yesterday?" I asked Mum, thinking she looked a hell of a lot better than I was expecting. She rolled her eyes.

"Oh, you know, like someone who's dying. But I don't wanna talk about all that. Tell your mum how all this came about. I mean, it was bloody obvious to anyone with eyes, but I want the details."

She folded her arms over her chest and waited for one of us to spill. I let Josie take the lead while I shuffled uncomfortably beneath her in the chair. Something about Mum hearing how we got together made my cheeks flush, and I looked at everything in the room but the two of them as Josie relayed the story, from us meeting by chance at the club to our camping trip and even the time we spent together last night. Mum took it all in, nodding in all the right places, but her expression was unreadable, and I could tell something was tick-tocking away in that brain of hers.

"Well, that's sweet. I couldn't think of a nicer girl for my Roxanne to be with. She's a lucky girl. Now, Josie, be a love and go fetch me a magazine from Milly, she should have my *Take-a-Break* by now."

Josie did as she was told, and widened her eyes at me as she left, I think in surprise at how well it was all going. The second the door closed, however, Mum shot me a serious look, thickening the atmosphere in the room instantly. "Have you told her yet?"

My neck pulled back. "Told her what?"

"Erm, I don't know. That you work in a strip joint?"

My heart leapt to my throat. "Mum! I–"

Mum held up a hand.

"Save it. I'm not stupid, I see everything. I'm your mother, and it's my job to know what you get up to, plus you really should get a better pin for that phone of yours. And don't think for one minute I'm happy about you doing that to keep me in this place because I'm not, but I love you and know you felt like you had to do it. But listen, kid, you better bloody be honest with that poor girl, or this thing is gonna be over before it's started."

I pinched the bridge of my nose and closed my eyes, not even knowing where to start. The conversation about her going through my phone and reading my messages was going to have to wait, Josie would be back any second.

"Mum, it's fine. I know what I need to do."

"What do you need to do?" Josie asked, stepping back into the room with the magazine tucked under her arm.

My eyes shot to Mum. Without missing a beat, Mum responded. "She needs to pull her bloody finger out and get writing again, that's what she needs to do. I was just saying at least now she has someone to get on her case and get her arse into gear."

My stomach unclenched, and I blew out a breath but my heart continued its gallop. I really thought for a minute Mum was going to drop me in it, and the violent thudding that idea caused in my chest let me know just how invested I had become and how urgent it was that I do something about the cause.

Josie smiled and handed the magazine to Mum. "Oh, you can be sure of that." Then she winked. I smiled weakly at Josie, feeling the guilt consume me like rust under Mum's watchful eye. I turned to Mum and nodded, silently telling her I had this, I would sort it.

~

AFTER SAYING GOODBYE TO MUM and a drawn-out goodbye to Josie, I headed back to my place and found Clara in the kitchen chomping on a fish finger sandwich.

"Wonders will never cease." I tried to keep the snarkiness from my voice but failed. I hadn't seen Clara for a few days and couldn't help but feel that she had been avoiding me.

"Hey, Biatch." She spoke through a mouthful of sandwich.

"You're disgusting." I kicked off my Converse and walked the kettle over to the sink.

"Uh-huh, one of the many things that make me so endearing. Where did you get to last night anyway?"

"I was with Josie." I put the kettle on to boil and felt my face betray me by shifting into the beginnings of a sickly grin.

Clara's eyes popped. "Oh, shit! Are you in love? You love her, don't you? Has Roxanne Mackenzie actually been pinned? Well, I guess wonders *will* never cease." Clara's tone was over-enthusiastic and mocking.

"Calm it down there scrappy, it's early days." I hoiked my bum onto the counter and dangled my legs. "She's a raging hippy, you know; candles, incense and pointless cushions scattered everywhere."

Clara shrugged. "Whatever floats your boat, I suppose."

I looked at the grout lines between the kitchen tiles. "I don't know, I kind of like it. She's different from anyone I've met before, you know?"

"You told her yet?"

I shook my head and sighed. "Nope, but something's gonna have to give."

"You leaving the club?"

I shrugged and sighed again. We were both quiet for a while.

"So, what the hell's going on with you anyway? I haven't seen you in forever. There's been no one around to abuse me, and you know that doesn't bode well with my masochistic tendencies."

Clara rolled her eyes. "Well, you're not the only one around here who can get laid, you know."

"You haven't? I bloody knew it. You've met someone. That's why you were acting all shady. So, what's he like?"

Clara jammed the remainder of the sandwich into her mouth and made a noise resembling the rhythm of the words "I don't know" and shrugged.

"What do you mean you don't know? Of course, you know. Please tell me you didn't meet him at the club?" Clara rolled her eyes once more and hitched herself onto the opposite end of the counter. She pointed to her puffed cheeks while she finished chewing. Her procrastination techniques were frustrating, but I could wait if she was finally about to open up.

"His name's Adam," she said through a splutter of crumbs and fish finger, "No, I didn't meet him at the club, and he's...I don't know, fit, I guess."

I eyed her. "You've been with fit men before, and they've never made you go AWOL from work, you've never stayed out this much, and you've certainly not ignored my texts."

Clara looked up to the ceiling, swinging her legs against the drawers. "Fiiine. He's more than fit. I actually really like him. There, you happy now?"

Because I knew how much it pained Clara to show any speck of vulnerability, I chose to be a good friend and not go on about it. I did, however, demand I get to meet this new guy as soon as she knew it was going somewhere. I couldn't help feeling a little dubious given Clara's history with men, and I hadn't forgotten how upset she had been the past couple of times. I just hoped he wasn't an arsehole. She could be an arsehole but she deserved better.

~

CLARA CHOSE TO TAKE THE RIGHT night off work. Two months of dry sunshine had given way to torrential rain which seemed to have appeared from nowhere. I had to make my way to the club in it alone. I shook out the umbrella and sat at the window seat on the train. After taking my phone from my pocket and plugging in my headphones. I selected a folk playlist on Amazon Music and some band called First Aid Kit rang out a mellow tune in my ears. I had to admit, as I stared through the wet window at the blur of graffitied walls and business blocks whooshing by – a sight I had seen a thousand times – the easy listening soft beat of the music made even London seem chill.

A text bleep came through on the phone interrupting the music and I hurriedly checked the screen to see if it was my sister returning the three calls I'd made to her since leaving Josie that afternoon. It wasn't. I was disappointed, but only for a second because the text was from Josie and simply said: *I miss you xxx*

I grinned at the screen. Apparently I was no longer in control of what happened to my face any time I thought about her. I tapped back a message.

I am listening to folk! FOLK! The lesbian 'urge to merge' has begun. I miss you too by the way xxx

When I left the train and began my sodden fifteen-minute trudge to the club, I called Emma again. The only thing standing in the way of what I needed to do that night was my sister's inability to pick up her phone. It was typical of her not to answer, especially if the call hadn't been planned in advance, so I wasn't especially worried, but still, I was eager to speak to her before my shift started so I would be able to catch Paul before he left.

I arrived at work, slumped at my dressing table and began the ordeal of fixing my now wet hair and getting my face looking as far away from my actual face as possible. I piled on the foundation, lilac eyeshadow, dark lipstick and false-lashes and reached for my phone once more. Again, Emma didn't answer my call. Frustrated, and bordering on desperate, I left a voicemail.

"Em, it's me. Seeing as you're not picking up, I'm going to have to do this by voicemail. I have something important to ask you." I looked around to make sure none of the girls or Paul could hear me and pressed on. "You know when Mum first went into the home, and you offered to help with my share of the fees? Well, I was an idiot for saying no. I'm not going into detail about what I've been doing to get the money, but it isn't pretty, and for reasons I'll tell you about later, I can't do it anymore. So, my question is, if you think there's any way you and Jake could cover the remainder of Mum's time there? And I promise I will pay you back every penny as soon as I can. Okay, let me know. And don't worry if you can't, I completely understand. I thought it'd just be worth a shot, that's all."

I hung up the phone, laid it on the dresser and gave myself an affirmative nod in the mirror. There, it was done. Whatever happened now was in the hands of my younger sister and she was literally my only hope. I had no plan B. And if Em called me back within the next ten minutes and said "yes", I wouldn't even have to go out on that stage.

I spent the next ten minutes doing nothing but stare intently at the phone until those dreaded three words hit me like a slap to the ear: "Rox, you're up."

"Shit." I picked up the phone and willed it to ring. "C'mon Em, call me back damn it." Still nothing. It was no good. I sighed and tore myself away from the dresser. It looked as though tonight wouldn't be the night. As I sauntered out onto the stage, I was struck by how packed the place was. Paul had already briefed us there were a heap of football fans in, but I hadn't realised there would be quite so many. The barmaid was rushed off her feet, juggling glasses, trying to take two orders at once and although the atmosphere was a little more boisterous than usual with pints being downed and the guys egging one another on, it all seemed in good spirits.

As I began my routine to The Pussy Cat Dolls "Buttons",

thoughts of Josie occupied my mind. There was no doubt anymore that quitting this job was the right thing to do. Whatever the consequences of no longer earning big money, I was prepared to take them, not only for my own sense of self-worth but *for her*. I know it was fast, probably way too fast, but I had fallen for her. There was no other explanation for what I felt. It *was* like we were meant to be together, and I couldn't imagine my life without her in it. I had to do whatever it took because being with Josie, I felt safe. The world felt real and right. I knew if I had Josie by my side, whatever hardship or heartache followed, I would be able to get through it, we would be able to get through it together.

The music merged from one sexy beat into another as I tugged suggestively at my bra strap and leaned back from the pole. Although I could see the guys staring back at me, my mind was off making plans of a solid future, one that included a stunning redhead with the most beautiful dimples I had ever seen. And although I was a little apprehensive about how things would pan out, the overriding feeling I had was utter excitement. The thought of being able to give Josie my all without a blanket of guilt hanging over my head felt liberating. I was ready. I was prepared to give myself to her completely. A small smile began at my lips, and for the first time since working at Chace's, I knew the smile had reached my eyes. I was able to give the routine some gusto. I had pretty much convinced myself this was it, the last time I would have to flaunt my naked body to a room full of men. The thought of not having to perform again gave me a new sense of freedom, and it showed in my set. My body had a powerful grace to it as I swung around the pole, I flicked my hair purposefully, and the mischievous expression on my face that usually felt forced and unnatural came to life as the words "I'm out of here fuckers" ran out through my mind. I was giving the best performance of my life, and the guys loved it, and the more animated and vocal they became, the more energy I put into it. I was going out with a bang.

Fully naked, I turned my back to the customers. I stretched my arms above my head and bent forward so my hands were touching the stage. I looked at the crowd from between my legs. This ignited some loud whooping noises from a group at the bar. They were a younger group of lads who had just walked in, definitely a stag-do I thought, given the guy with the shaggy blonde hair was wearing antlers. I smiled at the group as antler guy stepped aside. Then I turned to stone. Every part of my body froze dead still as blood rushed to my head and my vision blurred. Just past the shaggy blonde, an unmistakable female figure had her back to me. She was wearing a scarf and chatting animatedly to the barmaid who pointed over in my direction.

CHAPTER 22

FROM THAT SECOND, TIME RAN in slow motion. Me, naked, bent over, looking between my legs. Josie, turning around with a dimpled smile on her face, stretched on her tiptoes attempting to search me out in the crowd and then her eyes locking onto mine as the realisation kicked in and the colour drained from her face. Our eyes remained fixed on one another's for a few seconds before either of us were able to comprehend what we had seen, but once we had, there was no hitting the rewind button. Josie couldn't un-see my naked body, and I couldn't un-see the pain of betrayal in her expressive eyes.

"Shit, fuck, shit." I shot up and scrambled around the stage, grabbing at my clothes as she headed for the door. I rushed out back and threw on a black lacy robe which I swiped from the clothes rail. Paul tugged at my arm as I passed, attempting to stop me. I shook him off and dashed past and out the fire escape into the heavy rain. Barefoot, and with the rain whipping at my face, I ran up the back alley and out onto the main street. I frantically searched left and right. I couldn't catch a glimpse of her. I was immediately soaked through, and my hair stuck to my face as I continued to search for her. Kicking out time at the pubs made it impossible to see past the sea of umbrellas from where I stood. I had no choice. I jumped on the bonnet of a parked black cab. The driver blasted his horn repeatedly, drawing instant attention from drunks who stopped and stared. I didn't care. The robe I wore barely covered my arse, I pulled it tight against me. Now on top of the taxi, I stretched up onto my tiptoes and frantically searched the street. The driver blasted his horn some more. I still didn't care. The only thing I cared about was Josie. I couldn't see her at first, but just as I was about to give up, I caught a glimpse of her. She was crouching in a shop doorway with her head in her hands.

"Josie!" I yelled, tasting the rain.

She slowly lifted her head and scanned the streets before her tear-filled eyes settled on me. My heart ached for her and the pain in her face. She shot up and began to weave in and out of the crowds.

I jumped off the cab, ignoring the abuse from the driver who had now left his car and was threatening to call the police. With my bare feet stinging from the rough concrete, I ran as fast as I could down the street.

"Josie, wait!" I called after her. The rain still whipped at my cheeks and mascara ran into my eyes. It stung. I could just make out the top of her head as she picked up her pace, stretching out her thumb at each passing taxi. I ran faster towards her as people nudged each other as I passed. I *still* didn't care. With gravel in my heels, I caught up to her and grabbed her shoulder.

"Josie, please, let me explain." The words were gulping gasps.

She spun to face me. Mascara ran down her cheeks from tears, not the rain.

"What?" she snapped, and her dark eyes cut into me.

"Please, let me explain." I desperately searched for words.

She wrapped her coat around her and widened her eyes impatiently.

"I...I..." I struggled for words.

She shook her head rapidly, her eyes widening even further into an expression not far from horror.

Still, nothing came out.

Josie laughed sardonically. "Oh, do you know what? Just forget it! I don't think I want to hear it." She turned to walk away.

"No, Josie, wait!"

She spun to face me. "What? What could you possibly have to say to justify your lies?"

"I'm...I'm sorry." My throat closed around the words.

Josie scoffed. "You're sorry? She shook her head. "You're sorry?"

I nodded pitifully.

She pinched the bridge of her nose and shook her head again. "And what exactly is it you're sorry for Roxy? Lying to me repeatedly about your job? Pretending to be someone you're not? Making me trust you?" Her voice cracked.

"Yes. All of that. Everything. What you just saw in there, that's not me. I'm not that person."

"Oh, right. Well, who the fuck was it then? Because from where I was standing, it looked a hell of a lot like you." Her voice had risen to a shout.

"Well, it was me, but it wasn't me. You know what I mean–"

"Do I?" She closed her eyes and laughed. It sounded bitter. "Do you know why I came here tonight? I came to surprise you. To tell you I'd spoken to Jefferson, the dean at my uni. He has a contact at Warwick and he's willing to pull a few strings to try and get you back on your scholarship, so congratulations." She looked me up and down. "Little did I know I would be the one getting the surprise, eh?"

I sniffed as my tears combined with the rain. I didn't know

what to say. My thoughts were drowned out by the thud of my heart and the pounding in my ears. My bottom lip quivered as I remained voiceless and overcome by shame.

Frustrated by my lack of response, Josie again turned around to walk away.

Panic took over. "It was for my mum," I called out. "I did it for my mum."

She stopped dead and turned slowly to face me. "Well, I'm sure she would be really proud of her little girl." Her eyes had a coolness to them that was unrecognisable.

"Don't...Don't do that."

A hint of guilt flashed across her face as she swallowed.

"I needed to pay for her care," I went on.

"And I'm sure there was no other way to pay it, right?"

"Not that kind of money, no. You really think I would be doing that in there if I didn't feel like I had to? You really think I had a choice?"

Josie shrugged. "Well, you know what they say Rox, if you're not changing it then you're choosing it. Maybe it was for the money and maybe it wasn't. Perhaps your daddy issues run so deep that you'll do anything for some male attention. How would I know either way now? I can't trust a thing you say to me. You lied. You've lied all along."

She attempted to turn, but I grabbed hold of her arm.

"Please. Of course, it was only for the money. It's got nothing to do with the blokes. Tonight was my last night. Tonight was going to be my last night. I never have to do this again. I choose you. Josie, I choose you!" My voice cracked into a tortured sob.

She shook her head repeatedly. "You're missing the point here. It's not what you're doing for a living. I mean, let's be honest, it leaves a lot to be desired, but I always knew you were a little rough around the edges. If you had told me the truth, I would've got past it because that's how much I liked you. But it's the lies. You know how important trust is to me, in fact, I couldn't have made it any clearer, and yet you still chose to keep this from me." She shook her head and frowned. "You know, you're desperate not to be like your mum, you see her as weak, but I'll tell you something, at least she knows who she is, what you see is what you get, no bullshit. You could learn something from that."

My eyes fell to my bare feet as every word ripped me open a little bit more.

"Don't sweat it anyway. It's me I'm angry at. How could I have been so fucking stupid? Again! All that crap, toasting to trust and how amazing I thought you were for holding down two jobs." She scoffed. "Do you know the worst thing? The worst thing is I sensed something. The second time I came to your flat. There was a weird look you and Clara gave each other, and my instincts told me something was up, but I ignored it like the idiot I am. I can only imagine you had a good old laugh behind my back. Stupid, clueless Josie."

"No! It wasn't like that. I didn't want to tell you because I was ashamed. I didn't want you to see this side. I couldn't bear the embarrassment. I was..." I shook my head, reaching desperately for the right words.

"Peeling off the blue and white labels, pretending to be better than you are?"

I swallowed. "I was ashamed. I *am* ashamed."

For the briefest of moments, something in Josie's eyes softened, and then just as quickly, as though she was tallying up all the lies I had told up until this point, they flared in anger again. She pulled her arm away from my hand. "Just leave me alone, Roxanne."

"Josie, please, you're breaking my fucking heart here?" I held my hand out to her, and she looked at it then settled her eyes wearily on my own.

"You've killed it." She nodded. "We're done."

And with those final words, I watched her disappear into the crowd.

We're done.

I guess the problem with relying on someone else to make you happy, is when they inevitably leave you, they take your happy with them and you end up left with gravel in your heels and an emptiness inside the size of the universe.

STACY WRAPPED A TOWEL AROUND my shoulders and guided me to my dresser as rain dripped from my sopping hair and splashed to the floor. I sat in shocked silence while she went to make me hot chocolate – or whatever it was she said she was getting – I hadn't been listening. All I could hear were Josie's words replaying on loop in my mind. "You've killed it. We're done."

I had just put my head in my hands when Paul stormed into the dressing room. "And what the fuck was that?"

I looked up at him wearily.

"Do you remember what I said the last time you pulled this stunt?"

I blinked at him. It's all I had the energy for.

"I can't have it Rox, it's bad for business and–"

"Paul, I get it." I stared at him for a long moment, then nodded. "I'm done."

He nodded back, almost regretfully. "Yeah, kid. You're done."

Well, it was certainly the night for things being done. Before I had time to even process what had just happened, Paul left the room and a flashing light on my phone caught my eye. For one crazy moment, I thought – hoped – it might be Josie. It wasn't. It was Emma. She had returned my call from earlier and left a voicemail. Deflated, I lifted the phone to my ear:

"Sis, whatever weird-arse mess you've got yourself into, we're letting you off the hook. Of course, we can cover you. Jake's earning loads at the moment anyway so just stop doing whatever it is…oh my god, it's not illegal is it? Because none of us need that right now, Roxanne, what if you got arrested or worse, prison? Anyway, I'm glad whatever it is you're stopping. I'm sure you'll tell us all about it. Call me back. Love ya and be safe."

I blew out a long breath and slung the phone on the dresser as the realisation of the evening's events gripped me. I looked at the reflection of my mascara-smudged face and shook my head.

"What the fuck have you done?" I asked out loud before the mirrored vision of my face blurred, and my eyes slowly rolled to the back of my head.

I never did get that hot chocolate.

"ROX, ROX, ROXY!" MY HEAVY lids lifted, just enough to make out an out of focus Clara kneeling beside me.

"You okay, Rox?"

"Erm…" I squinted my eyes and tried to work out where I was. I looked around the room; it was familiar. I seemed to be lying on my own sofa. Someone must have brought me here when…shit…Josie! The image of Josie's face shot into my mind: the anger, the disappointment, the hurt. I groaned as the images pieced themselves together. I dropped my face into my hands and sighed. "Oh, Clar, I have fucked up so badly."

Clara slid onto the sofa and squeezed me into her arms as tears trickled into my palms. I leaned my head against her shoulder and sobbed. Eventually, the tears ran out and I grabbed the offered tissues and blew my nose.

"How did I get here?" I asked between blows.

Clara flipped the top off a bottle of Bud and handed it to me.

I took a swig then handed it back to her. I was still far too rocky for alcohol.

"Paul called me, freaking out; said he was going to call an ambulance. I told him not to bother and drove over. I found you limp at your dresser, so I slung you over my shoulder, chucked you in the car and brought you home. You're welcome."

"You didn't lift me over your shoulder." I smiled half-heartedly.

"No, you're right. You're really heavy. You might wanna consider laying off the pancakes for a while. Paul helped me get you into my car, and followed me back so we could get you in here."

"Right."

"Sooo…You gonna tell me what's been going on? Paul said you've lost your job and you've been acting properly weird." Clara took a swig of the beer.

I threw my head back against the sofa and closed my eyes. I didn't even know where to begin, but I did recognise the time had come to open up to my funny friend. I spent the next hour filling Clara in on everything. I started right at the beginning from Mum's first diagnosis and worked my way up to the scholarship, moving to London, getting the job at Chace's and through to how I thought I had fallen in love with Josie and thrown it all away because of my cowardice and pride. I told her everything. Then I waited. Her response wasn't long in coming.

"I just can't believe you kept all this from me. You must think I'm a right arsehole if you didn't feel like you could share this?" Clara's hurt was evident in her pout.

"Clar, no. It's not like that at all. I love our friendship and the way we snark together; I was just worried if you knew about Mum, you would get all sympathetic and start treading on eggshells around me and I didn't want that. You took my mind off everything because you're so normal with me and I didn't want that to change."

Clara downed half the bottle of beer before speaking. "I bloody knew there had to be a reason why a brainiac like you worked at the club. Do you remember? I told you right at the start you must have a story and you denied it."

"Yeah, you did, and you were right. That was never me you know, working at the club. I was never meant to be *that* person. I'm not saying you are or anything. But I don't think any of us should be making our money that way. We're all so much better than that."

Clara sniggered. "Speak for yourself. I could never get a job that paid this much money, I didn't even get two GCSE's."

We fell silent for a minute.

"What was the one you got?"

"Huh?"

"You said you didn't get two GCSE's, so you got one? What was it in?"

"Oh, right. I got a C in Spanish."

"But you speak fluent Spanish."

"Exactly my fucking point. I'm going to be stripping my gear off until my tits touch my toes."

I laughed a genuine laugh and Clara smiled, pleased that her humour had cheered me up, if only momentarily. She knew how to do that, and I found myself wishing I had told her sooner. She handled it well, with no sarky comments or witty retorts, just sincere compassion. At one point, when I spoke about what Mum had said about me not getting with Josie, I thought I saw a tear in her eye. She didn't let it drop, though. I think she knew I needed her to be strong.

"Let me call her and explain." Clara grabbed my phone after picking up on my not-so-subtle phone watching.

"There's no point, she won't answer. I've ruined it. She won't forgive me for this. I've lost her, and I've screwed up the only chance I had of going back to uni in the process." I groaned and threw myself face-first into the cushions. "Argh. Why did I have to be so stupid? I should have just told her right from the start."

"That's bullshit, I'm not having that. We're not giving up on you that easily. What was that guy's name who had the contact for your scholarship?"

"Jefferson or something, he's the Dean at the University of London," I answered meekly into the fabric. I was finding it difficult to muster up the same level of enthusiasm as Clara.

"Well, Mr Jefferson's not gonna know what's hit him."

CHAPTER 23

THE FOLLOWING TWO WEEKS WERE the longest of my life. Having lost my job at Chace's, I had surplus time on my hands to dwell on the what-ifs and if-onlys and spent my time hopping between berating myself for what I'd done to Josie and watching one Netflix series after the other.

Losing Josie had dismantled me in the worst possible way. She had left my life and taken all hope with her. I tried to contact her more than a handful of times, but each call either muted within the first couple of rings or rang through to her messagebank. As a result, memories of how she felt in my arms begun to evanesce, and I truly had no idea how I would bounce back. I only left my flat to visit Mum, and when I did, it just served to make me feel worse. She was deteriorating fast. The nurses had her hooked up to an oxygen machine to aid her breathing, and the obscene amount of morphine they were pumping into her had doubled in just a week. Some days, when I visited, she barely recognised me, and each time I walked into the room and saw that same distant look in her eye, it crucified me. She had started having the priest visit her once a week, and I encouraged it, given her newfound faith and the hole that must have been left by Josie's absence. And I knew how bad Mum was because she didn't ask me one question about what had happened.

Josie had not visited the home since our split. Every day, I made a point to check the visitors' log for her name, and each time I was more deflated. Milly would offer a sympathetic smile, and I would return it with a half-arsed smile of my own. It didn't take a genius to work out something had happened between Josie and me, I wore it like a badge, and I'm sure Milly didn't have to listen to the sound of my footsteps to judge my mood. She only had to look at the state of me to know I hadn't been sleeping or eating or doing much of anything for that matter. I would rock up to the home in a pair of jogging bottoms and a hoody which would always be pulled over my head in an attempt to hide the greasy hair, un-plucked eyebrows and dark eye bags.

Occasionally, Clara would come to the home with me, she didn't go in but would wait outside in my car as moral support for when I came out. She had become my rock; the silver lining in everything that had gone on. Sharing all that had happened with her had brought us much closer. She had hardly seen her new boyfriend between working extra hours at the club until Paul found my replacement, and looking after me, making sure I ate and bathed and slept. She even took on the cleaning, clearing up *my* mess. Somehow Clara knew the right time to drop a crude joke and make me laugh, even against my will. But more than that, just like when I first met her, and she saved me from the lechy punter, she had my back, she was protecting me, and I needed that.

I guess I shouldn't have been surprised then, when two Wednesdays after my opening up to her, she came charging into our flat like she had been chased.

"Here, take it." She held out a white envelope, panting for breath.

"What is it?" I stared at her blankly.

"Just fucking open it."

I took the envelope from her and did as she said. In the far-right corner, the typed letter showed the address for The University of London. For a millisecond, I thought it might be from Josie until I began to read. The letter was addressed to a Peter Burgess, Professor at Warwick University. True to his word, Jefferson had called in a favour from an old friend and had pleaded my case to be accepted onto a scholarship for the next term. The letter shook in my hand as I read it and re-read it to make sure I had it right. I looked up at Clara, who grinned. "What the…? I mean, how the…? I don't understand." I stared at Clara dumbfounded.

"Was no big deal. Went to see the man Jefferson you told me about, wore a low cut top, smiled sweetly, swayed my hips, rammed your sob story down his throat and all for nothing apparently as he had the letter written and sealed in his desk drawer. Said he intended to send it out the next day anyway. He made some boring speech about talent not being overlooked because of money or some bollocks and handed it to me. You should've seen the way his eyes lit up when he talked about the teacher chick too, the guy clearly has a boner for her. I'm guessing that had something to do with it. Oh, and he said it might be a good idea to put some samples in there just to seal the deal. Looks like Josie has a heart after all and didn't stitch you up."

I shook my head. "Clar, I don't know what to say, I can't believe you–"

She cut me off as she removed one of her high heeled boots. "Yes, okay, I get it. I'm great blah blah blah, but you can save the dramatics because as I said, I didn't actually do anything because it was all written up, so you need to thank old Jaffa cake, not me."

"Jefferson," I corrected.

"Yeah, whatever. So, are we going to get pissed and celebrate or what?" Clara headed straight for the kitchen. I followed behind her and looked over the letter once more.

"Well, I haven't actually been accepted yet." I leaned against the worktop.

"Have you read that letter? He owes him! And people like that always keep their word, it's the gentlemanly thing to do. Rox, you're in!"

I swallowed and allowed the smile I'd been holding back to take over my face. "I am, aren't I?"

"Yes! Now, how much of that gin do we have left?"

IT WAS AUGUST 19th WHEN I took the call, just four days after I sent Jefferson's letter off with some carefully selected samples of my work. The prospect of going to university and having something to focus on had finally begun to sink in. I knew to succeed, I needed a severe shift in how I approached life. Although I still hurt over Josie, I had reached a point where I could dig deep for the positives. It wasn't the easiest thing to digest, but I considered the possibility that maybe I *was* meant to meet Josie and perhaps all along it had nothing to do with romance and everything to do with getting my life back on track. One thing was for sure, I had made a firm decision that I wasn't going to let it all be for nothing. Josie once told me a Rumi quote that said, "S*et your life on fire and seek those who fan your flames*." I remembered it by heart because I knew that's what she had done for me all along; fanned my flames. I had learned so much from her about the best ways to approach life, and I would hold on to that. She had made me believe in myself again, and for that, I would always be grateful.

So, after weeks of moping, I convinced myself to leave the flat and do something, just for me. I took the tube into the city and spent the morning wandering around Covent Garden. I loved it there, watching the street performers while sipping coffee at an outside table of an expensive café. It was easy to get lost in imagining what went through the minds of the gold-painted-mimes as they expressed themselves through nothing but their eye movements.

At midday, I went to the hairdressers where I had both a colour and a cut. The stylist tried to talk me into a complete re-style, but I'd had enough change going on in my life that I figured a makeover would be a step too far. After the hair-dressers, I jumped on a tube to Oxford Street and did a bit of shopping, buying a couple of pairs of jeans, a few tops and a yellow halter neck dress. The dress, although outside the box, was meant to be symbolic of the whole "new me" thing I was trying.

Exhausted, yet satisfied with my retail therapy, I headed back to Greenwich. I had just reached the bottom of the steps to the front porch when my phone vibrated in my pocket. I laid my bags down on the steps and fumbled around until I found it. The care home flashed on my caller ID. My heart clenched. My arm turned to jelly as I lifted the mobile to my ear. The nurse's voice told me everything I needed to know. I knew what would follow.

"Hello, am I speaking to Roxanne?"

I scrunched my eyes closed in the hope that I could make it disappear or better still, make *me* disappear. I wanted to say no. I didn't want to be Roxanne. I wanted to be anyone but me at that moment. I would have traded places with anyone. Literally anyone. I took a deep breath in and braced.

"Yes, Roxanne speaking." My voice shook as I dragged out the words trying to delay the inevitable.

"Hello Roxanne, it's Mandy from Princess Park. Are you sitting down dear and do you have someone there with you?" Negative and negative.

My eyes clouded over, and my legs felt as though they would give way any minute.

"I'm standing, and I'm alone, but I'm sure I already know what you are about to say." My words caught in my throat. I moved my free hand to the top of my head in an attempt to steady myself as the fuzziness took over. I abandoned the bags and moved in the direction of the front door. If I could just get into my flat, I could sit. I took a few tentative steps, aware of the acid bile that had appeared in my mouth. My body, collapsing from the inside out made me dizzy.

"Just say it," I said through my constricted throat. I laid my head against the front door.

"I'm so sorry to have to tell you this Roxanne but..."

I didn't get to hear the end of her sentence.

ONCE AGAIN, I CAME AROUND on the sofa in the living room. There was no need to ask Clara what had happened. I knew the drill. My head hurt, my throat burned like I had gargled sand and my heavy chest ached. Clara sat at the end of the sofa with my feet resting on her lap.

"Please tell me it was a bad dream?"

She placed a hand on my leg and gave me a sympathetic smile with tears filling her eyes. "I'm so sorry, Rox."

And with those four words, Clara's tears, and the pain I felt in my heart, I knew it hadn't been a bad dream.

"I stopped by at Manney's to get us both dinner and found you out like a light on the steps. I couldn't bring you round but this lovely stranger passing by helped get you up here. The home called your phone again because they were concerned about you, and that's when they told me what had happened. I'm so sorry Rox"

"Thanks Clar, so what did happen?" I did that thing they call steeling yourself and waited for Clara to tell me.

"Your mum had an internal bleed in the afternoon, it took her quickly, and she didn't suffer in those final minutes. The nurses said her last words were "tell my children I love them" and then she smiled and slipped away."

I took a deep breath and nodded. Her time had come.

I closed my eyes, doing my best to absorb what I'd just heard. It's not like I hadn't expected it. I'd been waiting for months, but even though I thought I had mentally prepared myself; nothing quite readies you for that wave of pure agony that sweeps through your heart no matter what. No one warns you of the gaping hole that gets left. The hole where someone used to be. The hole in the back of your mind. The hole in the front of your mind. The hole in your heart and the hole in your life. Time stood still. None of it seemed real. If it weren't for the way Clara kept looking at me, I would never have believed it.

"I don't know what to say, Rox. You know what I'm like in these situations. I'm bound to say or do the wrong thing, but if you need anything and I mean *anything*, please just ask me okay?"

I looked at my friend, who was wide-eyed and out of her depth.

"Clar, I think you're better than you think you are…and thank you." I nodded and managed a weak smile.

Clara came from a good place, but realistically, there was nothing she could do to fix the pain. Mum had gone. And as a result, I had become home to grief gremlins who strummed at the nerve endings of my heart, each note sending an entirely different stabbing sensation my way. In my moment of immense darkness, when everything was crumbling beneath me, one person drifted into my consciousness, someone who would understand exactly how I felt and someone who could lessen my despair, if only they knew what had happened, and that, of course, was Josie. For the briefest of moments, I considered calling her. Pouring out my heart to her and begging her to come and be with me. Deep down, I knew she would come too. She had shown how much she cared by not messing up my scholarship potential, and I know that Josie would have done anything she could to help, but I couldn't ask that of her. I needed her to be with me because she loved me and couldn't imagine her life without me in it, and not because guilt and pity brought her to me. I would have to get through this one alone.

CHAPTER 24

"HELLO, EARTH TO ROXY, COME in Roxanne." The silhouette of my sister's hand waving in front of my face snapped me from my daydream.

"Huh?"

"I said, Jake's going to Waitrose, do you want anything?"

I rubbed at my tired eyes. "Oh, right. Yeah, ask him to pick me up a pack of Buds, please. I'll give him the money when he gets back."

Em had her hands on her hips and was judging me with her eyes. "You seriously need to think about how much you're drinking lately, perhaps it'll help you make better life choices."

Although Emma was eight years younger than me, she had always been the more serious one. She had inherited Mum's authoritarian tone and given it a whole new twist of her own. Her HR position at a large automotive company in Romford could not have been more suited to her, but it would have been nice if, at times, she didn't talk to her family like we were staff being called into the office for reprimanding. I had already endured a heavy lecture for working at Chace's and wasn't prepared to sit through yet another one on the effects of alcohol.

"Okay, Em, I get it. Just not right now, okay?" I gave her a look that warned her not to push. The next week was going to be hard enough, and all I wanted was for something to take the edge off. I had to give it to Emma though, because of her, the funeral preparations were well underway. She had spent the past week busying herself with the details – place, times, which vicar to use, and finding out from family and friends who would be attending. Em's ability to take charge came as a tremendous relief. Other than picking out the flowers for the service, I hadn't done much of anything. My brother Ben had been even more useless than me, spending the majority of his time watching sports on the telly, also drinking way too much beer and saying very little.

When Em wasn't organising the funeral or lecturing me on the way I lived my life, she busied herself baking victoria sponge cakes and brownies, both of which were Mum's recipes. She would never admit it, but I think it made her feel close to her. The funeral was set to take place in Southend. Mum had spoken to the three of us about her wishes to be buried there. It's where she had grown up and she had fond memories of fooling around with her friends at the beach in the summer during her teenage years. I had a vivid image of a picture taken of her and those friends. She was on the rocks wearing a striped bikini, with her long '70s hair flowing over her shoulders and down her back. She laughed with a friend as a good-looking man, bombed off the rocks and into the sea. The picture caught it perfectly, the essence of that summer's day and Mum's genuine smile. I don't think I ever saw her smile like that in all my life with her.

With me living in London and Ben working on the rigs, Em was the only one that remained in Essex. She and Jake owned a modernised farmhouse on the outskirts of Southend, paid for by Jake's shrewd eye for investments, and although at first, I couldn't wrap my head around someone like Em living on a farm, I soon understood the appeal once I visited. And because Em lived closest to where the funeral would be held, it made sense for us all to congregate there until the day.

As the week progressed, the pain had lessened a little. Still there, of course, but waking up in the morning had become more tolerable. Behind all the heartache and pain I felt, just below the surface, there was a small current of relief: for the ones left behind and relief for our mum. She wasn't suffering any more, and we were no longer waiting for the worst day of our lives to arrive. It had happened and, I realised, we would survive.

One of the best things about the farmhouse was the stars at night. The place was just far enough from town that the sky was surprisingly unaffected by streetlights or city glow. In the short time I had been there, I'd made it a ritual to have some time alone outside just staring up into the black. The night before the funeral was no exception. I stepped outside with a thin blanket wrapped around my shoulders and took in the warm air. The night, perfectly still, was blessed with a sky freckled with stars. The sheer beauty of the scene reminded me of Mum. Everything reminded me of Mum. I sat on the porch step and crooked my neck to the sky just in time to see a shooting star flash by overhead. I convinced myself it was Mum letting me know she could shoot across the sky if she wished. I thought about Josie too. Every day I thought about Josie.

Em's and Jake's wellies leaned against the wall on their porch. Em's were pink with black spots, and Jake's were camo green with small tears down the back where he had tried to force them on one too many times. I stared at them, long and hard, thinking about what could have been with Josie and me. What was once a beautiful analogy, given by one of the most remarkable people I had ever met, was now a harsh reminder of how I had let her slip through my fingers while she had hold of my heart and took it with her.

I jumped from my thoughts to a text bleep. I drew my eyes away from the wellies and slipped my phone from my pocket. It was a text from Cayden:

Rox, please call me when you get the chance xx

I hadn't spoken to Cayden since Mum's passing. He had texted a few times asking how I was but he was going through such an exciting time in his life with the release of his book that I didn't want to bring him down and make it about me. I knew I couldn't keep avoiding him though. I got Cayden's caller ID up and hit green. He answered after two rings.

"Ah, Rox. I'm so glad you called." His tone was sympathetic.

"Sorry, I just needed a bit of time. How's the promo going?"

"No way! We're not talking about that. How are you? How are you coping with all this?"

I shrugged. "I don't know. Crap, I guess."

"I bet you are sweetie. I'm so sorry you're going through this. I wanted to come and see you last week. Clara said you were at your sister's. That's why I called a few times."

"You speak to Clara now?"

He laughed. "Yeah. She makes me laugh and keeps me informed."

"Does she now? Should I be worried about you replacing me with her?" I wrapped the blanket closer to me and smiled into the phone, happy for the distraction.

"No one could ever replace you, my gorgeous. I *was* surprised to hear about your money making venture though and even more surprised that I never got to see you shaking your fine arse up and down that pole."

"Oh my god! I will kill her!" I closed my eyes embarrassed but smiling, I didn't really care that Cayden knew.

Cayden chuckled. "She was worried about you. She told me what happened with Josie."

I blew out a breath. "Yeah. Not my finest moment."

"So, you guys are definitely over?"

"Yep. It certainly looks that way."

Cayden's sigh came through loud and clear. "That sucks. I wish I could give you a big hug and tell you everything's going to be okay."

"Me too."

"Good. Because I'm coming to the funeral."

I sat up straighter. "No, Cayd. You don't have to do that. You've got so much going on with your book and–"

"I'm coming! Clara's offered to drive me so, I'll be arriving with her. I have an early start the next day with a writer's conference in Nottingham so, we'll have to head back after the wake, but I'm coming. I know you've wanted your space and I get that, but you need your friends around."

I smiled and dropped my shoulders, thinking that actually, it would be good to have him there for moral support. "Well, if you're sure?"

"Of course, I'm sure. Nothing's more important than knowing my friend's supported through this horrible time. I'll see you tomorrow okay?"

I pointlessly nodded, knowing he couldn't see me. "Okay. And thanks, Cayd. I can't wait to see you."

"You too my lovely. Now, you get a good night's sleep, you've got a big day tomorrow."

I hung up the phone and after staring at those damn wellies and thinking about what might have been for a while longer, I took Cayden's advice and got an early night.

I ARRIVED AT THE SMALL church an hour before everyone else. Em thought we should all go together, but I needed some time alone before people arrived. I needed to keep my composure during the service. If I allowed myself to get too worked up, I would end up flat on my back, which would take away the focus from what actually mattered.

I placed the last gladioli at the end of the second row of flowers and looked around the church. It hadn't turned out to be the overcast day the BBC had predicted. Instead, it was blue skies with the occasional white fluff of a cloud which gave way to beams of light that flooded in through the stained-glass windows and made the church appear light and airy. That, coupled with the floral aroma, made it seem more suited to a wedding than a funeral.

Mum had not been religious most of her life. She believed in something, more superstitious than anything else, saluting magpies and not walking under ladders, that sort of thing, but it wasn't until her final weeks she began reading the bible and praying. I'm not sure if she had an epiphany towards the end, or whether she merely tried to find comfort in the promise of something more. I do know, though, it helped her to not be so fearful. And I had Josie to thank for that. A week before her passing, Mum told me Jesus came to her in a dream and told her she would be with the angels soon. At the time, I brushed it off and put it down to her meds. But as I stood there, in that holy house, a gentle warmth brushed my shoulders and sent a tingling sensation down my neck, and I swear, I could feel her.

I looked up at a wooden carving of Jesus on the cross by the altar, and pleaded under my breath: "You better be looking after her and delivering those angels you promised." I waited, as though an answer would come, of course, it didn't. Instead, I jumped at the church door as it flew open behind me.

I smiled. Clara and Cayden had arrived.

"Hey, biatch." Clara wore black knee-high boots, a short pencil skirt and a black blazer which cut off at the arms. Only Clara could look that hot in what she would call funeral attire.

Cayden looked really dapper too in what looked like an Armani fitted suit. His brow was furrowed and his eyes tearful as he came towards me with his arms out wide. "Oh, Roxy." He pulled me into a hug so tight I thought I was going to crack a few ribs, but my god, it was good to see him,

I pulled out of Cayden's bear hug and looked at my watch. "You're early," I said, realising we still had an hour before the service.

Clara shrugged, looking absently around the church. "Yeah, well, we wanted to make sure you were okay. Let's not make it weird." She smirked.

"Did you do the flowers?" Cayden lifted a yellow lily to his nose and sniffed.

I nodded. "Yeah, they're her favourite." I corrected myself. "They *were* her favourite.".

He smiled at me and replaced it. "Ah, I dunno, sweetie. I think you had it right the first time."

Clara rested her arm on my shoulder. "So, how you holding up?" Her concern was evident in her voice.

I blew out a breath. "I'm doing okay, I guess. I just..." I hesitated for a moment, "I just miss her, Clar." I sucked in my bottom lip, as fresh tears formed a mist.

Clara pulled me into her and squeezed me tight. "I know you do," she whispered, "I know you do."

The door opened and interrupted our embrace. Em, Jake and Ben had arrived.

"Huh-hum." Emma cleared her throat, in a way that was so reminiscent of Mum, it startled me. "Interrupting something?" Her tone was weirdly snarky.

I cut her a look. "No. Emma, this is my friend and house-mate Clara. Clara, this is my sister Emma, her husband Jake, and my little brother Ben."

Emma winced and held her hand out to Clara. "God, sorry, I thought you were that Jodie."

"Josie," Clara corrected, and it was weird hearing her say the name. Clara shook Emma's hand. "I'm sorry for your loss."

"Thank you. And thank you for looking after Rox over the past few weeks. She said you've been amazing through everything, and it's good to know she's got someone keeping her on the straight and narrow."

I rolled my eyes at my sister, and Cayden widened his eyes at me. Clara keeping me on the straight and narrow? Jesus, what had happened to me? Clara introduced herself to Jake and Ben while Emma turned her attention to Cayden.

"Cayden, it's so good to see you again. You look amazing. Thank you for making it today. I know it means a lot to Rox." They both gave me a sympathetic smile. "Rox says you're a big author now? I've been meaning to read it but I just never seem to find the time and now, with Mum and the funeral preparations and…" Emma's voice cracked and she fanned her face. I hitched a breath seeing her show such emotion.

Cayden didn't miss a beat and pulled her into one of his rib-cracking hugs.

Once the introductions were out the way, it didn't take long before others began to arrive. Everyone made a point of saying hello to my siblings and me and giving their condolences. People came from all over. Even the local corner shop owner from the street we grew up on turned up. I was grateful that Milly and a couple of the nurses had made the journey from Princess Park too. Everyone had something to say about Mum, lovely things, kind things, things that were…not exactly ringing true. After a short time, I was starting to wonder if I was at the right funeral. It's like they had forgotten her already and the person they were now talking about was someone even I didn't know. I guess it's a bit like when a celebrity passes away, all of a sudden, they become a hero, and the whole picture gets forgotten. The more people I spoke to, the more it niggled me, no one was actually talking about my mum.

Other than that, I was holding up okay. I regularly checked in with Emma and Ben, who seemed to be doing okay too. I guess it's times like these when people find hidden strength or at least pretend to have hidden strength. Until one day in the not too distant future, when washing the dishes or taking out the bins, that's when it hits and, that's when you give yourself permission to fall apart. But on this day, among friends and family, the three of us were holding up. Ben, my uncle John, uncle Geoff and Jake carried Mum's coffin in, as "Angels" by Robbie Williams rung out from a CD player at the back of the room. Cayden squeezed my hand as they laid her at the front, and I gave my brother a "you did good" kind of nod.

After that, the minister delivered a short speech about Mum. He talked about how she turned to Jesus at the end and would be welcomed into Heaven as one of his children and how she was a proud mother who spent her life devoted to the three of us. He made her sound like a true saint before thanking everyone for coming to celebrate her life. Then he introduced me and asked me to come to the front. It was my time to speak. I hadn't wanted to talk at the funeral, but as the eldest and the supposed writer of the family, it fell to me.

"Mum would have wanted it," Em said when dishing out the roles, and damn it, I knew she was right. I downloaded a poem from the internet, "Remember me" by Christina Rossetti. The words were beautiful.

I made my way to the front and took the place of the vicar, suddenly very aware of the sympathetic eyes on me. I took the sheet of paper from my trouser pocket, and it trembled between my fingers as I unfolded it. My eyes found Em and Ben, who looked at me encouragingly. Seeing their expectant faces made me realise the words I got off the 'net simply weren't going to cut it. Not today.

I scanned the church while the paper still shook in my hands. A lot of the seats were occupied, which was surprising, given the number of people Mum had managed to upset throughout her life. I glanced around at those who were there, not knowing what to say but knowing I needed to say something. I looked down at the paper and back at the faces. I drew in a deep breath and prepared myself.

"I..." My voice trembled, and it took me by surprise. I swallowed and tried again. "I..." I scanned the room looking for an encouraging face. Anyone that could help me through what was sure to be the most difficult speech I would ever give.

I stopped searching, and my heart almost ceased to beat. Tucked away at the back of the church, partially hidden behind unfamiliar faces, was a face so familiar to me, the only way to describe it was "home". The distinct contours of her face, the red of her hair and those eyes; filled with more compassion than I thought I could comprehend. I was transfixed. Josie had come to the funeral and was giving me a nod of encouragement, willing me to continue.

CHAPTER 25

WITH A SLOW NOD TOWARDS Josie, I folded the paper and slipped it back into my trouser pocket. The entire time my eyes remained on hers. Josie being there gave me strength and I needed it, not to read someone else's words but to say what I really wanted to say.

I cleared my throat, and the sound echoed through the church.

"Yesterday, I printed a poem from the internet to read to you and it was beautiful, but it wasn't written for my mum and I think she deserves the respect of having her own personal words."

My voice was small, and I wondered if everyone could hear me. I straightened my back and stood taller. "So, if it's okay with you, I would like to just talk about my mum." I nodded at Emma and Ben. *"Our mum."* Ben nodded back, and Em gave a small reassuring smile. I went on. "Our mum was not like anyone else I've ever met. She was one of a kind and I'm sure she was someone different for me as she was for each of you."

I took a steadying breath. "She could be funny and had a

way about her of managing to make a joke of any situation, no matter how bad." I smiled. "I'm sure if she were here, looking at us now, she would call us all morbid saddos and tell us to get a grip, or something to that effect. She certainly didn't have time for slushy bullshit, as she would put it." A few amused sniggers rang out around the church and Josie smiled knowingly.

"I think everyone here would recognise Mum for her love of a good old gossip. You could pretty much guarantee if she wasn't gossiping to you, then she was probably chatting about you. I suspect everyone in this room has been on the receiving end of one of these sides at least once."

"I remember once when I was about thirteen, a man came out to fix our boiler and after finding out his surname, Mum realised he was a cousin of a girl she knew. This girl had planned to elope to Gretna Green with a teacher from my school and Mum was so excited about sharing this news that even when the man went to the toilet, she continued the conversation from outside the door until eventually, he had to ask her for some privacy."

Family and friends smiled and nodded their heads in recognition of Mum's lack of social awareness.

"She was beautiful..." My voice cracked with emotion but determined to get through it, I pressed on. "It didn't matter where we were, people would always turn their heads to admire how gorgeous she was, and it made me proud. The vicar was right, she loved the three of us, me, Emma and Ben probably more than we knew. We were her world…"

My jaw set in a hard line as I tried to be calm. I looked at Josie for encouragement, and she wiped her eyes and mouthed the words: "Go on."

I sighed. "But let's get real for a minute here. Mum was no Maria Von Trapp. She could be rude and awkward and sometimes even quite cutting. When I think about it, I'm not sure any of us really knew the real her. She did love us, I don't doubt that for a second, but she was a hard woman most of the time, her life had made her hard. And although she might've been able to fool everyone with her jovial banter, making light of everything as though she didn't have a care in the world, the truth was…" I took a deep breath. "The truth was…Mum hated life." A stir rippled out around the room and I caught aunt Carol tut and shake her head in disbelief. I continued over the muffled disapproving voices.

"You may think it's somehow inappropriate for me to be talking about this now, that we should all gloss over the fact she was so miserable she attempted to take her own life, but I disagree. I don't want to replace my memories of her with a false idea of someone who wasn't my mum, and I don't think any of you should either. She was who she was – all the good and all the…not so good and, let's be honest, we loved her for it anyway. So, the vicar thanked you all for coming to celebrate her life, and I understand why he did, but she wouldn't have wanted that. Mum didn't see her life as something worth celebrating. So, Instead, I'd like you all to celebrate with me, in her being put out of her "bloody misery" as she described it. She's now been given the freedom she so desperately craved." I blew out a breath. "Mum, we love you and know wherever you are, it's better than what you had to experience in this lifetime."

I stepped down from the altar to a mixture of both shocked and confused faces. I don't think anyone knew what to do with what had just been said. I glanced at Em and Ben to check they were okay with my speech. Ben gave me a tightlipped smile and Em nodded her agreement. I had told the truth, and it mattered. Once satisfied my siblings weren't upset, I looked at Josie to make sure she was still there. She was. I took my seat next to Clara and Cayden, who each took one of my hands in theirs. I wanted to speak to Josie, but Mum's send-off had to come first.

There were still hymns to be sung, another reading from the bible and a closing.

Eventually, the service came to an end and Mum was carried out to "Supermarket Flowers" by Ed Sheeran, which left everyone wiping at their tears. I headed to the back of the church. Uncle Jerry attempted to get my attention and talk to me as I passed, but I pretended not to see as I wiped at my mascara-smudged face with my sleeve. By the time I reached Josie, I could only see the back of her hair as she walked away.

"Josie, wait." I ran to catch up to her. "Please, wait." She stopped and turned slowly to face me.

"You're leaving?" I didn't care about the desperation in my voice.

She tucked in her lips and stared into my eyes for what felt like an eternity. After an agonising wait, she spoke.

"I'm so sorry about your mum, Rox. I know I should have called you, I wanted to, but I just..." She looked at the pavement and then back up at me. "You gave a good honest reading up there, I think she would have liked that." My jaw clenched, and I didn't let my eyes drift from hers.

She studied me with a pained expression, and I said nothing. She looked back at the ground and shook her head to herself as though internally debating something and then to my surprise, she held her arms out to me and shook her head again.

"Come here."

I didn't hesitate. I fell into her and wrapped my arms tight around her back. We fit perfectly together, just like we always had. I buried my head in her neck, and I got lost in her familiar scent as my tears slid down my cheeks. My body remembered her. Every part of it tingled at having her so close, and my heart must have remembered her too because regardless of the day, it danced in my chest. Everyone else around us dispersed as I surrendered to my pain in her arms until my silent tears turned into a not-so-silent sob. With each burst of release, she pulled me in that little bit tighter. I came undone. Her presence gave me permission to come undone. After a while the tears subsided and I brought my mouth to her ear.

"I've missed you," I said simply.

Josie stayed quiet, but the tight grip she had on me seconds before loosened a little.

"I'm not working at the club anymore," I went on. "Because of you, I got the scholarship into Warwick, and I start next term." Again, silence. "Say something," I pleaded.

She released me and held me at arm's length. Her eyes were apologetic.

"Roxy, my being here, it doesn't mean anything's changed between us." Her hands fell from me completely and found their way to her jacket pockets. I immediately felt the loss.

"Josie, Please?" I barely recognised the desperation in my voice.

She shook her head repeatedly. "I can't, I'm sorry, but I can't."

The blood rushed to my face and I covered my eyes with my hands, unable to believe what was happening. What did she mean she can't? I tried to digest her words and the utter panic they sparked in me. It didn't take long for my hurt to turn to rage. The anger I could deal with, more sadness I couldn't begin to comprehend.

"So why did you bother coming?" The words were spat through my tears.

"I wanted to see if you were okay."

I sniggered. "Well, I'm not. I'm not okay, Josie. In fact, if you want me to be completely honest, I'm so far from okay, you wouldn't believe it. And let me tell you this, you showing up here at my mum's funeral of all days, has just made things a million times worse."

She flinched and laid her hand gently on my arm. "I wasn't

trying to upset you. That was never my intention. I care about you, Roxy, and I just needed to know how you were."

I pulled my arm away. "And at no point in this master-fucking-plan of yours did you think seeing you here today might give me false hope?"

A tear fell down Josie's cheek, and she made no attempt to disguise it.

I shook my head, trying not to be affected by the sadness in her eyes.

"You're a hypocrite, you know that? You talk about living in the moment and believing anything is possible, but you're stuck in the past and you're letting it ruin your here and now. I'm not your dad, Josie and I'm not Kaz. Please believe me when I tell you, I would never hurt you like that."

She bit the inside of her cheek. "I'm so sorry." Her expression was a mix of regret and sadness.

I reached out to touch her arm. "I miss you, Josie. God knows I've screwed up, and I know you find it hard to trust, but I promise I would never lie to you or keep anything from you again. Please, I'm begging you, can we just–" Aunt Carol butted in then, asking for directions to the burial site. I dismissively pointed in roughly the right direction as Josie took the opportunity to move my hand from her arm and step back.

"Please don't go…Please."

"You're right, this was a bad idea. I should never have come. I'm sorry." She regarded me for a second or two and turned away.

As I watched her walk from my life for the second time. I knew exactly what was happening, I think there was even a conscious part of me willing it to happen.

The contours of her body began to take on the characteristics of an out of focus picture, and it became a blur until she had disappeared entirely, along with everything and everyone else around me.

"BASICALLY, HER BRAIN'S A PUSSY. The second the going gets tough it shuts itself down and knocks her out."

Clara's animated voice dragged me back to the land of consciousness. If I hadn't been so shattered, I would have mustered up a giggle at her use of the word "pussy" around the likes of aunt Carol and uncle Jerry. I didn't open my eyes straight away.

"Should we pour some water on her?" Okay, aunt Carol was officially starting to piss me off. Reluctantly, I lifted my eyelids and groaned. It was the only way to prevent a soaking. I was sure that no matter how inappropriate and unnecessary, and just for shits and giggles, Clara would let her do it.

"Ow." I touched the back of my head, and a small lump pulsated against my fingers. I checked to see if I was bleeding, thankfully I wasn't, but it throbbed.

"Okay, okay, move out people, there's nothing to see here." Clara shooed my family away, including Em, which again, if I'd had the strength, would have amused me.

"You okay?" Clara knelt beside me.

I sighed. "Best day of my fucking life."

Cayden came up behind Clara. He took my hand and pulled me to my feet. "Come on, you. Let's go say goodbye to your mum."

The burial went as well as these things do. It was sweet and straightforward, and although I watched a piece of my heart go into the dirt with her, I somehow stayed in control and kept upright, so that was a relief. The wake, however, was another story altogether.

I know people say you shouldn't get plastered at wakes, that regardless of how much you're hurting, it shows disrespect to the loved one you're sending off, but I suspect those people hadn't said goodbye to both their mum and the love of their life on the same day. By 6pm, my whole swearing off alcohol rule was officially out the window and I was utterly shit faced. I would like to be able to say it wasn't my intention, but that would be a lie. I was on a mission.

We had all congregated at The Wood Pecker pub, a cute thatched building with wooden beams and a selection of real ales on tap. Emma had chosen it for its proximity to the church and the fact they were willing to give us exclusive hire, which was probably not a bad thing given the spectacle I was making of myself. I was propped up at the bar and becoming more agitated by the bartender by the minute.

"This is the best birthday party ever." My sarcastic slur was directed at the lad who inappropriately wore a 21-Today badge to a wake. The bar-boy looked down at the badge and back up at me with an embarrassed smile. Em must have heard me as she appeared from nowhere and swiped my neat Jack Daniels from my hand.

"Okay, Missy, I think you've had enough." She slammed the glass down on the bar and gave me her best-disappointed stare.

I reached over to grab my drink back and turned back to the bartender. "Haappry birthdaaay to yooouuuu. Happry…"

Clara came up behind me and draped an arm around my shoulder. "Let me deal with her. You've all been through enough for one day. I think she just needs some fresh air."

My head wobbled about on my neck.

"Fresh air? Oh, yeah? That's what I need? Fresh air. You don't know what I need, none of you do. I'll tell you what I need, I'll tell you all what I need." My voice was raised enough to grab the attention of everyone in the pub. "I need my mum to be alive, I need the love of my life to forgive me, and I need aunt fucking Carol to learn some manners."

"Rox that's enough." Emma's warning came through gritted teeth.

I leaned against a bar stool, and it gave way behind me.

Cayden caught me just before I hit the floor. "Right." Clara pointed behind the bar. "You, birthday boy, help him out here."

The barman dashed from behind the bar, and the next thing I knew, I was being carried from the pub by Cayden and the bar staff while Clara mumbled under her breath something about Josie being a stupid bitch who should have known not to show up today of all days.

"Shush." I attempted to focus on Clara. "I love Josie."

"Yeah, no shit. But she shouldn't have come here today, Rox, it was a dick move."

The guys lowered me to the ground in the car park where the air immediately had a sobering effect. As the bar guy made his way back inside, I mumbled a barely coherent apology to him, already feeling like an arse for the way I had treated the poor boy and Cayden slipped him what looked like a twenty pound note, to better emphasise the apology. Clara pulled her car up next to me and Cayden helped me into the passenger seat and got in the back.

"Right, I'm going to drop you back at your sister's where you can sleep it off, then we're gonna head home, okay?"

"Clar, I don't want to go back to Em's. Can I just come back home with you two?" I was whining and clearly not in any fit state to know what I wanted.

Cayden reached over from the back seat and placed a soothing hand on my shoulder. "Rox, you need to be with your family right now. They need you as much as you need them."

I turned to face him. "But...I need to see Josie."

Clara scoffed. "That's a definite fucking no then. Christ, what do you even see in her anyway?" She widened her eyes and waited for my drunken explanation.

"I just love her." The words came through a hiccup.

"Yes. I think we've established that. But why? What is it about her you love so much? 'Cos from where I'm sitting, she's done nothing but break your heart and piss off when you need her most. She's a knob."

I spun to face her. "Easy…" I overly stressed the word. "Don't cross that line Clar. I may be hurting, and I may be pissed, but I still won't hear anyone bad mouth Josie, even you."

Clara banged her hands on the steering wheel. "Well, fucking enlighten me then! What's so great about the teacher?"

I covered my eyes with my arm and let out a frustrated groan.

Cayden squeezed my shoulder once more. "Rox, I think we're all trying to understand where your head's at and why you're so affected by this. In all the time I've known you, you've never been that fussed about being with anyone." His tone was a lot softer than Clara's and I felt more inclined to share what was going on inside my head. I let out a heavy sigh.

"I just don't think you two get it. Since meeting Josie, for the first time in forever, I believed in myself. She reminded me who I am and what I could be. She made me feel special, not just some piece of shit from a council estate. I felt like something more with her, she made me feel like I was something more and that feeling is something I've longed for all my life."

"Is that what this is about? You not feeling good enough? Because if it is, you've got it twisted. No one sees you like that. No one! It's in your head." Clara was beginning to soften.

"She's right, Rox. This low self-esteem thing you have going on is not in any way warranted and it shouldn't take another person to make you see your worth. That needs to start with you and how you feel about yourself."

I shook my head. "It's not just that. She made me realise what I want from a relationship. She's kind, funny, intelligent as hell, and she gets me, like the real me. She makes me dig deeper to see who I really am. I just honestly believed we could have been happy together."

Clara stared out the windscreen and drew in a deep breath. She remained silent for a moment or two and eventually nodded. “Okay, fine. Have it your way. I know what I need to do.” She turned the key in the ignition and sped out the car park.

“Huh? What are you going to do?”

“Something I should’ve done weeks ago.”

CHAPTER 26

"HARDER, HARDER, HARDER, THAT'S IT. I'm nearly there. Roxy, harder!"

"Alright! I'm doing it as hard as I can. Jeez."

"Nearly there. Nearly there. Yes!" Clara fell and landed on her back with a thud.

We had just spent the past ten minutes trying to squeeze every hoody I owned into the last suitcase. I was in charge of bouncing on top while Clara had the impossible job of zipping the case shut. I looked around at my now empty room, consisting of only brown boxes and suitcases piled up in the middle. I must have let out an unconscious sigh.

"Look, you brooding bitch, you can come back and visit whenever. It's two hours away. Well, unless I like my new roomie more of course, then you'll probably not see me again." Clara's mouth curled, but I could tell she felt the weight of the moment as much as I did.

Clara had been my rock these past six weeks, and I don't know how I would have got through it all without her. She was there during the darkest of times. When I just wanted to hide away and give up on everything, she made it her job to consistently remind me I still had a life, albeit without Mum and without Josie.

Like a true friend, she intercepted all my attempts at late-night phone calls to Josie, snatching my phone from me and hiding it until the morning. She watched crap TV with me and knew when I needed a Chinese takeout or an entire tub of Cookie-Dough Ben & Jerry's. She even cleared out the drink cupboard to stop me spiralling down that road. She had me covered, and I would always be grateful to her for everything she sacrificed for me. She had barely been out on her own. Her boyfriend had dropped off the side of the planet, and on top of that she worked her arse off at the club to pay the rent, so I could take the last of my savings with me to get me through until I found a part-time job in Warwick.

I still thought about Mum every day, and sometimes the pain of losing her felt unbearable. The little things were the worse, catching myself thinking "oh, I must tell Mum..." before the realisation kicked in. Any time something like that happened, I would remind myself – she's in a better place and no longer in pain. Sometimes this helped, sometimes it didn't.

I thought about Josie too. The hurt from seeing her at the funeral had faded, leaving me able to reflect on all the positives she had brought to my life, rather than dwelling on what could have been. There would forever be a scar on my heart with her name etched into it, and although it stung, I wouldn't have it any other way because the sting reminded me of how real it had been. Before meeting Josie, I had no concept of what I looked for in a partner. I knew what I didn't want but spending time with her, getting to know her and falling for her made me see how good it could be, and I hoped one day I would have that again, and next time I would get it right.

Josie and I had not had any direct contact since Mum's funeral. The week before I packed up for Warwick though, I made the trip to Southend and visited Mum's grave, knowing I wouldn't be able to get there for a while. When I arrived at the cemetery, a stunning bouquet of orange and red chrysanths had been placed next to her headstone with a small note attached that read:

It looks like the end
It seems like a sunset
But in reality, it is a dawn
When the grave locks you up
That is when your soul is freed
Have you ever seen
A seed fallen to earth
Not rise with a new life
Why should you doubt the rise
Of a seed named human.

There wasn't a name on the card, but I knew who it was from, and my eyes pricked at her gesture. If it's true what she says about each of us having a soul, then she has the kindest one of all. Josie Calhoun had driven a four-hour round trip to visit my mum's grave to leave her that poem.

At the time, I had taken the card and slipped it into my back pocket, knowing Mum wouldn't mind. I wanted to keep the words as a reminder that she still lived on even though I couldn't see her. It was also a reminder that wherever she was and whatever she did now; Josie still cared. For the first time in a long time, I felt a sense of hope. Finally, my words were beginning to hit the page again and what I was writing was good. I had found my flow, and between that and getting myself prepared for uni, I was pleasantly distracted. Moving to Warwick was undoubtedly not going to be easy, but it was all I had and I sure as shit wasn't going to stuff it up.

"Well, let's get this show on the road." Clara's words snapped me from my daydream as she lifted the first box. I took one last look at my bedroom before helping her. Once we had crammed the car with as many boxes and cases as we could, the time had come for me to leave.

"Okaaay." Clara rocked back and forth on her heels, taking a drag of her cigarette and looking everywhere but at me. I considered letting her off the hook with a fist-bump but decided against it.

"Get your arse over here." I held my arms out to her and reluctantly she fell into me. Her body was stiff at first, but soon she surrendered and hugged me back. My eyes glistened and I was glad I could hide behind my shades. I knew Clara would hate it if I cried, so I did my best to hold back the tears. But, as I pulled away, there was a definite glisten in her eyes too.

"What's this? Clarita Martinez cries?"

Clara swiped at her eyes, removing all evidence. "I've no idea what you're talking about, but I do know if you call me Clarita again, I will end you. Now, listen, call me when you arrive and don't work too hard. All work and no play makes for a sad celibate bitch, okay?"

I nodded and held out my fist. Clara bumped it with hers and held it there for a second.

"You're a good egg, Clar." Thoughts of what a good friend she had been to me surfaced, and I smiled. "And it's good to see you back to your old self. You weirded out for a bit there and I missed you."

An expression settled on her face resembling something like embarrassment, but I'd never seen Clara embarrassed so I couldn't be sure.

"Clar?" I pressed. Whatever was going through her mind, I wanted in.

"Nah, don't worry, some things just don't need saying."

"Clar, come on, tell me."

She blew out a loud breath and stretched her arms in front of her. "Okay, fine. I'll tell you, but don't get all dramatic about it because it's nothing and stopped being a thing weeks ago, okay?"

"Okaaay."

"And before I say this, you should know that I love cock. You must know I love the cock, right? Like, a lot."

I laughed. "Yes, Clar, I know you love cock. Where are you going with this?"

She looked at her fingernails for a moment. "Okay, so, there's the ever so slight possibility that I was crushing on you for a while. There, I said it." She turned on her heel.

"Clar, come back here!"

She swivelled slowly to face me but didn't look at me.

I took a moment to compute what she had shared. "You were crushing? On me?" I wanted to laugh because it just seemed so absurd but I refrained as I didn't want to upset my friend.

"Yes. But I'm not anymore so like I said, it's no big deal."

I frowned as parts of the puzzle began to piece themselves together. She had started acting strange around the time I met Josie. She disappeared whenever Josie was around. The time she left Cayden's party. The tears. The snarkiness. The damn right sabotage that night at the club.

"Fuck!" I was genuinely flabbergasted. The fact she would ever even think of me in that way blew my mind and also that I didn't see a single sign of it – not once. I'd been so blindsided by Mum and Josie that I hadn't picked up on all the obvious cues.

"Yeah, fuck."

I stayed silent and she went on:

"I'm over it now. I'm not thick. I know you and me would've been a complete shit show, but in my defence, you're the only person who's ever been nice to me or showed me an ounce of respect and I got it twisted for a minute there."

I shook my head and lifted my shoulders. "I just don't know what to say."

"Seriously, you don't have to say anything. I'm honestly over it. I know I'm over it because I wouldn't be telling you otherwise. I pulled some dick moves there Rox, especially when I saw you with the teacher chick that night at the club. You were looking at her all cunt-struck and I admit I was jealous. I thought I was going to lose my friend – my only friend – and I panicked. So, yeah, soz about that."

I stayed silent for a longer moment. "Soz?" I repeated the word back to her feeling my lip curl slightly at the side.

Clara shrugged. "Yeah, you know, soz. Soz that the first night I met her I told her you would fuck her and not call the next day. Soz for running out of Cayden's party the way I did. Soz for lying to you about having a boyfriend–"

"Wait. Adam was a lie?"

"Yes. Now let me finish. Soz for drinking too much and becoming a complete and utter baby, but more than any of that, soz for snogging that bouncer bird with the worst breath in the history of the world because I stupidly thought it would make you pay some lezzy interest in me. I'm definitely fucking soz for that one."

I brought my hand to my forehead and closed my eyes, taking it all in and then I laughed. I *really* laughed. I don't even know what I was laughing at, maybe just the ridiculousness of it all, or the way Clara was casually saying "soz" to a long list of things that really I should be fuming at her for but instead, it just amused me. I couldn't put my finger on it, but something about the whole situation tickled me.

Clara started to laugh too, and I was glad because the last thing I wanted was for her to think I was laughing at her. We continued to giggle together until one of us got to the point where we stopped and let out that last tremulous post-laugh sigh and then we started up again.

"Clar...I...Just...Can't...Even."

"I know. It's pathetic isn't it?"

I managed to calm my breathing and control my laughter. "No. It's not pathetic. It's actually quite sad." And then we were, off again, in hysterics.

"This is ridiculous. Why are we laughing so hard at this?" Clara said, wiping tears from her eyes.

I did the same with my own. "I don't know." Once again I tried to be serious. "Are you sure you're over it? I want you to feel like you can talk to me about it if you're not. Honestly, you can tell me anything."

Clara shook her head. "I promise. I am one-hundred-percent over it. It was actually at your mum's funeral when I realised. The way you talked about the teacher–"

"Josie."

"Right, Josie. When you talked about Josie and how you felt about her, I knew then it was a silly crush and nothing more, I'm not even sure you could call it that. I looked – look – up to you, you know?"

"You do?" I smiled a genuine heartfelt smile and continued, "I do love you Clar, but just not in that way–"

Clara stuck both fingers in her ears and started singing "La la la".

I stopped talking and pursed my lips, waiting for her to realise I wasn't speaking anymore.

"Have you stopped? Oh, god, please tell me you've stopped," she said, fingers still in her ears.

I nodded.

She dropped her hands. "Look, please, let's not make this weird. I had a silly crush, I don't anymore. We're just friends, that's all we'll ever be, thank god and I *really* don't ever want to have this conversation again, capisce?"

I held my fist out to her once more. "Capisce".

"Now, go. Be gone. That's enough soppy bollocks for one day." She turned me around, pressed her hand against my back and guided me towards my car. "I never want to talk about this again," she repeated as she pushed me into the car and closed the door. I started the engine and laughed. Clara crossed her arms over her chest and watched as I pulled away.

"Love you, bitch." Her voice could be heard over the engine.

"Love you too, Clarita."

And with a beep of the horn, and one seriously weird conversation to get my head around, I was on my way.

I'D BEEN ASSIGNED BLUEBELL STUDENT accommodation. It was located on the central campus and housed around five-hundred students. Because of my age and, no doubt, because of Jefferson's contact, the university had kindly upgraded my accommodation to one with an ensuite. Grateful to not have to share my bathroom with a bunch of eighteen-year-olds, the second I arrived at Warwick, I sent an email to Jefferson to thank him once more for everything he'd done and assured him I would make the best of the opportunity he had given me.

I still had to share cooking facilities with nine other students which would take a bit of getting used to, but although not quite the luxury I had become accustomed to, the five by three meter room with a bed, desk, wardrobe and bookshelf, provided everything I needed. For the first time since my childhood, I was beginning to understand it didn't matter how much material stuff I had or how extravagant my surroundings, the only significant thing was what I had to offer as a person. It didn't take me long to settle in. After exploring the grounds and sticking close to the campus map, I learned where each of my lectures were set to take place, and I soon made the library – which was famous for holding over a million books – my new favourite place to be. The other students who shared my accommodation all seemed nice enough. I think I had imagined sharing with a load of hooligans blasting heavy metal until the early hours, trashing the place and wiping out my food from the communal fridge, but I couldn't have been more wrong. Perhaps it was because I was staying in the more expensive digs, but from what I could tell, they were a good bunch, there to learn. This pleased me.

I laid back on my single bed after a tough but rewarding day of critical analysis and called Cayden. I had promised I would speak to both Cayden and Clara once a week at least.

"Hey Cayd," I said as he answered.

"Rox! Listen, I've got about two minutes before my meeting with *Attitude*. Tell me everything but be quick. How are you settling in?"

"It's good. I'm actually really enjoying it. It feels right, like this is where I'm meant to be."

"Aww, sweetie. That's amazing. I'm so happy for you."

"How about you? *Attitude*? That's huge!"

"I know. They're running an article on contemporary gay writers and I'm having a photoshoot and everything. I also have to talk about the book *again* but all I really want is to be at home writing the next one. I miss it. And I miss you." I could hear how rushed Cayden was and didn't want to take up any more of his time.

"I miss you too. Look, call me next week when you have a bit more time. Good luck with the magazine. Love you."

I hung up the phone and immediately called Clara.

"Hello, lover." Her tone was playful.

I snorted. "You wish."

"Nope. You had your chance, Mackenzie and you blew it."

"How will I ever live with myself?"

"You'll survive. So, whatcha been up to? You better not have been boring. You do know that place is literally made for sex, drugs and partying."

"Yes, that's exactly what the ancients said when they

invented the university: "This will be a place of drugs, sex and parties.""

"Right? So, how are you? Slapped down like a sack of shit lately?"

"Nope. I haven't passed out once. And I've even given up drinking completely."

"Yeah, me too."

"What?" I sprung up on my bed.

"Well, not completely. But I've cleared out the drinks cupboard and now just have a few when I'm out."

"And this is because?"

"Because, when I drink, I make stupid decisions."

"Hey! I'm not a stupid decision, I'm a catch!"

Clara chuckled. "Yeah, yeah, if you say so. It's not just that, I've also been seeing someone and he prefers me when I'm not all loud and drunk and twattish, and actually, I think I prefer me when I'm not like that too."

"So, this is a real person?"

"Yes, of course."

"And he's nice?"

"He's *really* nice. Actually, he's pretty fucking amazeballs."

I laughed. "Well, bloody hell. I never thought I would hear you say those words."

"People can change, Rox. You've changed, you're all writery and boring now, so I can change too, right?"

I laughed again. "I suppose. And I'm really happy for you, Clar. That's great news."

"Yeah, yeah, I'm gonna go before you start getting all soppy. Anyway I have a hot date tonight, he's taking me up the Shard for a posh meal. I'll call you next week and don't be boring okay?"

"Okay. Laters Clarita."

"Oi…"

I hung up the phone and chuckled to myself, wondering

who in their right mind would take Clara to an expensive restaurant at the Shard. I really needed to meet this brave guy.

I was glad Cayden and Clara seemed so happy and it felt good to be back on track with my own life. I did have the occasional bad day, where I missed both Mum and Josie, but for the most part, I remained optimistic.

~

IT WAS THE THIRD TUESDAY in October and the last lecture of the day had arrived: poetry – my favourite. I sat at the back and waited for the hall to fill while I doodled planes and birds on my notepad. I was alone as, against Clara's advice, I hadn't got involved in any extracurricular shindigs, so hadn't made friends at the university. There were people from my dorm who I said "hello" to in passing but being a considerable bit older than the other students, I knew they would only ever be acquaintances.

As the last student took a seat, and the buzz of animated chatter faded out, the projector at the front lit up. I glanced up from the notepad to see what the lesson had in store. Just one word, in large capital letters, filled the screen; RUMI. I laid down my pen and straightened, feeling the excitement build within me. Rumi; the poet whose words Josie would use time and again to express what was in her heart. The words I had grown to know and love and the words that, in some strange way, had helped my mum through her hardest times. The image stayed on the screen for a minute or so before switching to a slide show of one of the most beautiful poems I've ever read:

A moment of happiness,
you and I sitting on the veranda,
apparently two, but one in soul, you and I.
We feel the flowing water of life here,
you and I, with the garden's beauty

and the birds singing.
The stars will be watching us,
and we will show them
what it is to be a thin crescent moon.
You and I unselfed, will be together,
indifferent to idle speculation, you and I.
The parrots of heaven will be cracking sugar
as we laugh together, you and I.
In one form upon this earth,
and in another form in a timeless sweet land.

A single happy tear rolled down my cheek, and I wondered for a moment if it was a sign. If the universe was telling me to reach out to Josie, to try to apologise once more to the person I'd loved and lost, to send a letter or better still, to go to her…I stopped wondering as the air was sucked from my lungs. Descending the central stairs from the back of the tiered seating was a sight that made every hair on my skin sit up and pay attention. I crooked my neck to watch her.

"It can't be," I murmured under my breath. I squeezed my eyes shut and opened them, she was still there. Not a dream. Not a figment of my imagination. In all her glory, the beautiful scarf-wearing redhead who stole my heart was making her way to the front of the lecture hall. Waves of electricity penetrated my spine at the sight of her. My face burned from the adrenaline pumping through my blood and my breathing became heavy and erratic. Don't you dare pass out now, I told myself, I needed to know if it was real. I had to be sure Josie Calhoun was really standing at the front of one of my lectures looking more breathtaking than I had ever seen. Josie's eyes landed on mine before she drew in a steadying breath while our lecturer, Dawn Spencer, addressed the hall.

"Today, I have the great pleasure and privilege of introducing Josephine Calhoun. Josephine is a Lecturer of Psychology, who until now has been teaching in her field at the

University of London. She has kindly offered to speak to you today, as part of a series of guest lectures you'll be attending in the coming weeks, and my understanding is, she will be joining Warwick as a full-time member of the Psychology Department within the next month. Josephine will be talking to you today about the psychological impact poetry can have on the left hemisphere of the brain, which is sure to be a fascinating topic. I know you'll all make her feel as welcome as possible as our newest member of the faculty."

Josie's eyes subtly searched mine for a reaction. I sat like a dummy, unable to take in a word that had been said. What? How? But? My mind couldn't work fast enough. I struggled to understand what the hell was going on. It was her. My Josie. In front of me, right now. *My Josie*.

Josie turned to Dawn. "Thank you for that warm introduction. You can now take a much needed break." She smiled at our lecturer who returned the smile and took a seat at the front. Josie turned her attention back to the class and went on. "Hello everyone. Thank you for having me. Before we begin with the science, would anyone like to share their thoughts on what they think Rumi might be talking about in this poem?" She directed the question at me. I turned to my peers, waiting to see if anyone would speak. The hall remained silent. I slowly raised my hand.

"Yes, Miss...?" She looked at me expectantly for my name, and there was a glint in her eye that only I could recognise. The entire class turned and stared at me then, unsurprising, given it was the first time I had raised my hand since I had been there. I overheard one student asking another, "Who's that?" I stared straight into Josie's eyes.

"Mackenzie," I answered, and my voice shook.

Josie chewed the inside of her cheek. "Go on, Miss Mackenzie."

I sucked in a breath, having no clue what I was about to say, but I knew it was an opportunity to let her know how I still felt about the single most important person in my life.

"I believe he's talking about soul mates." The corner of Josie's mouth gently edged its way up. "About two people who were meant to be together for eternity and regardless of everything else going on in the world around them, they manage to find happiness in each other. Two people who have not only shared this life but all their many lives before and fate keeps bringing them together in the most extraordinary ways. And now they're together again." I stopped and gave Josie a questioning look. She nodded once. "Back together and entwined in each other's love and I suspect they each have a pair of wellies lined up together on their veranda. Two people whose names are written side by side in the stars, etched into the cosmos because they are eternal and will remain eternally together. Two people who are crazy in love and regardless of their differences and ways in which they may have hurt each other, their love remains unshakable."

The room was silent, and for a moment I could see Josie had forgotten herself. Her eyes had glassed over as they locked on mine. After a short time, the rest of the class nodded, and a few even clapped, agreeing with what I'd shared. The sudden noise jolted Josie from her daze. She cleared her throat and nodded.

"Thank you for sharing, Miss Mackenzie. Your observations are quite profound, poetic even."

For the next two hours, Josie conducted herself professionally, delivering a lecture as good as any I had seen that month. On occasion, our eyes met, and I gave her a questioning look of "what the...?" And she smiled, seeming almost unsure.

Eventually, once Dawn had thanked Josie and headed off to her next class. I waited patiently for everyone to filter out. Five students lingered, wanting to ask questions, and others talked amongst themselves. Her class had caused quite a stir. She had mixed psychology and spirituality with poetry and writing, and it had ignited an interest in a lot of my classmates, which made me see exactly what she meant when she told me how rewarding her job could be once the students were engaged. Finally, we were the last two remaining. We gazed at each other for a long moment and I swear I could hear my own heartbeat. I spoke first.

"What? Just *what*?" I shook my head.

Josie shrugged. "Clara."

I shook my head. "What's Clara got to do with this?"

"She came to see me the night of your mum's funeral. She dropped you at your sister's, waited for you to fall asleep, raided your phone for my address and then once she'd taken Cayden home, she paid me a visit. She didn't hold back. She gave it to me straight and told me a few home truths about the kind of person you are. She told me you were leaving for Warwick and that if she was in my position she would be packing her bags already. She said I would never find someone else like you and if I'm honest, it's what I already knew, but I was petrified of getting hurt again and opening myself up to you–"

"But I don't understand–"

Josie cut me off. "Please, Rox. I've been preparing this speech for a month now. Please let me get it out."

I nodded and remained silent.

"When I lost my mother, I promised myself I would never knowingly get into a situation where I could get my heart ripped out again. Because for a long time, I felt as though anyone I ever allowed myself to love left me. But when I met you, I had no choice. It didn't matter how many times I told myself getting involved with you was a bad idea; I just couldn't help but want to be near you.

"When I saw you that night at your work, it took me back to my dad and to Kaz, and I felt betrayed. Like I was playing a part in some sick charade, and the universe was conspiring against me, and it was all too much. I said some really hurtful things to you, things I can never take back and I'm so sorry, but you hurt me too.

"It was torture for me after that, and no matter how much I threw myself into my work, I didn't stop thinking about you, not even for a second. I came to the funeral because even though I couldn't bear the thought of seeing you again, the thought of not seeing you tore me up inside. I wanted nothing more than to take you home and tell you everything was going to be okay, but I was scared to take that risk. Once Clara came to my house and gave it to me in no uncertain terms, I knew I had to take a chance, because I'd lost you, and nothing was ever going to hurt more than that." She paused and I could clearly see the rise and fall of her chest.

"I guess you're a pusher, and I'm a runner, and that makes for a tricky combination, but I refuse to let my trust issues keep me away from something I know could be everything. You're the one. I knew it from the very first moment I laid eyes on you and when I picture my life in five, ten or even thirty years from now, you're there. You're in that picture. In fact, you *are* the picture. It's only you and I'm not willing to lose you again." She paused for a moment and the tears in her eyes spilt over. "But Roxy, I need to know that you're never going to lie to me again–"

"I promise." I interrupted, not wanting to allow even a shred of doubt to creep in.

"I believe you. Which is why I'm here. I knew we'd struggle to make it work if I had to make a four hour round trip every time I wanted to see you, and I also knew after what I put you through last time a simple sorry wouldn't do. I had to do something big. So, I pulled a few strings, well actually, Jefferson once again pulled a few strings, and now, here I am, hoping you still feel the same and that leaving my entire life behind has been worth it?" She shrugged, and her eyes were filled with hope.

"You're here? You're actually here? You've left your house and your job to be here, with me?"

Josie laughed nervously at me being dumbfounded. "I told you I believe in you. I know how you feel about yourself, and I don't know if it was your mum, your lack of a father, where you grew up or what it was that made you feel less than perfect, but I want to spend the rest of my life bringing out the best in you and showing you every day how amazing you are. I need you to see what I see and you need this chance, this opportunity to live the life you deserve. I need this chance. I can make it work here, as long as I'm with you, we'll make it work together."

I got up, and with limp legs and tears in my eyes, I closed the distance between us until we were face to face. I laced my fingers around her neck.

"You're actually here." My voice was full of emotion, stuck somewhere between a laugh and a cry.

Josie nodded and smiled. "I'm here, baby."

Our lips came together at the same time, moving against each other in soft, tentative exploration and I savoured every second. After believing I would never be able to kiss Josie again, the power of what it did to me could only be described as magical. It was as though she was breathing life back in to me, it was a promise of hope, love and forever afters – it was everything.

She rested her hands on my hips and pulled me against her so I could feel her heartbeat against my chest. It beat as fast as my own. And every pulse sent us deeper into the perfect kiss, that would make everything right, a moment so beautiful and pure it became the glue to the tiny pieces of my shattered heart.

When I pulled out of the kiss, we were both breathless.

"Whatever happened to not fraternising with Faculty?" My tone was playful. Josie smiled against my lips. "You climbed the rope, remember?"

I smiled. "I'm so in love with you, Josie."

"I love you too, baby."

FOUR-THOUSAND WEEKS. AND THAT'S if we're lucky. I could never have imagined that I'd spend the first one-thousand six-hundred weeks of my life becoming the person that Josie Calhoun would eventually grow to love and want to spend her life with. But what I did know, with certainty, was that I was not going to waste a single one of the two-thousand four-hundred weeks I hoped we had left together and I was damn sure that during those weeks, I would do all I could to make Josie proud, to make my mum proud but above all else, to make me proud.

THE END

Thanks for reading. Please add a review on Amazon and let me know what you thought!

Amazon reviews are extremely helpful for authors. Thank you for taking the time to support me and my work. Don't forget to share your review on social media and encourage others to read the story too!

DEDICATION

For Helen. You brought me to life.

ACKNOWLEDGMENTS

A huge thank you to Diana. I think we both know what this book would've been (or not been) without you. Thanks to Daniela. I'll see you on the other side (Gen Q of the Lesfic world). Kiki, it is true, kindness does breed kindness, your guidance means the world. Clare Ashton, thank you for your wonderful words, I will pay it forward. Hannah (AKA spirit) you have read as many drafts of this book as I have. For all your support, not just in this venture, but in everything, there are no words. Craig, you are my constant. The Boggers, because I said I would! My family, for the all the ups and downs and many shades of colour, I love each and every one of you. And to you, lovely reader, for taking a chance on an unknown author. To the first of many.

ABOUT CRYSTAL CHARD

Crystal loves travelling, driving around in her Fiji green Z3, and singing (wailing) along to power ballads. Her early experience in the field of psychotherapy began an ongoing fascination with human behaviour and a need to understand what makes people 'tick'. She enjoys exploring this through her characters. Crystal hopes to sell heaps of books, so she can quit her day job, packing toilet parts in a dusty warehouse, which is really not that glamorous.

CONNECT WITH CRYSTAL

www.crystalchardbooks.com
www.instagram.com/crystalchardbooks
www.facebook.com/cchardbooks

OTHER BOOKS BY THE AUTHOR

When everything's at stake, how close is too close?

Forensic Psychologist, Grace Weatherford, wants her old job back with the Covert Intelligence Squad, but on her own terms. Yet when CIS offer up a case with a mysterious female perp at the centre, she can't say no. The catch? Grace's speciality is undercover guidance – she now has to go all in.

Nadia Florescu is nobody's fool. She's survived worse than the grim CIS cells and suffered in ways Grace cannot imagine. So giving up the names that CIS demands is a game she can play and win – no matter the cost.

When their worlds collide, and Nadia's shocking story begins to unravel, professional lines blur. But is Nadia really who she says she is? And how many boundaries will Grace cross for justice – and an uncompromising and beautiful suspect?

BUY NOW

Manufactured by Amazon.ca
Bolton, ON

28162638R00176